WAVES

From the Chicken House

Sharon Dogar's terrific first novel is taut, neurotic, edge-of-consciousness stuff. And it's not only me who thinks so – you can take Philip Pullman's word for it too. Somewhere between *Wuthering Heights* and *Lovely Bones,* it's almost a crime mystery, and certainly a love story. It's about life and death – literally.

Barry Cunningham
Publisher

WAVES

SHARON DOGAR

Chicken House

2 Palmer Street, Frome, Somerset BA11 1DS

Text © Sharon Dogar 2007
Cover illustration © Georgina Hounsome

First published in Great Britain in 2007 by
The Chicken House
2 Palmer Street
Frome, Somerset BA11 1DS
United Kingdom
www.doublecluck.com

Cover design by Radio
Typeset by Dorchester Typesetting Group Ltd
Printed and bound in Great Britain

1 3 5 7 9 10 8 6 4 2

British Library Cataloguing in Publication data available.

ISBN 978 1 905294 24 4

For: the brother I never had but always dreamed of

To Adder, for everything, every day, especially Jem, Xa and Ella, with love X

PART ONE. The Family.

Prologue.

Our holiday house is white. You can tell it's a 1930s seaside house because it looks just like a ship that's somehow strayed on to land. Our house is right next to the beach, but on a hill, so that when you look down you feel as though the whole world's spread out beneath you, just waiting for something to happen. We come here every summer. It feels like always, forever.

'You were here as a bump,' says Mum, if I ask her when I first came.

'As a twinkle,' smiles Dad.

I hope I'll come here with my children's children, if I'm lucky enough to live that long.

In the kitchen there are photos of the whole Ditton family clan: Mum's mum, Dad, Charley, me and Sara – and that's just on our bit of the wall. Spread out all around the kitchen walls are the other faces, faces of all the families who stay here – cousins, aunts, uncles. There are some I don't even know or recognize.

One of the weird things about a house like this is that we all think it's ours, but really it doesn't belong to anyone, or perhaps it belongs to everyone, I'm not sure.

In the photos you can see us all growing.

'Hair gets shorter, legs get longer,' says Mum, and then she touches us, a soft, light stroke, as though we were wood, and she is touching us for luck.

Sometimes I wish the photos weren't there at all, and then I look at my sister Charley on the wall. There are lots of photos of Charley. There's the Charley I never knew, aged one. She's fat, with red fluff on her head. Charley aged three stares at the camera, with eyes that look so like mine. I'm in the picture too, but I haven't got my grown-up eyes yet. Charley's smiling, but I can see her little fist squeezing my fat baby arm, and I can imagine feeling the pain of it. I don't think Charley liked me being born at all. In that photo her eyes are green. They dazzle. *'Look at me,'* they shout, *'look at me, not at that scrappy little thing on the floor.'*

Right next to that (surprise surprise) is another photo of Charley, aged four, but it IS a surprise, because in this photo she's standing in a rock pool, and her eyes aren't green at all any more. They're blue, as blue as the sky she's staring up at.

'Chameleon eyes,' says Mum, smiling, 'that change with the weather.'

It's true too, her eyes really do change colour. Mine do too. Underneath though, I think our eyes are grey, a nothing colour. A take-on-anything colour.

Fickle.

With each photo, Charley's eyes just get bigger and bigger, and she grows slimmer and taller, until the last photo.

I look at it. I don't have to see it for real because it's the picture I always have of her in my head, in my mind's eye, where our eyes aren't the same colour at all.

Charley is beautiful, and I can tell you that was a surprise. The real Charley was just Charley; irritating (often), kind (rarely), fun (sometimes), but mostly just a pain.

But the photo-Charley is beautiful – just like the sun going down on the beach behind her. It was Dad who took that last photo. I remember it. 'Just look at that child's hair in the light,' Mum said, and we all looked up, each one of us, all hoping that it was us she meant, but this time it was Charley. The sun does look like it's caught in her hair. It glitters in gold and red as it falls across her face. She's looking into a tin bucket, full of that day's catch.

'Come on, Charley,' said Dad, 'to the rock.'

Every year Dad took a photo, and ever since she was five all of Charley's photos were taken on the same rock. A huge rock, buried beneath the sea, and only uncovered by the tide. Year by year, she gets higher and higher up the rock, until that year, last year, she's finally made it to the very top: 'Charley fifteen years old,' the photo says.

She doesn't look too steady if you ask me – there's not

11

much rock to balance on up there. I know, I climbed it early the very next day, as though I might be able to see her from up there, spot her somewhere on the wide, empty, early-morning beach, the way Mum's never really stopped trying to do.

It's a hard climb to the top of that rock, but she's standing – that's Charley for you – standing straight up into the middle of the air, and you can see that she's laughing. Charley's laugh, the one that says: *'I've done it, look at me, I've done it.'* I used to hate that laugh. I won't look, I won't look, I'd think – and then she'd call out:

'Hal, look at me, Hal!'

And I'd pretend not to hear, and then when I did look, there she was, always at the top, always there, where I wanted to be, and waiting for me to be happy about it. Well, I'm waiting for you now, Charley, we're all waiting now.

The photo.

Her hair is as red as the sun, as gold. It flies right up into the air from her tipped-sideways head, it's as long as it ever got, just touching the elbow of her right arm. It looks as though her hair is just about to break free of her body, and fly away towards the dipping sun. The flipped-up ends of it are golden, the scalp of it a deep, deep, red. It's a burning picture.

It hurts me just to look at it.

Sometimes, when I'm alone in the kitchen with Charley's picture, I feel my head turning towards it, turning as though it's no longer mine, and I close my eyes, not wanting to see, but she's there just the same, there behind my eyelids: 'Hal, *look at me, Hal!*' she cries, and she's dancing, a little black demon of a silhouette on the rock, surrounded by red globes of light.

And she's alive, so alive that even the sun wants a piece of her, and that's what hurts most of all. That someone so alive could possibly be dying. And worse, that as she dies, we all seem to be dying too, somehow, especially Mum.

Sometimes, I think the sea that nearly killed her, loved her so much that it didn't want to give her back. Other times I just hate Charley for ever existing in the first place.

13

North Oxford. Now.

'How can we?'

Mum's voice comes up through the night-lit window, and into my room. This is always how it ends, every night for weeks, in Mum's wail of despair.

'How can we?'

Dad's voice comes back at her in a low, deep, wordless mumble. God, it's hot. I imagine I could open the window and be in Cornwall, hearing the sea, feeling the cool breeze fresh from the waves. It's so sticky and hot here. The midges dance around the candle flame on the garden table. Mum and Dad stop talking suddenly and look up.

'It's late, Hal,' says Dad.

'Yeah?' I shout back.

They wave and drop their voices. The lights at the end of the garden flicker and go out. I watch as the pale moon appears, and floats on the black river. Mum blows out the

14

candles and the smoky smell of wax drifts up to my window.

It's hot.

'Night, Hal,' whispers Mum, and the garden falls still and silent. I look up at the sky; it's never truly dark here. In Cornwall the sky's so deep and black and inky that it's just stuffed full of stars, all racing around the moon. Some nights there are so many that it feels as though some are closer to the earth than others.

3-D stars.

'How can we, Jon?'

Her voice comes up through the floor this time – it's so full of despair that I wonder why the moon doesn't drop an inch to hear her better, but it doesn't. I wonder if they'll ever stop. I wonder if they'll ever ask me what I think. I wonder where my sister Charley really is, and if she'll ever wake up. But most of all, I just wonder if we're going back to Cornwall for the summer.

'We have to, Milly.' Dad's voice is just as definite as hers, just as despairing.

'We can't . . . I can't . . .'

The long silence tells me that she's crying quiet tears, imagining that I can't hear them, can't see them anyway, in my mind's eye, where she never seems to stop crying.

'What about Hal and Sara?' he asks. 'They can't stay stuck in Oxford all summer.'

Mum mutters something – I think I hear my name and then silence. I can hear my heart thumping. And then Dad again, weary now.

'Right, I'll take them, you stay here with Charley.'

More silence.

'Can you manage that, love?' His voice is still gentle, but it's all sad and soft and definite too. It's like Charley being half-dead has sort of broken their voices up, so that they've got more ways of telling each other things, more ways of meaning things, only just not in words.

I try to listen, to hear between the gaps. There are so many now – gaps, I mean.

'No,' says Mum slowly, after an age of silence, 'no, Jon, you're right. We need . . . no, they need . . . to be . . . I just can't . . . I don't want . . . it's like . . .'

'Trying to be a family without Charley?' he finishes for her. He's not really asking her anything – he already knows that's exactly what she means.

I listen harder, and I can almost see her nodding her head, a head so full of feelings that they're beyond speaking.

'They need you too, Milly, Hal and Sara. They need to get away from all . . . all . . .' Dad almost whispers, as though he's afraid that just the sound of the words themselves might make her change her mind.

'I know,' she says, finally, and my heart fills with joy and I thump the pillow. We're going to Cornwall.

When I wake up the sun's shining on the ceiling and the birds have stopped singing.

It's late, must be, 'cos I can hear Sara in her room chatting away to herself.

'Look,' she shouts, 'it's not dark, it's morning. Time to get up, lazybones, if you're not down in five minutes I'll go without you. WHERE ARE YOUR SHOES?'

She makes me smile; she sounds so like Mum used to on a really late school morning. I go in to see her. Her room's a total tip, no floor space anywhere, just toys and clothes flung about all over the place. She looks up at me from the middle of it all and says:

'It's mornin' time Hal, the sun's come on.'

'Were we all asleep?' I ask. She nods and turns back to her dolls.

'It's time for breakfast, girls,' she says, and I watch as she puts two of her dolls around a small plastic table.

'Are you hungry?' she asks them.

'Are YOU hungry, Sara?' I ask her back. She nods and ignores me.

'Oh dear! No milk!' she goes on. 'Mummy and Daddy are too tired from all the shoutin' to buy milk.'

I stare at her, and she gives me a quick, freaky glance from under her lashes, before going back to pretending I'm not here.

'What did you say, Sara?' I ask.

'I was TALKING TO MYSELF, Hal,' she tells me, as if I didn't already know.

I scratch my head and yawn. I wonder what goes on in Sara's head? How much does she really know about

Charley? Can she really remember her being properly alive? Or has Charley always been someone who just lies in a hospital bed, in a coma, never talking back?

'Mummy and Daddy all gone now, all 'way now,' and her voice changes, something in it makes me look up. 'I know,' she says in an excited, secret voice, 'let's play sister-dolls!'

I feel the hair on the back of my neck stand straight up when she says that – it's like she can read my mind or something.

She sits back and stares at the two doll children sitting around the table. They stare back at her. She turns her big-eyed gaze on me, and gives me the long, slow look-over, before pointing to an ugly ginger-haired troll of a doll, and deciding that it's definitely me.

'Hal,' she says, 'that's a you-doll.'

'Hey, thanks Sarz.'

But she just goes right on ignoring me, exchanging a doll at the table for the me-doll.

'Mmm, now, Sara, let's see.' And she scans the dolls on the floor before quickly pointing to the smallest, prettiest dark-haired doll and grabbing at it, clutching it to her chest, as though someone else might get to it first.

'This is me!' she says. She makes me want to laugh; who does she think is going to take it away?

Charley? suggests a voice in my head, but I delete it, 'cos that's a crazy idea.

There's a silence as Sara scans the floor again, searching. 'Now, a Charley-doll,' she half whispers to herself, and I

18

watch as she reaches out for a tall slim doll, with dark red hair; I watch as she lifts it up in a kind of fearful half-stroke, and drops it into the third empty chair around the pretend table. There are three children around the table now, no gaps.

It looks so right it makes me want to cry.

'All finished!' she says suddenly and quickly, and she sweeps the dolls aside, knocking them onto the floor, as though she could make it all disappear. Not just the dolls, but the feelings too.

'Hal?' she asks.

'Yeah?'

'I'm a good girl,' she says, with a sense of wonder, as though she can't quite believe it. I wish I knew what the hell she means, and why, but it's still far too early in the day for me to think about.

'Sure you are,' I say, 'and a hungry girl too, yeah? Let's get brekker.'

She gives me this sideways look she does, like I haven't quite got something, and right away I get the heart-lurch. It is so what Charley used to do, that freaky I'm-a-girl-and-you're-just-a-poor-boy-who-can't-possibly-understand thing, but Charley was older, and Sarz is just a kid. Where does she get it from?

It's in the genes, sucker, I hear Charley say. I hear Charley a lot these days. It's as though a bit of her has crawled out of her hospital bed and lodged itself straight into my head. I delete again.

Life's hard enough.

'Were you awake a long time, Sarz?'

'Time to get up, when the sun comes on.'

She sings the words as we go down the stairs, and points at the sun through the hall window.

'It's not a light really, Sara, the sun – it's a big ball of fire.'

She thinks about that one all the way through pouring out her cereal, and then she stirs her Weetabix and laughs out loud at THAT crazy idea.

'Bouncy ball,' she yells with delight. Her face is full of Weetabix, and for some weird reason I suddenly remember how small she was when she was born. How Mum never seemed to have any time for me and Charley then, either. Now it's like it's me and Sarz who are the ones on the outside, and Mum's locked away in hospital with Charley, or if she's not actually in the hospital, then she's locked away in her own head, thinking about Charley.

It's a bit like I'm seeing Sarz for the first time. Here she is, eating breakfast and staring at me again, staring at me like she's making her mind up about something.

'We're goin' to Corn-wall,' she says, managing to get her tongue round the word after a while. 'Shall we go swimmin' in the sea?'

'Sara can go swimming with Daddy,' I say firmly.

'Not Daddy, wanna go with Hal,' she pouts.

'Hal doesn't swim in the sea any more,' I tell her. She does that to me: suddenly I'm talking as though I was her version of myself. Her Hal, not mine.

'I know.' She carries on staring at me with her big blue

eyes. 'Why?' she asks.

Good question, Sarz, only I can't answer. Seems like I don't really trust the sea any more, can't seem to see the surface of it without imagining just how dark and deep and dangerous it might be underneath.

'Are Sara's eyes blue like the sea?' I ask back, but for once she isn't distracted.

'Hal's eyes are like the sea,' she says, and then she sighs deeply. 'And Charley's in the sea.'

I feel my mouth fall open, but no words come out.

Sara just carries on spooning in the mush, as though what she's said is completely normal, which for her it is, I suppose.

'Who's in the sea, Sara?' I ask, just to make sure I heard right. 'Charley's in the hospital, not the sea.'

'Fish and crabs and Ariel the mermaid and the big fat lady and all the little fishes and Guppies and Daddy and Sara, but not grown-up girls, grown-up girls can't go in the sea. There's a man in there with a fork an' temper . . . and sea flowers . . . that gets you!' And she's gone, just slipped away into her own world, where I know there's no point at all in trying to follow her.

Mum comes in then. 'Morning you two, cuppa tea?'

She looks as tired as ever. She isn't really brown any more, and she isn't young-looking either. She's a weird grey colour, like she lives in a cave underground all the time; or maybe that should be in a hospital. She lifts the blinds and lets in the sunlight.

'Guess what?' she says.

'We're goin' to Corn-wall?' says Sarz.

'Family grapevines, eh?' laughs Mum, but somehow still manages to look sad.

'Hey!' I say.

'Hey Hal-boy, what are you up to today?'

'Dunno, bike maybe? Boat? Mates?'

'No going out on the river without Dad around, ok?'

'Sure,' I say, keeping it light and cazh. 'You?'

'Just the usual, Charley. Shopping. Cooking, and—' she looks at Sara, 'and a little bit of cuddling might be nice.' Sara leaps into her arms, right on cue, and Mum sinks her head into her shoulder. I watch her as her eyes close in the sunlight, and it's truly weird, it's like Sarz has some special secret thing that Mum just has to breathe right in, all the way down to her very soul. She opens her eyes and sees me staring. She winks at me, including me, but I know I can't ever make her feel quite so good as Sara does.

'See ya later,' I say.

'Hal?'

'Yeah?'

'Hal, will you come and say goodbye to Charley?'

'Sure.'

'And Hal?'

'Yeah?'

'Think of something to leave with her, something special the nurses can chat to her about, something she can remember you by.'

'Sure.'

'And Hal?'

'Yeah?'

'Love you, only-boy.'

'Yeah. You too.'

I open the kitchen door. The sun's so hot, and the river's all the way to the bottom of the garden. I get out the fishing line and rods and hooks, and set myself up under the willow tree with a book. Truth is I don't want to say goodbye to Charley. I don't even really want to see her again. She's just not there, she's hit her head on a rock and can't move, can't speak, can't talk, can't even breathe without sounding like a machine! Call it coma, call it PVS, call it what you like – if you ask me, she's dead already, though, and the worst thing about it is that Mum and Dad just can't see it.

I start to think about what I could possibly leave her – a new brain, perhaps?

I drag my way through the hot dusty streets all the way to the hospital, but Mum's already there, sitting by Charley's bed. She's talking. She talks as though Charley's just asleep, not in a coma and definitely not dead. She talks as though the whole world is sitting up, waiting, holding its breath and just waiting for the moment when Charley finally sits herself up, smiles, and shakes out her long red hair. Her hair keeps on growing.

How gross is that?

Anyway, I know what Charley would do if she did wake up. She'd stretch and yawn and say something. I try to imagine what she might say. 'Sorry', that would be quite good if you ask me. Sorry for being such a totally self-obsessed arsehole. Sorry for going out and falling off a wave and not quite killing myself. But sorry's not really Charley's style. Hers would be more like this:

The scene: a hospital. A beautiful girl's eyes flutter awake.

'Oh, I've been in SUCH a wonderful place,' she'd say, and then she'd smile her secret smile (*'Look at me, Hal, look at me'*) and she'd look straight at me, and I'd know she'd seen things I'll never see, been to places I can't even begin to imagine.

Still, even that would be better than having to look at her the way she is now. Now I don't want to look at her at all. I hate it. She doesn't even look like Charley. She looks like someone dead. Her mouth slips. I sit outside the door on the sweaty plastic chair and listen to Mum.

'The sun's out, sweetheart,' she says. Yeah, right, Mum, scintillating stuff, that'll bring her right back to life! 'And I've brought you some gorgeous snapdragons to smell. Why is it that the yellow ones smell so pale and the orange and red ones so hot? Here, try.'

I peep, urgh, she's holding them up to Charley's nose. I wait to see what happens, but Charley's breathing doesn't change at all.

24

Great response.

Up. Down. Up. Down.

It's not normal-sounding, her breathing, but that would be because she's not really here – because somehow it's only a machine doing the breathing, not her.

'Remember,' Mum goes on, 'you used to press the petals to make them speak, and you called them bee-houses, and they smell so beautiful and look so bright. Always out in June, just before you were born. I still can't walk past a snapdragon without thinking of you. Gosh, it was hot the year you were born . . .'

She's holding Charley's dead-looking hand and stroking it, whispering something – her name, probably. She does it all the time, over and over, as though just by saying it she could call her back to life. If I was Charley it just might be enough to kill me off, hearing Mum sound like that.

'We're going to Cornwall, Charley, just me and Dad and Hal and Sara. We're going to miss you so much, love, but I'll be back every week, and Sally and Jenna said they'd visit, and Hal and Sara need to . . . they need . . .' she trails off. When she starts up again her voice has caught hold of itself – it's all bright and cheerful and lying.

'You're in a special hospital, Charley. You've been here a long time. You hit your head on the rocks – at least, that's what we think – we won't know fully, darling, until you can tell us, will we? Hal found you in the waves on the rocks . . .'

'Didn't!' I say quickly. 'Didn't!' and for a second it works, and the word's stronger than the memory, wiping it out, but only for a second. I say it again, as though saying it could make it true. 'Didn't,' but it's too late, the mind's eye's already kicked in, and I can see the wide, tide-out, golden beach, full of the morning's emptiness. I can hear my own breath running, and feel my eyes searching. 'Didn't, didn't, didn't!' I chant the words over and over, but it's like they don't work any more, because I know I did find her. I found her lying on a flat rock in the shallow waves, where her body had landed, and it looked so broken, so like a left-over doll that she didn't need any more, so like a . . . stop!

'What were you doing there? Why were you looking?' The question leaps out at me before I can kill it.

I take a breath. I don't have to do this, I tell myself. I focus on the walls. They're the exact same colour as puke. I feel the plastic chair beneath me, I hold on to the world around me, solid and real and here. I hold on to Mum's voice.

'This room's so lovely,' she says, 'the sun shines in every afternoon. It's a bit white, but that's because it's a hospital. We wish you were at home.'

Even Mum can't make the words sound new and alive, she's said them so often. We all have, but Charley just can't hear us.

'Oh, Charley!' Mum cries out, and her voice sounds so sudden and new and true again – and full of pain. It's like she's leaving Charley for ever; and that's when I get it, I finally get it. I get that maybe Mum really does think that

Charley will die without her visiting every day.

Maybe she will, I think. Maybe she should, is what I don't think. I creep away, before Mum sees me, away from the smell of the flowers in the dead white room, like bleached bones. Away from that thing they still call Charley.

Next time it's Dad on duty. But I want to say goodbye to Charley alone. If I have to do this, then I'm not doing it with either of them watching.

I can see the stone he's brought for Charley to 'remember' by. What a joke. It's lying next to her dead-looking hand, on the bed. It's grey. It's pure Brackinton, smooth and wave-washed, with a few grains of sand miraculously still clinging to its surface. Just a glance and I can already hear the sea rushing over it. A white line of quartz rises up in a ring around it, breaking up the grey smoothness. It reminds me of so many things: of hot pebbles beneath my feet, of watching a skimmer bounce out to sea; but now, I think, it will always remind me of Dad's hands as he holds it.

'Hi Hal,' he says. I leave, before he tries to get me talking to her, but I can still see him through the square window. I watch as he gently fits the stone into her palm, and folds her fingers over it, clasping her hand. When Dad holds Charley she looks so small again. It reminds me of bedtime and picture books.

Here's a little baby,

One, two, three,
Stands in his cot,
What does he see?
Peepo!

He holds her hand over the stone, wrapping it up in his own.

'So Charley can't come to the beach? Well, the beach'll just have to come to Charley, then. Do you remember the stones?' he asks her. 'And the rock where we take your photo every year?'

His voice is like the waves themselves, it rises and falls, it lulls. If I was Charley, I wouldn't want to wake up, ever, when I heard it. I'd just want to go right on sleeping.

'We're going back, Charley, and you'll be with us. We'll watch the sun sink over the sea, and I'll climb to the top of the rock for you.'

His hand gently strokes hers as he talks, but then he stops, as though suddenly just holding her hand isn't nearly enough, and he heaves her into his arms, where she flops in his lap like a great big ugly baby, and I wonder how they can do it, Mum and Dad, even though I already know what they'd say if I asked.

'We love her, Hal, just as we love you.'

Well, I love Charley too, but it doesn't mean she doesn't look revolting.

She does.

Listening to Dad I suddenly know exactly what to bring her – even if it is ridiculous.

He tucks her head under his chin and rocks her. Her toes look blue and cold, sticking out of her jeans. They dress her every morning, just like she cared. Just like she was HERE, for Chrissake.

'I can't surf for you, love.' Dad's still talking, and he laughs for a moment, at the thought of himself on a surfboard. It makes me smile too.

'You'll have to come back and do that for yourself. Oh, Charley,' and he runs out of words at last, and just sits and holds her. Rocking and rocking – and somewhere, deep under his breath, I think that maybe he's chanting her name, like a charm. Like it's a chain that could hold her to him: like it's all that they have left between them.

I leave them to it.

OK, it's finally my turn to say goodbye, and I'm here, at the gates of hospital hell with a surfboard in my hand. People are staring. So? I stare back. Who cares? Not me. I've got a half-dead sister. I don't have to care about people staring. I hit the door hard with my hand and prop the board against the bed.

'Wotcha, gravy bum!' I reckon Charley's had it with everybody being nice. I've listened to them all telling her where she is, and how much we all love her. I reckon there's one thing, and one thing only, that'll bring Charley back, and that's her knowing that right now I've got something she hasn't.

A life.

'Hey, I brought you this.'

I put the surfboard next to the bed. She doesn't move. Her sheets go up and down, up and down, marking out where she's breathing.

'Can't you see it?' I ask.

Up. Down. Up. Down.

No answer.

'Have it your own way, shit-face.' Still no answer, not yet.

I grab her hand and flop it on to the tip of the board. I don't like touching her, it feels like the taste of warmed-up leftovers. It looks so stupid now it's here – the surfboard, I mean. It looks so huge in the tiny room, and it's impossible to believe that the dead-looking Charley in the bed ever stood on it and rode the waves.

'Didn't get much use out of it, did you?'

She just carries right on breathing, but suddenly I'm sure she's there. She's right behind that freaky breath and those closed eyes, and she's listening and she loves it, all of us crowding round to say our goodbyes, begging her to still be alive.

Before I know it I'm up close, right next to her empty face, and I'm angry, really angry.

'Bitch!' I hear myself say. I'm horrified, but I can't stop.

'You just don't give a toss, do you? Mum, Dad, me, Sara. You just lie there breathing. WAKE UP.' Just as I'm shouting at her, a nurse walks past, looks in through the window and goes off.

I lean over again, and hiss in her face.

'Wake up, Charley, and if you can't do that, at least have the friggin' decency to die.'

This time the nurse does come in. She checks Charley's pulse and eyes me over.

Easy, I tell myself.

'All right?' she asks. I smile and nod.

'Tough, saying goodbye to your sister?'

'It's only a month, give or take.'

'Hard for your parents, though.'

'Yep.' I get up.

'Gotta go. Sayonara, sis,' I say to Charley, 'sorry we won't be seeing you on the waves this year.'

The nurse gives me a strange look, and then she catches sight of the surfboard, with Charley's hand still pretending to touch it, and her eyes go all soft on me.

I know exactly what she's seeing; haven't I been looking in mirrors all year, separating out all the bits into mine and Charley's?

Hair: all my own, as dirty and blond as Charley's is clean, red and golden.

Skin: olive. I'm browner than Charley. She was always pale and cold in winter, brown and freckled in summer. Now, she's always white, like a permanent winter – and her skin's like snow, covering her bones in silence. I'm 'ruddy' as Dad calls it, but personally I prefer 'olive'.

Height: hey! I'm pretty sure I'm taller than she is now, but it's hard to really know without lying right down beside her.

31

No thanks.

Eyes: same shape, same horribly long girly lashes, and same desire to just blend in with their surroundings. Looking into her eyes was like seeing my own.

'You could be twins,' Mum used to say, 'born back-to-back!' and it feels like that sometimes, with Charley being gone. Like I've had to shut the door on a piece of my own soul.

'Hey!' says the nurse. I look up at her, and I realize I've been staring at Charley, staring as though if I could only take the picture I have of her in my mind – if I could only drag and drop it from me to her, lay it over her, like a blanket – then she might re-animate, might wake up, might BE here.

'You have a good time, now,' says the nurse, 'and don't you worry about Charley at all, we'll take good care of her.'

I stare at her. And you can sod off, I think, I've had enough of sympathy, I've had sympathy till it's coming out my arse. Know what? It doesn't work. It doesn't change a thing.

'You're the gravy bum!' I'm sure I hear Charley say it, it sounds as clear as day, and the nurse seems to flicker and jump too, but there's nothing doing. When I look up Charley's still just lying there breathing, same as ever, and the rest – well, the rest is nothing but imagination and wishes.

Charley: Hospital. Now.
'Wotcha, gravy bum!'

Who said that?

I'm in a cupboard. A dark cupboard, and it's too small for me. The walls press against my flesh, stilling me, and something's holding my head, holding it so hard that I can't turn my eyes to see.

The whole cupboard lurches, rocking. Oh no! It's beginning to fall, I can feel it all around me, falling, but I can't move.

My stomach drops.

'Wotcha, gravy bum!'

The words separate and stand right up, pushing themselves up out of the dim hum of sounds.

The cupboard I'm in hits the floor with a bone-jolting crash, and through a chink of light where the door is barely open, I think I can hear voices.

So many voices.

'Help me!'

Hal. Now.

I walk through the hospital corridors. I'm on a mission to escape; if I can make it to the doors without stopping, none of this will have happened. But just as I'm about to clear the revolving door, Sara arrives with Mum. She's carrying a plant. There's only one red flower on it: a deep red, tightly curled flower. It reminds me of something, but I can't think what.

'I buyed Charley a flower.' She smiles up at me.

'Can you take her in, Hal?' asks Mum. 'I want a last word with the nurses before we go.'

'Mum, I've already said goodbye, I—' I take one look at her face and back off. 'Come on, Sarz, let's hurry!' I want her to be quick, I want it to be over. I can hear the sea calling.

Sara's surely a natural when it comes to talking total nonsense to someone who can't even hear you. She just gabbles on and on at Charley, happy not to be interrupted for once. She doesn't ask the difficult questions now, like: 'Why doesn't Charley wake up any more?' or 'Mummy, why is Charley so tired?'

She dumps her flower on the floor, where it nods on its narrow stem, as though it's about to break.

'It's for Charley,' she says.

Sara sits by Charley and holds her hand, just as she's been told she always should.

'Charley,' she begins, as though she was a teacher in small school, 'I found a flower that's better than all your dreamin'. Mummy took me to the shop an' we looked an' looked an' we found a flower . . . look! You can touch it! If you open your eyes, you can see it . . .'

I begin to day-dream; Sarz can go on like this for hours.

Sadly, Hal Ditton has failed in his mission to escape; he has been caught and tagged by the system, he will now have to forfeit the rest of his life to the—

It's a while before I notice the silence. Sara's looking at Charley, really looking at her, and she's not saying anything at all.

'Do you want to wake up and touch the flower, Charley?' she asks after a while, and shoots me a look, like she's done something she shouldn't. She looks scared.

'Hey Sara, it's all r—' I begin, because it has to be all right for Sara. Sara's the one who keeps it all normal, who doesn't really know what life's like without a half-dead sister. It's Sara who says all the things we can't say, in her bright crazy voice, like none of it matters.

'Is she dead, Hal?' she asks after a while, and she begins to shake, even though it's still boiling hot.

'I don't know. We don't know, Sara.'

She looks at the beautiful flower she's bought for Charley. (*'You could at least say thank you, bitch.'*)

'It won't hurt her, will it, Hal?' she asks.

'No, Sara. It won't hurt her,' I promise.

A new nurse comes in then. She's all kind and lovely to us, but she speaks to Charley like she's a doll, or a pretend person, and that makes me sad and angry all at the same time.

'That's my sister,' I say. What a dork – like she doesn't already know that.

'An' mine,' joins in Sara, 'and I buyed a flower an' it will look after her when we are goin' to Corn-wall.'

'We'll look after her. Don't you worry,' and the nurse strokes Charley's brow, just like Mum does when we're ill and feverish.

The nurse's hands look cool and soft as they tuck a stray strand of hair behind Charley's ear. I turn away quickly.

Abort Mission! Abort Mission! Get out of there, Ditton!

'You all have a good holiday, now, and look after those

parents of yours.'

'We DO!' Sara's back now, and in full flow.

'Come on, Sara, we've gotta go.'

The nurse looks up sharply, Charley's limp wrist still hanging from her hand.

'You haven't said goodbye.'

Sara grabs Charley's limp hand and kisses it. I feel sick.

Your time is up, you have thirty seconds to leave the room. Leave the room . . .

'Bye Charley, love you,' she shouts.

'Sayonara, sis, the waves are calling.'

'They'll be back before you know it,' the nurse says to her blank face.

Up. Down. Up. Down, goes the breath.

'Not if I can help it,' I laugh, but the nurse doesn't smile, just gives me that sad look that people give you – you know, the one where you're in such a shit place that no one's even allowed to actually feel angry with you.

Charley: Hospital. Now.
So many voices . . . beyond the door . . . voices shouting and broken . . . words that don't match or make sense.

Why is it so dark?

Because my eyes are shut? They are – tight shut and squeezing. I try to open them.

I can't.

I push hard at the sides of the cupboard all around me, I lean

36

on them with all my weight, but nothing moves.

Am I moving, or am I just imagining it?

It's as though the earth is holding me down, packed tight in gravity.

Words hang . . . somewhere just beyond memory.

'Sayonara, sis,' *they say.*

'Get lost, gravy bum!' *says a voice inside me.*

I feel a smile.

A smile is like sunshine.

Hot.

Someone, somewhere beyond me, is crying.

Mum! I can hear her voice! She is saying my name over and over again.

'Charley!'

'Charley!' *I am a little girl sniffing flowers.*

'Charley!' *I am hiding. Can't find me.*

'Charley!' *She rocks me, I am sleeping.*

So many Charleys . . .

'Charlotte Mary Ditton, where are you?'

Mum!

Open! Please, open! I push and push against the sides, but nothing moves, only inside me.

'Charley!'

'Mum!' *I answer, but she doesn't hear me.*

'Oh Charley,' *she whispers, and my heart stops beating at the sound of something in her voice. She's turned my name into a long, drawn-out, desperate, unending cry, and I can see it. See it behind my eyes: my own name, stretched out in letters, wide across the empty sky.*

'Charley!'

She calls my name so that it streaks across the sea and through the night. A shooting star, a lengthening shadow that goes on and on, until it's stretched as thin and fine as a fishing line . . . about to break.

No!

'Mum!' *I shout back, but no sound comes out.*

'Mum!'

Somewhere outside a door closes . . .

Darkness . . .

My name is silent, its light's gone out.

She's gone.

'Help me!'

Hal. Now.

'Help me!'

I hear the words as clear as day. We're standing outside the hospital waiting for Mum. The air seems to shimmer and shift through the sunshine and dust, as though the world isn't solid any more, as though it's lifting before my very eyes, as though the massive grey hospital is about to slide aside and reveal something. I feel my throat close up tight, like it's gasping for air. The heat feels sudden and real, as though it's deliberately draining the power of movement from me, and I hear my lungs heave a great big sighing breath out of air. Then the blood leaves my head, and everything goes small, like I'm seeing it through the wrong end of a telescope.

'Don't,' I whisper to the feeling, but it doesn't feel stoppable.

'*Charley!*' Her name comes up like a punch in the gut, just as Mum appears through the swing doors.

'All done,' she says, and the sound of her voice feels like bones breaking. We walk to the car. I'm shaking and holding on to Sara's hand. Mum opens the car door and collapses inside. It's like she's been hit by an invisible fist – I can SEE the life draining out of her. It's frightening – it's like suddenly she's having trouble staying alive too.

Maybe that's what happens, I hear myself think. Maybe when their children are dying, mums start to die too. She tries to come to life again, for me and Sara, but she can't do it.

'*Help me!*'

Charley's voice, definitely Charley's voice. I look around as though I might see her, sitting in the car next to me, scowling.

'All right?' asks Mum.

'Fine.'

I look at my watch. I listen to it ticking. I concentrate on it, hard. It says the day is Friday. It says the time is 4.15. It says the month is July. The date is July 15th, the day we always go to Cornwall.

But never without Charley.

Charley: Hospital. Now.

'*Help me!*'

But they've gone.

'This one's not going anywhere.' *The voice is outside the cupboard.*

I try to move away from it, but I can't. I'm trapped tight. Hurts; voice has hard, sharp edges, it tears. Makes my head ache to hear it.

'And where are the family again?' it says.

Where am I?

I'm trapped in a cupboard.

Locked in tight.

'Help me!'

'They've gone somewhere called Brackinton Haven . . . go every year apparently, can't imagine it myself, going to the same place every year . . .'

Brackinton Haven . . . the word clings, connects with something inside . . . and . . .

. . . suddenly I'm in a kitchen, a bright white kitchen, with sunshine falling through the windows. . .I watch the two people talking . . . is one of them me?

Charley. Then.

'Let's just see, Charley,' says Mum.

'Mum! C'mon, even Julie's going to Greece this year.'

'No!' says Mum. 'I don't care what Jenna, Sally, or Julie for that matter, are doing. You, young lady, are coming with us to Brackinton.'

'Please, I'm begging. I'll wash up for a year.'

Mum's laughing, she holds the glass that she's cleaning right up to the light, and it shines all the way through.

'No, sweetheart, the answer's no. You are not going to Italy with Jenna, you are coming to Brackinton with us. Maybe next year.'

'Next year, next year's forever away . . . I could be DEAD by next year.'

'Charley!'

Charley: Hospital. Now.

Am I dead?

Is it a cupboard holding me tight? Or is it a . . .

'Mum!'

But I'm too late, the sunlight is dissolving her face. New faces shiver in the darkness; shiver and take substance . . .

Jenna, and Sal, and me . . .

The sunlight falls on us . . . we're sitting under a tree in a wide green field. Somewhere below us, a river sparkles.

Charley. Then.

'She says maybe next year. NEXT YEAR! Can you BELIEVE it?'

'Don't whinge,' says Jenna. 'The thought of all those surfers!' And she pretends to shake with pleasure, and roll her eyes, and knock her knees together.

'For you, maybe, Jenna!' 'Cos Jenna's built like Marilyn Monroe, only not blonde.

'I dunno,' she says, 'they seem to quite like the skinny look, and you should thank your lucky stars you're in Cornwall. Have you ever seen Italian boys on the beach?'

'No, worse luck – and no chance either, thanks to my dinosaur of a mum.'

'Charley,' says Jenna, 'if only you knew, Italian boys are far more interested in how their own arses look than any woman's.'

'And how do they look?' asks Sal. Jenna bursts into giggles, and when she laughs, we all laugh, it's just impossible not to. It's like the bubbles in the Italian Prosecco she drinks – irresistible!

'Tell you what,' she suggests, 'I'll take notes and we can compare. "A comparative study of the posteriors of three nations: England, France and Italy." How do you think Mrs Shirley-Browne would like that one as a project?'

'As long as it was well researched she probably wouldn't mind,' I say.

Sal bows down before me.

'Oh, so sorry, forgot your little crush on old S-B.'

'Text us. Promise you'll text.'

'I'll text.'

Charley: Hospital. Now.

. . . and they begin to fade, to fade away to darkness, slipping through my mindless fingers . . . no . . . no . . . please . . . wait . . .

Then I hear the noise of an engine, the shift of a gear; the car is grinding up a hill. I hold on to the noise and slowly, so slowly, the picture comes . . . Brackinton.

Charley. Then.

We're over the hill and I can see the sea, the bright blue sea. The sun dances off the white caps, and my heart leaps, and I'm glad after all that I'm here, I can't help it. I love Brackinton, and this year I'm going to take Sal and Jenna's advice.

They are sooo right. So Mum and Dad love not having to socialize for a month – doesn't mean I can't. No more looking out over the valley from the terrace, no more being stuck in the garden dancing with Hal, watching the bonfires on the beach – I'm out there.

I'm scared.

'I'm not staying in all the time,' I say to Mum.

'Quite right,' she agrees, 'you need to join in more.' That takes the wind out of my sails a bit.

'I want to go over to the camp site, make friends.'

'Yes. Look Charley, we just hadn't realized you were getting older, OK?'

'Too right.'

'And we don't want you disappearing for the whole summer.'

'Fat chance.'

'All I ask is that you don't forget Hal completely.'

'Look Mum, it's very not OK to have your little bro hanging round 24/7.'

Mum gives me that look she always gives me when I talk school.

'Very cool,' she says, and her own voice is cool, as cool

as minted ice. 'I think you forget sometimes, Charley, just how very much you like Hal's hero worship.'

'OK, Mum. But I mean it. No Bluebeard's Castle this year.'

Because what Mum always says when we step into the kitchen at Brackinton, is this:

'What bliss, no friends and no strangers.'

She's not horrid or anything – it's just that at home it's so completely non-stop all year, and Brackinton's their couple time, and our family time.

Mum and Dad.

Mum and Dad REALLY like each other. I mean REALLY, like they still stay up at night chatting and laughing, even though they're ancient. In Brackinton my earliest memories are of hearing the sea, and their voices in the night, all mingled together with the waves rushing over the stones.

Charley: Hospital. Now.

Dad . . . Dad.

I can hear his voice as it chants my name . . . rocking me in my sleep. He folds my hand over a stone, cool-ridged . . . smooth . . . still sandy. I touch it, and slowly I begin to hear the sea pounding against the beach.

I'm holding a stone.

The waves rise and crash and the air smells of clean fish and salt, only there's something missing, something in the air . . . that's . . . I reach for the sound, and slowly it comes to me. A high call on the air, a lonely keening over the water, joined by another and another. Wings beat in my ears, and a word drops from the sky:

'Gulls,' and as soon as I catch it, I hear his voice.

'Aggressive things, shoot 'em, I say.'

'Dad?'

Beard against my face, like pressing myself into warm, warm sand, my cheek sinking into its soft prickliness.

Are the tears I feel inside me actually falling, falling to turn it wet?

No, it's the stone that falls, from my hand, and with the fastest flick of a fish tail the words and memories are gone.

Dark.

'Where are you all?

I'm alone.'

Hal: Brackinton. Now.

'I'm alone.'

The words arrive inside me just as we clear the hill-top, and I can see the sea spread out below us. The sudden sight of it takes away my power to breathe, to move. I look at it; I remember how me and Charley always wanted to be the first to see it. Then it hits me: everything looks exactly the same, everything – the cliffs, the sea, the beach – only Charley's not here. No one's racing ahead of me to be there first.

'I'm alone.'

I watch the gulls swoop up and away from the garden, the way they always do when we arrive.

'Shoot 'em, I say,' says Dad. Doesn't he ever get tired of

the same jokes?

The house stands waiting, quiet and empty up on the cliff, and we all look up at it, as though we can't quite believe it's still here.

'C'mon Hal, don't just stand there, grab a bag and get moving.'

We climb up the thirty-two steep steps up the cliff, over and over again, until the car's finally empty, and our legs are shaking.

'Here we go!' says Dad, and he lifts up the old key from the tin by the door and fits it into the lock. Sara's jumping up and down and asking if she can sleep in the blue room.

'Shh, Sara!' says Mum, suddenly, and she turns and looks right past me. I wonder for a moment what she can see, because I can feel something. Something behind my shoulder, as though Charley's standing behind me, right behind me, and her voice is whispering in my ear.

'*Get on with it, Dad, for Chrissakes,*' she says.

'Charley?' I turn around, but there's nothing – nothing but empty space. Have I said anything?

Dad turns the key in the lock and opens the heavy oak door.

'Hello. Hello, we're here, we're here, house!' yells Sara, disappearing up the stairs.

The sun falls into the house, lighting up the wooden hallway.

Home.

I can't move.

I stand on the terrace with the sea in my ears and the sun shining on my face. From somewhere far away, behind the sound of the sea and beneath the heat of the sun, I think I can hear Charley's breath, her hospital breath, falling over me in waves.

In. Out. In. Out.

It blocks out the house, the door, the sea and the sand. It wipes out everything around me.

'Hal?' asks Mum, questioning. I smile at her as she stands in the hallway with the sun all around her, like a halo, but I can't answer her. All I can hear is that mechanical, machine-like breath, and the inaudible hum that surrounds it. I notice that my legs aren't just shaking any more, they aren't working at all.

I can't move.

It feels like the whole world has just stepped right back and left me stranded.

It's still revolving, but somewhere else, simply moving on without me.

'I'm alone.' The feeling fills me, echoing all around the hall, and inside me.

'Hal!' Mum shouts, irritated. 'Stop standing around like a dropped divot,' and it's as though she's turned a lock, or something; somehow she's freed me.

'Hey!' I grin at her, 'cos the motor's back and the legs are moving.

'You are so . . . so . . . TEENAGE sometimes!' she finally manages.

'Easy, Mum!' I grin again, and she smiles back.

'Put this stuff in the fridge and then go and unpack.'

'Sure.'

And we both pretend we haven't noticed the spasm of pain that flits across her face at the sight of all the Charley photos still hanging on the kitchen wall.

Charley: Hospital. Now.

'I'm alone.'

I can see them all – but I'm not there.

Dad puts the old rusty key in the lock. 'Here we go!' he says.

'Get on with it, Dad, for Chrissakes,' I snap at him, but he doesn't answer – just carries right on, as though I'm not there. Only Hal turns, turns and looks at me, staring at the empty space as though he might have seen me.

'Charley?' he whispers, like I'm a secret.

And then he moves into the house, and they're gone again.

Dark.

Suddenly, I'm lying on my back in the warm sand. The sky above is so blue, blue, blue . . . my body sinks deeper and deeper into the warm sand, until I can feel each separate grain, holding me up to face the sky.

Get up, says a harsh voice inside me, get up, now!

'I can't!' I shout back, and as soon as the words are there I know that it's true.

I can't move. I can't move. I can't move.

'I can't move.'

There is no cupboard . . . I am not trapped . . . there is only me, not moving.

I scream and scream, but there's no sound coming out of me, and all I can see is an endless, free-wheeling, gull-less sky above me.

'Hal!' I see his eyes staring at me.

Our eyes, that change like the weather.

I lock on to them.

'Oh, Hal! Where am I? Help me!'

Hal: Brackinton. Now.

I can't sleep. Our room's exactly the same. Same beds, same covers, same window looking straight out to sea – but no Charley. Outside, the stars hang and the sea's high and wild; somewhere above the roar of the waves I think I can hear her voice mixed in with the wind and the surf and the dark, scudding clouds.

'Hal! Where am I? Help me!'

When morning finally arrives, it's hard to believe this is the same sea as last night, or that I'm really here. I open the window and breathe it all in, fresh and alive. The sharp, salt tang of it is so different from the dead Oxford air.

'Over there, Hal,' says the whisper in my head, 'look over there.'

'No.' I say it firmly. I don't want to look at the rocks where I found Charley. I do not want to remember. I look away from the rocks, and the sand, and the memories that I'd somehow forgotten would still be here, waiting. I look out over the village instead.

The surfers chill into the Cabin Café, fresh from the

early morning tide, and eat Brooke's huge breakfasts. I watch, and for a moment it's as though Charley's right beside me.

'Hey Hal, six o'clock,' I hear her say. I look. Straight ahead is a surf god.

'I'm too tasty for my breakfast!' The words just land in my head, but I know that they're not mine, really, that they're Charley's. They say it all. There's a guy who thinks he's better than a cooked breakfast.

I look away.

Mum's standing on the terrace, scanning the sea. I watch her step up on to the low wall, her hand raised to block out the early sunlight. She stares out to sea, all alone against the sky, like a sailor in a crow's nest, searching. I'm surprised by how thin she suddenly seems, surrounded by all that blue. She looks as though the lightest breeze could lift her up and carry her away, far away, across the sea. I watch as her head swivels on her neck and her arm lifts and waves. She's found what she's looking for, Sara and Dad in the sea. She smiles to herself with relief. She's always watching now, counting us in, gathering us up like sheep, as though that could somehow save us from harm.

'I hate you, Charley. You did this.'

I find this thought in my head a lot these days. I hate what she's done to all of us. Here we are, stuck in a half-life, like some nuclear dump, with millions of years to go before the poison burns itself away. I know then what I wish Mum would say, and it's this:

50

'She's dead, Hal, she's gone.'

But she doesn't; she just spots me up at the window, and waves, turning away now, as though once she's caught me, pinned me down and numbered me, she can forget me. She's muttering to herself:

'I wonder . . . and if . . . oh, I don't know!' she ends, with a sigh. The half-words float up past me, and I wonder what the hell she means. What decision could any of us possibly make that would change anything? What, I suddenly hear myself wonder, what the hell are we doing here anyway?

Dad and Sara run up, yelping from the cold and the sea.

'Come on out, sleepy head,' yells up Dad.

I go down. The air is beginning to warm up; it's going to be hot. Sara leaps into my lap – she pushes her cold wet head under my chin and snuggles in. Her hair slips so neatly over her scalp, sleek and wet, like sealskin.

'We was swimmin' in the sea, Hal.'

'I know.'

Dad smiles down at us both like his face will crack with pleasure at the sight.

'I think it's going to be hot,' he says. We all look up, and the sun stares back at us, and there's this moment, a moment when we're all still, and everything feels perfect; there's the warm, warm sun, the white-wash hum of the sea, and the feel of the air, all dropping and still.

Then the moment passes, and we're silent, each of us not saying what we know to be true: that it can never really be perfect for any of us, ever again, and that Mum can never sigh in that old way she once had, of being full-up and happy, just because the sun's shining.

'Are you alnite?' Sara asks, anxiously.

'All night what?' asks Dad, and we all laugh.

'All rrrrr-ight.' She pushes her mouth and tongue around the word, pushing the moment away from us, but not before Mum catches it.

'No, Sara sweetheart,' she says suddenly, 'we're not all right.'

We all stop and stare at her. Sara moves over to sit on Mum's lap, and tries to fit her small arms all the way around her.

'There, there,' she says. 'What is it?'

'We miss Charley,' says Mum, getting up. 'Anyone want a cup of tea?'

And the words come down across my mind again, like a shutter.

'Where am I, Hal?

I'm alone!'

'We all are, Charley,' I whisper, and it's true. Sara is standing staring after Mum's retreating back, Dad's looking out to sea, his eyes squinting against the light, and I'm noticing that my hands feel suddenly empty and useless.

I pick up the binoculars, and for one crazy moment I think I might see Charley through them. I wonder if her eyes are somehow guiding me as I look out, over to the camp site, away from Mum and Dad and Sara.

From our side of the valley, the tents seem to string

themselves out in different colours across the hillside. The pattern shifts all the time; some tents are just there for a night and gone before you know it, others are whole tent-empires. There are bikes, windbreaks, kitchen areas, kids' tents next to adult tents, even washing lines. They're here for the whole of the summer, just like we are.

I zoom in on one tent that's been here for years, just like us. It's not really a tent as such, it's a yurt – a round tent with a flue coming out of the middle of its pitched roof. That's how we first noticed it, early one morning, years ago, when we saw the smoke drifting out of the metal flue.

'Cool!' I remember Charley saying.

'Help me! Hal, don't leave me!'

I shake my head, focus in on the tent, but it's weird, it's almost like Charley's with me, watching. Watching like a high hawk, far above, just waiting to swoop. I shake my head again, refocus the lenses.

The family has two children, a boy older than me, and a girl; well, it's difficult to tell how old she is. There she is! She comes out of the door and looks around. She's laugh-ing, and she glances up at our house and turns away, calling to someone inside. She's tall and thin with a chain around her ankle. It's like she senses someone's watching, and she turns back and looks straight at me. I spin a dial and her face nearly fills the circle.

Whoa! Talk about freckles, they're all over her nose. She's scanning the hillside, looking for something. I watch her as her eyes graze across the sky behind me, and she gasps.

I turn around – what's she seen? A buzzard, an eagle? Charley? But when I look up, the sky behind me is empty. I swing the binoculars back up to my eyes, towards her, and there she is, right in frame, laughing.

'Made ya look!' she says, or something like it, and she waves at me, a friendly wave. I wave back, but I can already feel my face burning under my skin. Div! I hear Charley's voice again.

'How many times do I have to tell you, duh-brain? Make sure the sun's behind you before you use the binocs.'

'Seen something you like, Hal?' Mum's back with the tea, and grinning away at me like a lunatic.

'Well, at least you're happy,' I mutter to myself, as she holds out her hand for the binocs. She makes as if to look over to the site.

'Muuum,' I wail, and she laughs at me, handing them back.

'As if I would. Hope she's good enough for you, Hal.'

'Why do you assume I'm looking at a girl?'

'Because I can see her waving at you?' She laughs.

'Glad you find it so amusing, Ma.' But she just gives me that annoying smile, like she doesn't actually find it amusing as such, oh no, she's just feeling a whole bunch of other things that I can't possibly imagine, me just being a kid an' all.

I see the girl again later, as early evening falls and the rocks begin to make long deep shadows on the sand, turning it from gold to brown. All the day trippers have gone, and the wind drops, quiet and relieved, as though it's finally managed to blow them all away.

The older kids from the site build barbies high up on the rocks, under the cliffs, and play music. The girl is heading down to the beach. Her wet suit's folded down around her waist, and her skin's touched golden by the sun. I wonder if she's got freckles on her shoulders too.

'Hey, Jack!' someone shouts, and she waves.

'On my way,' she shouts back. The sound of her voice carries up above the soft push and pull of the sea, floating on the still air all the way up to the terrace. She glances up at the house again, but my head's turned away. I look at her out of the corner of my eye. I watch her all the way across the road and down the slipway, until she disappears towards the smell of charcoal and smoke, is swallowed up by the sound of the waves and the music.

God! I wish I was with her; I wish I was anywhere but here.

'Drink, Milly?' Dad asks Mum, as he throws Sara high in the air, in between shifting coals and sausages. Sometimes I look at him and think: what would you do, Dad, if we all disappeared, and you had no one left to care for?

Right then he decides to stick a fork in a sausage, and the thought of us all disappearing, leaving him standing there with an empty fork in his hand, looking around for his sausages and his family, makes me laugh out loud, makes me feel needed. He looks up and smiles.

'Penny for 'em, Hal?' he asks, as he always does.

'Cost way more'n that,' I tell him back, like I always do.

'You go off, love,' he says to Mum. 'I'll hold the fort here.'

She looks up at Dad digging around in his sausages, and she laughs too. I look up, 'cos it's a real laugh, a proper Mum chuckle. It's not loud, more like something inside her is smiling at something else inside her, that no one else can see.

'Do you know, Jon, I don't think I feel like a walk on the beach tonight. I'd rather stay here.'

And it makes me feel that I should stay here too, even though I wish I was out on the beach, with the girl and the faint drift of music; but maybe, I think, maybe for tonight, just the one child missing is enough.

That's when I see someone crossing the road beneath the house. He looks up and stares, and I'm wondering what he wants, because there's the weirdest look on his face, and I'm about to ask him, 'Yeah, what is it?' – but something stops me. He's stand-up-knock-down–drop-dead-gorgeous, even I can see that, and he's staring right at me in a seriously freaky way. I open my mouth to speak, but there are no words in there, just this sudden, surprising feeling of blood pressure falling, and it's like there's a wave under my feet, dragging me out to sea. My head's dizzy and fractured, and the world's only visible through the smallest pinprick of light. I hear Charley's freaky breath:

In. Out. In. Out.

And by the time I look up, he's gone.

'Hal?' asks Mum, 'Brain wave?' 'Cos clearly I've sat down

too suddenly in the grass, even if I can't remember doing it.

'I'm fine,' I tell them.

'Growing pains!'

They both say this at the same time, and I stop myself saying, 'Make a wish.' Instead we just look at each other, and smile over at Sara.

Sad smiles.

She's picking up bits of grass and looking them over carefully, before stuffing the best bits down her trousers. She looks up and sees us all smiling at her.

'Me too!' she says, and Mum and Dad laugh, and just for a millisecond we almost feel like a whole family again.

Hal. Next day.

The sea breeze lifts the thin curtains at the window, and the salt-fish smell of it reminds me that I'm here, here in Cornwall, in Charley's bed. I wake up sweating and panting and gasping for breath as the last pieces of the dream fade away. I'm chasing . . . chasing Charley, hard, but I can't catch her. There's a river ahead, and she dives in, arcing into the water in a flash of light so smooth and sure that there isn't even a ripple.

I'm at the bank, searching the fast-flowing water, but it moves on, as if she was never there beneath it. I'm taking my shoes off, but I can't control my hands, I can't make them hurry.

I dive into the water, just where I think she went in. I

can't see anything; the mud swirls around me, hiding her. I panic – I won't be able to find her and she'll die, and it will all be because of me. And that's when I see it, her plait, waving in the water just ahead of me, all red and lovely. And I grab hold of it and pull, and she's so easy to carry through the water, so light, as light as my heart feels, now that I've finally found her. And we burst out of the river together, gasping for air and laughing.

I call her name out loud into the raindrops of sunlit water.

'Charley!' I turn to look into her face. I know that I'm going to see her green eyes, alive and wide and dancing with laughter.

'Got me!' she'll yell, and we'll start all over again, the way we always have. Me and Charley. But when I look up it's only her plait that I'm holding; there's no Charley at all, just her lovely, long red plait, flopping in my hand like a dead fish.

She's gone.

'Hal! Help me! Find me!' The words echo through my head, in her voice, but I push her away. I feel like Sara. 'Me too!' I want to say. 'Alone too!'

I look out of the window.

Somewhere inside myself, I still believe that I might see her on the beach, running towards the waves, with her surfboard tucked under her arm, its black cord stretching up from where it's anchored to her ankle. Somewhere inside myself I feel like it must be my fault that she's lying in hospital, with mush for brains.

My eyes sweep across the empty sands, as though if only I could think hard enough – could somehow see clearly, drag and drop, or flick the right switch – then I could surely bring her back to life, wake her up, somehow.

And something, something almost comes to me. The beach is empty, but something in the picture doesn't quite fit, and I'm left with that feeling you get when you know you had something in your hand just a second ago, but suddenly it's not there any more, and you can't remember where you put it – or sometimes, even what it was.

I don't hear Mum come in and stand beside me; I just feel her hand land on my shoulder. God, it makes me jump.

'Whoa there!' she says. 'It's only me.'

'I – I – I –' I stutter, and I can't speak, because for one stupid second I thought, I really thought, that she was Charley, and then the words are tumbling out, before I can stop them, before I can protect Mum from them.

'I dreamt of her, Mum, and when I woke up she was still gone.'

I watch as the words go in. Words are like bullets some-times. Bam, bambambam, and Mum's face crumbles. Boom! Her insides rip apart, and she's just not around any more. That's what it's like. That's why I keep quiet. But this time it's different. This time she sighs and sits on the bed.

'I'm sorry, Mum, I didn't mean . . .'

She takes hold of my shoulders and turns me to face her, like she used to when I was a kid, and gives me a little shake. Her eyes are so sad.

'YOU'RE sorry! Oh, Hal, I'm sorry,' and she puts her arms around me. 'Breakfast?' she says, but I shake my head, I'm not hungry right now; I want to be on my own – get out on the cliffs, where I hope the wind might blow the memory of Charley away. And Mum leaves, quickly, hoping I won't notice the tears already building in her eyes.

I look out of the window again. The tide's turning, the sea's coming in now, racing up the beach and covering the rocks. The thought comes again, much stronger this time, but still just out of reach. Something's missing, what is it?

'Hal!'

That's not my voice. It sounds urgent, desperate. It's as though for a split second I'M Charley, and that I'm calling my own name, trying to tell me something. I need to get out more, I mutter, and I pull on my Quiksilvers and get myself out on to the cliffs before any more weird stuff can happen.

The early morning surfers are out on the sea. From up here, they look like seals relaxing on the waves. Again, an almost-memory leaps and fades; too many surfers, I think, but there are only two or three.

I look out over the cliff tops. I look at the villages, dotted about like Lego. I look at the cows, so high on the hills that the horizon cuts them in two. I look down at the sea. I even look at the cowpats, to see which ones are just right to get a good slide on: crusty on top, smooth underneath.

I look at anything, rather than face the sick feeling of guilt and pain in my stomach every time I remember that red hank of hair in my hand, with no Charley attached. Round and round it all goes in my head, like a merry-go-round, only with pictures and memories instead of horses and music, and somewhere underneath it all, as though she's the one keeping it all turning, is the memory of Charley. I can feel her, ghost-like on my shoulder, following along in the empty space that I've felt beside me ever since we left her in Oxford to come back here, an empty space that's somehow filling itself up with her voice.

'Help me.'

'What do you want?'

I wonder if somehow she's guided me here. I feel a shiver of fear; what if she's waiting for me, hidden somewhere amongst the gravestones of St Juliot's?

As I drop down from the cliff, the wind drops with me. Huge dark green yew trees lean over the lych gate. The grassy pathway to the tiny church muffles my footsteps. The churchyard's deserted and silent. I look around. The old gravestones lean in upon each other, sharp and paper-thin with years; lichen creeps across them, like age. I wish someone was here; anyone, anything, other than the memory of Charley.

'Can you hear the voices?' she used to whisper, creeping up behind me on the sound-deadening grass, a disembodied voice in my ear. I can hear her now, and I turn, scared that I'll see her shadowy form over my shoulder, but it's just another memory, just another Charley game.

I get lost in the memory of her, until I find myself

standing in front of her favourite headstone, wondering: how did I get here?

The headstone's carved on a piece of smooth grey slate, set in the dry-stone wall. It has a picture on it, a stick with a snake curling around it.

Dr. Tregothick
1876

I stand and stare at it. I remember Charley touching it, reaching out as though she could smooth the snake's curves into a straight line, bring it back to life, and make it slither away. And I can hear her voice.

'The story goes like this, Hal,' she groans, in a voice that scares me so much that all I can do is stare at her, waiting for the next bit of the story, longing to know what happens next, waiting for the ending that will set me free.

'It is coming to me through the stone – the voice!' she says, and she stops and stares at me.

'Aha! I almost have it, yes, Dr Tregothick . . . can you hear me, Dr Tregothick?' She nods to herself, as though she's listening hard, and then she holds up her hand, as though to stop an invisible voice in its tracks, and translates for me.

'Dr Tregothick, you are a . . . she was . . . a . . . a WOMAN!' she screeches, and I start to laugh at the anti-climax, and Charley laughs too.

'She was . . .' she goes on, 'she was . . . a FAT woman.'

We're helpless by now, neither of us knowing why, just rolling on the grass with laughter, clutching hold of each other, unable to even hear Mum and Dad telling us to have some respect, to keep quiet.

I reach out and touch the stone myself. I feel the warm curve of the snake's back, cut into the slate, and I wish so much that Charley was here, and that we weren't both so alone. I wish she was here with me, seeing the same things.

'Where are you, Charley?' I ask the still air and the memories, but all I can hear is her terrible breathing in my ear.

In. Out. In. Out.

It fills my head, until there's no room for anything else, until there's only me and Charley, and somewhere at the end of a long, turning tunnel of vision, there's my own hand, touching a piece of smooth grey slate, cut with a stick and a snake.

'Charley!' I hear myself call. 'Where are you?' I hear myself ask.

Because that's what no one can tell me.

Charley: Hospital. Now.

'Charley!'

I hear his voice. I hear it reaching through the darkness and fear that hold me tight and still.

'Where are you?'

'I'm trapped, Hal! In the dark where no one can find me. I can't see.'

Lonely . . . I'm lonely . . . but there's somebody close by, somebody always breathing.

Who is it?

In. Out. In. Out.

'Can you see who, Hal? Are you there?'

'Where are you, Charley?' His voice echoes.

'I don't know! I don't know. I only know I'm trapped here, with the breathing that sounds like waves.'

In. Out. In. Out.

In the darkness.

'Charley!'

His voice pierces the darkness like torch-beams – calling my name back to life, and at the sound of it a picture forms: a picture of a gravestone, and a snake, and a dry-stone wall. I hold the sound of him close, cradle it in my stiff cold hands, and blow on it with hope, until it grows . . . and he is here . . . in my mind's eye . . .

'Hal!'

He stands and stares. I can see him so clearly, his hand flat against the warm stone, staring at it like a lemon. He looks nearly as old as me now, and his hair's darker than it was, a sandy gold, just brushing his shoulders and curling up at the ends. I can't stop looking at him. He looks so sad with those huge grey eyes, as sad and grey as the staring stone.

'Hal.'

I whisper his name, and I reach out for his shoulder, but my hands feel nothing – are empty. I try to trace the curves, feel the warmth of the stone snake's back as it curls around the stick, but it's as though I'm tracing air, as though my hand is only imagining the shapes. I can't feel anything, except perhaps . . . a longing

. . . a longing for him to turn, to turn and to see me.

'Hal! Look at me, Hal!'

That's what I used to say!

Oh, please.

The longing burns, the loneliness stretches out across the empty, aching air that lies between us; and although my body is trapped, rooted to the earth and clinging tight, unable to let go, yet somehow, a ghost of myself, of my loneliness and fear and longing to be seen, rises up and reaches out to touch him.

'Hal?'

Hal: Graveyard. Now.

'Hal?'

'Charley!' I whisper back. I must be mad, standing in a country churchyard, whispering after my dead sister, but just the sound of her name on the air brings her alive somehow, makes her feel real again. If I stand very still I can definitely hear her.

'Hal!'

That's just how she really said it, impatient, demanding: listen to me, Hal. Listen.

'Hey, Hal,' she says again, and this time it sounds so different – it sounds like she's pleased to see me.

Charley: Hospital. Now.

'Hey, Hal.' *I watch as he slowly turns to the empty space at his shoulder.*

He can hear me!

'It's me, Hal, hey, Hal, look at me, Hal. Hey, Hal! But he just stands there, staring, not really believing.

'Can't you see me? Somebody, see me.'

Hal: Graveyard. Now.

I can feel her, over my shoulder. I turn slowly, full of fear and longing. It's her eyes that I imagine, floating in the air behind me, watching – but when I turn, there's nothing there, nothing but another piece of empty space.

'Charleyyyyyy!' I call her name until it echoes over the fields and bounces back at me off the gravestones, and for once it feels so simple: I just want to hear her answer, that's all. I want her answer to fill the air, so that there's no space where she used to be, but it's pointless. I know that the space she's left behind isn't just beside me, it's *inside* me, and it's forever.

Before I know it the tears aren't just hiding behind my eyes any more, the way they have for months, just threatening to fall; they're actually falling, falling down my face like rain, and splattering onto the grass.

Charley: Hospital. Now.

He can't see me!

'Hal, Hal, I'm here. Look at me, Hal. Look at me.'

Oh, please.

His eyes open wide as he turns, and then I watch them empty . . . like watching myself dying in his eyes, until they are a cold empty grey, and he closes them, because it's too unbearable.

I turn away. I can't look at him.
I'm alone again.
Trapped.
Dark.

'No! Hal! Don't leave me! Help me! Why didn't you help me?'

'Why what?' *I hear myself ask, and before I have time to stop it, a picture dances at the edge of my vision. I try to shake it away, but it dances anyway, and I find my head is free, and it is turning, turning to look at the picture, so that I can see . . .*

Charley: Brackinton. Then.
The night it all happened.

I'm in the sea, the waves are high and grey and cold, and I'm caught between the swells as they tower above me.

What am I doing here?

A wave picks me up and lifts me to its height, and I stare out into the endless grey of the world before morning, before the sun has risen and separated the sea from the sky.

Far away, upon the floating grey, a flash of light shines out. Hey! That's our bedroom, its light outlines our house, way up on the cliff, a mass of dim white, sailing out proud against all the grey. Thank God! I'm here, Hal, here!

'Hal!'

The light goes out.

'I'm here, Hal!'

But the light stays off.

The wave drops me down, down, down, and somewhere above me, a dark shadow rises on the waves.

I turn away from the memory, but not before the feeling has me in its grasp.

'Help me.'

Hal: Graveyard. Now.

'Help me, Hal.'

The sound of her voice fills the whole valley, so that even the cloudless sky seems to tremble and shiver before releasing her voice. And I think I can feel her fingers, her horrible hands all nerveless and dead, graze across my face, light as cobwebs – I feel them linger on my eyes, full of longing.

'Get off me!'

I can't help it, I don't want to be anywhere near her dead-looking body under the white sheets. I don't want her to touch me, but I can hear her voice, as clear as a bell, on the sudden breeze from the sea. Charley's voice, only distant and lost and desperate.

'Remember, Hal,' she calls.

And I begin to run, retracing my steps as though I could escape her, as though somewhere at the top of the cliffs, the world will have returned, righted itself, and remembered to have Charley in it.

Anyway, remember what?

I lean against the old wall, high on the cliff. I'm panting for breath, my heart racing as fast as the white-capped waves below me.

Remember what? The question hooks itself in, won't let go.

'Look, Hal,' she says, and far out, somewhere on the sea, a fleck moves: a seal dances, nose up to the light, clears a wave and disappears.

And it's like the trigger's finally gone off, the switch has been flicked.

The memory arrives, complete and whole, as though all it's been doing is waiting for me to see it.

'Remember.'

And I do.

I remember. I remember that night, the night that I woke up and found Charley wasn't there. I remember turning on the light, and just as quickly turning it off again. I remember thinking how it would shine out, like a beacon, telling everybody: something's wrong, she's not here. I remember looking out of the window. The sea was huge, and there was someone on the waves.

I start to run.

When I get home I can hear Mum and Dad's voices on the landing; they're shouting.

'How much longer can we go on like this?' says Dad.

'As long as it takes,' says Mum, steely and cold.

'But for what?' I hear him say. 'And how do we know what she's going through, Milly?' he begs. 'How do we know what it's like for Charley—?'

'Stop! Stop it!' shouts Mum suddenly.

I want him to stop too. Sara's shouting, in the kitchen.

'Don't, Daddy Rabbit, don't,' she shouts, 'it is very dangerous and you'll be put in a pie by Mrs McGregor!'

'Mum! Dad!' They come running down the stairs at the sound of my voice.

'Hal! Hal?' Mum gets to me first. I'm feeling sick with the run and the memory.

'Mum, I remember—' I can't get the words out.

'What?' Their faces are sharp with anger and fright. Mum's white; her hands are gripping my arm so tight it hurts.

'Daddy doesn't mean it, Hal, it's just something we're thinking about. You mustn't worry, this isn't—'

What?

'No, it's me, Mum, me, you don't get it.'

She doesn't hear me. She turns away and walks into the sun room, her fists clenched with anxiety, her breath jagged.

'Whoa there, Hal, hang on a minute,' says Dad. He puts his arms around me, and leads me after her. She turns from the window; behind her the sea's grey and empty, high-sided and heaving. I have to close my eyes not to see, not to remember.

'See?' Mum hisses at Dad, her teeth tight.

'Wait, Mill, let him get his breath, he's had a fright, he hasn't heard us. Slowly there, little man, one breath at a time, now.' He takes off my rucksack.

'Bloody hell – weighs a ton, son, no wonder you're breathless,' and when I don't laugh, he sits me down on the sofa. Sara's voice floats through from the kitchen:

'Stop frightening the children, says Mummy Rabbit, or I'LL put you in a pie myself!'

None of us laugh.

I can feel Dad's hand over the thumping of my heart. Black and red globes are dancing across Mum's back, and the sound of Charley's horrible breathing fills my mind:

Up. Down. Up. Down.

Like losing sight of her in the waves.

I hold on tight to Dad's arms, my head rammed into his chest, but the picture still comes . . . I close my eyes, but the memory just plays itself on, behind them, although all I want to do is to turn the other way.

'Remember.'

In my mind's eye I watch as Charley, lifted by another wave, then falls back and disappears, floating in the gap between the rollers.

'Hal, it's OK, Hal.' Dad's doing his chanting thing, saying my name over and over, 'Hal, Hal, Hal,' and it makes me shiver, it reminds me of how he is now with her – with Charley.

'Put his head down, Jon, he looks like he's going to faint.' I throw up then, great gobs of it splatting onto the floor. Mum's hand is on my forehead, holding me up.

'It's all right, love, better out than in.'

'But Charley, I saw her, that night—'

'I've told you, Hal, nothing's been decided yet.'

What's she on about? Why won't she listen?

They work like a team then, Mum untying my gruesome trainers and Dad holding me against him, getting my fleece off.

'Come on, upstairs, clean clothes.'

'But, Mum, it was me! I woke up. I saw her that night, I could have told you, I could have—'

'Enough, Hal! One thing at a time.'

Dad hauls me up the stairs, Mum goes to get fresh clothes. God, I feel tired, like I could sleep forever. Mum comes in smelling of disinfectant and sick. I sit on the edge of the bath and close my eyes, but the picture just keeps on coming: a small black shadow on the heaving waves, a dot between night and day.

Charley.

'Mum?'

'Oh, Hal!' she says, and I look up at her. At her face that is so like and so not like Charley's. She looks so sad and old. She's sad for me, and I can't bear that; it's bad enough watching her be sad for Charley. She sits beside me and wraps her arms around me.

'Only-boy,' she whispers. 'What is it?'

'Oh, Mum, I just—'

'What's this?' Dad appears in the doorway, filling the frame. 'You,' and he points at me, 'a couple of hours in bed, and then we'll see if we can still make it to Tintagel.'

I brush my teeth, longing to collapse into bed, but longing

72

as well to tell them what I'm seeing. I try one last time:

'Dad, that morning, Charley—' I begin, but he isn't hearing me, he's looking at Mum.

'All right?' he whispers to her, so gently that the air barely stirs at his words, and she nods back at him, her green eyes so big and full of unshed tears that she can't speak. And I know then that they're together, and I am alone. Alone in a place where they can't even seem to see me, let alone hear me.

'Yes, but, oh Jon, I can't even THINK about it, not yet, and look at Hal . . .'

'Hal?' asks Dad.

'I'm all right, Dad.'

And he believes me – he turns back to her.

'Milly.' He whispers, but I can still hear every word. It's as though the whole world has stopped spinning for a second, and held up its hand for quiet, just so every single word has crystal-clear edges:

'I just want us to be able to think about it, Mill, not necessarily to do it.'

She holds her hand up to his lips, stopping him, and smiles over at me, worried.

'Not now!' she says, and she turns away from him, to me. 'C'mon, young man, rest!' she says, and I wish I was five again, and could be carried up the stairs, knowing for sure that when morning came, everything would be all right again; but I'm not, and it isn't.

They're hiding something from me. What does Dad

want Mum to think about? I stand up and walk away from them, ears wide open and waiting, but they follow me silently, wait till I'm in bed and then disappear.

I lie down. As soon as I close my eyes I can see her, not the usual picture of her on the rock, happy and laughing. She's alone on the sea, riding the hugest wave I've ever seen, a smudge of a shadow, darting across a wall of darkness, on a sliver of white board, as it rolls towards land.

I know that I could never do what she does, that I'm not brave and wild like Charley. I'd much rather just watch and have a cup of tea, like Dad.

And that's when I see something else. I look hard at the picture in my mind as it shifts across the beach towards the street light. I hold my breath tight as my eyes slow and focus, focus on the darkness cast by the orange light. Can I see someone, a shape deep in the shadow? The darkness seems to move, and the picture fades.

So Charley wasn't alone! Who was it? Did she know someone was there? Who was watching her on the waves?

'Help me!'

Maybe she didn't get picked up by a wave and land on a rock.

'Remember.'

'Right,' says Mum, appearing suddenly. 'What's going on, Hal?'

'I – I don't know,' I stutter, 'but I remember something, Mum.'

'What do you remember, sweetheart?' she says, and it

feels a bit weird, the way she's talking; it feels like she's been expecting this all along, is ready for it.

'I saw Charley, early that morning, I saw her in the sea on the waves.'

'Yes?' is all she says, waiting for me to continue, as though she knows there must be more.

'You don't get it, Mum, I could've woken you up, I could've saved her!'

Mum smiles at me and reaches for my hand. 'Oh Hal, we could all have done things differently, darling, don't you realize we all blame ourselves?'

I pull my hand away.

'No, I don't,' I tell her, totally freaked. 'She was alone in the sea, and I didn't come and get you, I didn't save her.'

'You didn't MAKE her go out there, Hal.'

I don't understand it! I want her to scream at me and ground me for a whole year, I want her to make it all right, but she doesn't, she just goes right on being kind.

'Listen, Hal, it just doesn't do to go on thinking that it could be any different. Charley WANTED to be out there, and if anyone should have known that she was going to do something so stupid it should've been me and Dad, OK?'

'But I could've told you,' I yell at her, because I want her to say, 'Yes, you could, and I wish you had.'

'What if she wasn't alone?' I yell at her, but she just takes a deep breath, and when she speaks, her voice is firm and hard, and much more like the old Mum.

'Hal, listen to me. Charley had an accident. Hard though

75

it is to accept, she went out at night onto the waves and fell onto a rock. No one could do anything. No one saw anything. Believe me, Hal, everybody was asked at the time. The police were very – and I mean this, Hal – very thorough. There was nothing on her, or with her, to suggest that she wasn't alone.'

Except a shadow in the streetlight?

'What about that boyfriend she was meant to have?'

'He was questioned, as was his family.' Her voice is cold and hard.

'Why didn't you tell me?'

'Hal, you don't remember what you were like after you found her, sweetheart.'

She stops. Her eyes fill up all over again and she bites her lip, hard.

'It was like losing both of you for a while.' She stops for a bit, and it's as though I can see the memory taking her away, far away from me, to somewhere I can't follow. And it's so irritating, 'cos it's me she's thinking about, and I'm right here, right next to her – not a million miles away, somewhere in her head. Slowly, she turns back to look at me.

'We were told to leave you to recover in your own time, to talk about Charley as normal, not to push or pry, and we haven't, and you are remembering, so—'

'So what?' I ask her. I can't quite work it out; Mum and Dad have been asking people what to do about ME as though I'M the one with a problem?

'You mean you already thought I might know something about what happened to her all this time and you didn't tell me?'

'No, Hal! It was just that the police did think it was a bit odd that you couldn't help with any information about her friends on the beach, and it was obvious that you were traumatised, upset. You, you—'

'I WHAT, Mum?'

'You kept saying you should have found her sooner, that you could have saved her if only you'd found her sooner.'

'I could have.'

'We can only know that if you tell us what you remember.'

But suddenly I don't want to tell. What else does she know that she's not telling me about? 'What wasn't I meant to hear?' I ask. 'What were you and Dad talking about earlier?'

'We're talking about you now, Hal, and what you remember,' she says gently.

So I give it to her.

'I remember seeing Charley,' I say, 'and it was like she was dancing on the waves.'

'Oh, Hal!' she says, and sure enough, the tears begin to fill her eyes, and she smiles at me through them, somehow.

'Yeah, and Mum?'

'Mm?'

'I don't think she was alone. I think there was someone else on the beach, watching her.'

Tell me, I'm thinking, tell me you already know all this. Tell me it isn't me I'm seeing, me standing there watching: but all she does is stare at me for a moment, her eyes full of tears and confusion, before she finally turns and stumbles away.

It's not long before Dad arrives. He stands in the doorway for a long time, just looking at me. Dad does that. He waits and looks and hopes you'll crack, but I don't. Not any more. He moves to the end of the bed, and up close it almost looks like he's scared to sit down.

'We need to talk, Hal.'

'Yeah, right – you mean I need to listen to you, yeah, Dad?'

'No. Perhaps we should have reminded you sooner, Hal – about the investigation, I mean, and our worries about you – but you were so stricken, son.'

I look at the wall.

'I don't want to talk to you, you an' Mum, you just—'

'Yes?'

He does that too: asks a question and waits for you to hang yourself.

'Nothing.'

'So you think it's nothing that your mum's downstairs in tears?'

'No.'

'Hal, you can't just let off a bomb like that and not expect there to be any mess.'

'What?' I feel seriously confused.

78

'Look, you've just suggested to your mother that some-body saw Charley in the sea. So what do you think that means to Mum, to all of us?'

He says it so gently, as though he's speaking to a friggin' moron.

'That somebody saw her in the sea?' I suggest.

'That there could be somebody here, Hal – think about it for just a moment, will you? – somebody, maybe, who we live near every summer – either way, somebody who hasn't bothered to tell us, or the police, how or why our daugh-ter is . . . is . . . in the state she's in. How do you expect your mother to feel about that, eh?'

He waits again.

Shit! I didn't think about that. I say nothing.

'How can she not wonder who it might be? How can she feel . . .' he bangs on.

'RIGHT Dad!' I'm beginning to yell, I can't seem to help it. 'So I'M the one who's upset Mum, am I? I'm not the one who went out at night, I'm not the one who ended up in hospital, so how come this is my problem? Upset Mum? Well, it's not difficult, is it?'

'You little—'

For one mad moment I hope he'll hit me. Go on, go on, I think, do it.

'Hal,' is all he says in the end, his hand dropping to his side. 'Hal, it's so hard to know what to do for the best.'

'HARD? HARD, DAD? FOR FUCK'S SAKE, COMING HERE ISN'T "HARD". IT'S MENTAL.'

'Hal, don't speak to me like that!'

'Don't speak, that's right, Dad, don't speak. Don't upset Mum, don't worry Dad, don't speak, don't exist, don't dare talk about how SHIT it all is.'

'Hal! Language!'

'Stop saying my name.'

'Hal.' He sounds so hopeless.

'Stop it.'

'We're trying, son. I know we haven't always got it right.'

'Too right – you KNEW I might know something and YOU'RE the ones who didn't tell ME, so you can get off your pony about Mum for a start.'

'Look, let's go down and talk to Mum.'

'Yep, that's right, Dad, then it's two against one. Me and no Charley. How crappy is that, Dad?'

There's a long and horrible silence.

'I don't know what to say,' he says at last, and I can see that it's true; for a split second he looks so truly old and defeated. 'Everyone said you were doing OK. What can I say, Ha— son? We thought we were doing the best thing.'

'Who for?' I ask him, and I mean it. How nice that him and Mum can just look after each other, and forget all about me.

'For all of us, son,' he says.

'Yeah, right.'

'I won't have you speak to me like that.'

'Right, then how can you hear me, Dad?

He shakes his head.

'Always got an answer, son, just don't be too sure it's the right one, eh? And your mum, Hal, she's trying so hard to think about what the next step is, we need to be – together on this – as a family – we need—'

What does he mean?

'What next step?' I ask, and it's as though an ice-cold fist has grabbed hold of my heart, and is squeezing the blood out, slowly, just a little extra with each beat.

'What, Dad?' I ask again, but he just shakes his head at me, can't seem to see or feel or hear the fear in my heart, squeezing away.

Can't seem to help me.

He reaches out his hand for a shake, but I pull away.

'And, Hal?' He looks back from the door.

'I know,' I say, truly tired now. '"Go easy on your mother."'

'No, Hal.' He hesitates, and that makes me look up. 'I love you,' he says.

And I can see that he does, but it only makes me feel madder, like it's a winning counter in a game, and only he has it.

When I get downstairs Mum's bustling in the kitchen, trying to pretend everything's normal.

'Tea's on the table.' She ruffles my hair, and I shake her off. I sit down; the teapot's huge. Oh, God, there's enough in there for hours.

'I've put Sara in front of a video, so we'll have some peace.'

'I thought we were going to Tintagel?' I ask hopefully.

'This is more important.' Mum sits down, and they both look at me.

'You haven't paid an entrance fee.'

'What?'

'Well, you're both staring at me like I'm something out of the zoo; you could at least pay me for the privilege.'

'Hal, it's hard enough without the wisecracks,' says Mum. 'We're worried about you. You come back from that walk somehow believing that it's all your fault Charley had her accident, and now you're talking about remembering somebody seeing her? What's going on?'

'Why the sudden interest, Mum?'

She flinches a bit, and recovers.

'Hal, we can't help you if you just fend us off all the time.'

'You can't help me just because you've suddenly decided to remember.'

'Remember what?' She looks at me, confused.

'That I'm here.'

'Hal!' Mum's eyes just crumple up like tissues, in pain and horror, and I know that it's cruel, but it's true. She's always thinking of Charley, always crying for Charley, and I know she thinks it means she loves me and Sarz even more, but really it just means that she's dying with Charley, over and over again, and it makes it so hard for us – no, for me – to live.

'Hal, how can you think that?'

'Because it's TRUE, all you two can do is think of Charley. Me and Sara, we might as well just die too.'

I watch as they stare at me in horror before checking in with each other. Dad has a strange, 'told you so' sort of look on his face, and Mum drops her head into her hands, as though it's suddenly just far too heavy for her neck to carry.

'You miss her, Hal – we all do, but being so angry with us won't help,' Mum says slowly, in the end.

'Yeah,' I mutter, ashamed.

'And perhaps we do need to listen to you, Hal,' says Dad. I stare at him in disbelief. 'And perhaps you need to know something too – that we do know how hard this has been for you.'

It makes me shiver suddenly, the way he says 'has been', as though it was over, as though she was really, finally dead.

'But it's no one's fault, it just happened. It was an accident.' Mum repeats the words so slowly, as though she is holding them to herself, like a light in the dark, holding on tight, because she would be lost and blind without them.

'No, Mum, it wasn't!' I hear myself shout. 'No! There's a reason!' And Charley's voice is strong and sure within me.

I am right.

'Remember, Hal!'

I have to know what happened to her. Exactly what happened. And suddenly, I've got it, and this is the surest thing in the world to me.

It wasn't an accident.

'It's hard to believe, Hal,' Mum's still talking, 'but the world's a cruel, cruel place sometimes, and Charley being . . . in a coma, it feels so cruel and wicked, but it's just a terrible accident.' She stops for a bit, and then goes on as though she's talking to herself. 'And cruel things, well, I suppose—' she looks straight at Dad, and his eyes hold her up, as though they're willing her on, 'I suppose they ask cruel questions of us sometimes.'

'Help me, Hal!'

I stare at them both, but they don't notice, and the shiver inside me becomes fixed and cold, hard and frozen – I want to howl with laughter at the weird friggin' irony of it. Why now, why are they thinking about this now? Just when she's coming alive again for me? Why now, just when I'm beginning to remember? Perhaps that's why – because I'm beginning to remember something?

And Charley's voice comes back, stronger than ever.

'Remember.'

'What do you mean?' I say to them, in a panic, because I want answers, and I suddenly feel as though they might be about to take that away from me somehow. 'If Charley's body's lying in that hospital, but she's not dead, where is she?' I hear myself ask. 'And what was she doing out on the waves that night, why was she there?'

And suddenly, all the hidden-away questions are just giving themselves right up, tumbling right out of me, not caring whether or not they have a place to go.

Mum and Dad both seem to wake up, to come back

from some far-away, grown-up place that binds them together, and they stare at me as though I've only just arrived on the planet.

'I wish we knew, Hal,' says Dad at last. 'I wish she would wake up and tell us, but that's why it's so hard, son, because we don't know.'

Mum's eyes begin to spill over again, and I just wish so much that she could stop, stop, stop.

'It wasn't an accident, Mum!' and I can hear the panic in my own voice.

She nods, not hearing, blinded by tears.

'What are you going to do?'

They stare at each other, at me. Mum nods at Dad.

'We're thinking,' says Dad, 'we're wondering, Hal – just what it might be like for Charley to be the way she is?' He lets the words form slowly and clearly, as though he wants them to sink right in. They do; they land like stones in the pit of my stomach.

'She wants us to find out what happened,' I shout at them. 'She wants us to know why!'

But Dad goes on, like a slow steam train, stopping at no stations, taking no prisoners. 'And we will always remember her, Hal, of course we will, whatever happens, whatever decision . . .' and he looks at Mum, '. . . we come to. But you asked us what we were thinking, and we are wondering if she would be happy for us to keep her the way she is, when the thing about Charley was – is – that she was so . . . so full of . . .' the word sticks in his throat, and I wish I could say it for him, but I can't, I can't say it either.

I can only watch, as he swallows, and finally manages it.

'Life,' he says. 'She was so full of . . . life.'

None of us can speak, and for a moment it's as though Charley is right here with us all again, not half-dead Charley, but the real Charley, the one who laughed and danced and drove us all crazy. It's as though she's watching us. Dad holds out his empty hands, as though he wishes he could wrap us all up forever, and make it all better, but the saddest thing in the world right now is knowing that he can't.

PART TWO. Hal's story.

Hal. Now.

The freckly girl, the one from the yurt, is in the phone box, nattering away. She looks like she'll be in there for hours. She flicks me a look and then turns her back, as though she thinks I might be interested in what she has to say.

I sit on the wall and wait for a breeze, any breeze, but the sea is as still as the air. The sun burns, but I can't get warm; it's like Dad's words have solidified into a frozen fist of fear and loneliness, locked in my gut, and I can't get away from it; even the sea and the sun can't burn it away, an endless ache where Charley ought to be. What will Mum and Dad do to her? Stop feeding her? Switch her off? How will they let her die? I think of Charley, I think of how it used to be: of always feeling as though I knew what she was thinking; of how she'd sometimes start a sentence and I'd finish it; of how it still feels so sudden and shocking, her breaking away from us all like that, never being around, never telling us anything. And then I found her lying in the waves, and she wasn't in a fit state to answer any of our questions any more.

'Where were you, Charley? Why were you on the beach? What were you doing? Who was with you?' The questions just whirl around inside me, and I want answers.

The girl's back is long and lovely. Her shoulders are peeling, flaky red petals of skin parting to reveal a smooth new brown beneath. Her hair looks all crunchy with sea-salt; it's almost the same colour as Charley's, only a more orangey gold.

God, she's going to be in there for ages.

I REALLY need to talk to Jenna, Charley's best friend. She's the one who'll have the answers, and it's one of those days when mobs don't work in the valley, and I just can't wait any more.

I bang on the door. The girl turns around. God! Her eyes are so zingy-green. I mean green like a tropical wave just before it breaks, when you can see right through it; they sparkle, even though she's got that knackered been-up-all-night-and-can't-get-the-sand-out-of-my-knickers look that they all get after a few weeks on the site.

'Keep your hair on,' she mouths, and the sight of her eyes just knocks me to the ground. I drop to my knees and pretend to pray, holding up my fifty p and longing for those eyes to see me, and only me.

She smiles and says something down the phone. Then she's laughing and opening the door, and I realize that I really can't get up, even though the pavement's burning and scraping my knees.

'I'm stuck!' I say, as though it isn't obvious, and she laughs and holds out her hand to help, not realizing just how much I really need it to get off my knees. Her palm's sweaty from where she's been holding the phone, and our hands slip, but she manages to hold on.

'Hey, thanks,' I say.

'You're from the big house, aren't you?'

'Yeah.'

I know I'm staring, but I can't stop, can't seem to help it

at all, and I can't seem to speak in whole sentences either.

'Summer-only, like us, aren't you?' she says. 'Listen, I just want to say I'm really sorry about your sister. I mean Charley.'

'What?' It's like someone's suddenly turned the sun off. I'm cold – I'm sweating, but bone-cold – and the questions inside me have just doubled. Who is she? How does she know about Charley?

'Didn't you know that—?' she begins, and then she looks at me, as though she can tell I'm cold. 'Forget it, sorry, hey, anyway, look, I, oh shit—' She stops in the end, but I don't help her, I just go on staring.

'Anyway, you're Hal, aren't you?'

'Yeah.'

'I was wondering, Hal, why don't you lot ever come down to the beach, to the barbecue?'

'Never been asked,' I say. Well, I haven't, I think, but Charley went loads last year. It was practically all she did. I remember sitting on the low wall, watching the camp fires on the beach, feeling lonely. And then it strikes me. What else was Charley doing that I don't know about? That none of us knew about? How does this girl even know my name?

'Well, you have now,' she's saying.

'Have what?'

'Been asked,' she says, 'to the barby.'

'Hey, great!' I manage. She laughs again. She seems to laugh a lot.

'I'm Jackie, since you ask,' she goes on. I manage a nod this time.

'See ya, then?' I nod again, and she turns away after giving me a quick, speculative glance. Does she realize that I can do words sometimes? I imagine peeling the curly skin off her shoulders and kissing the soft new skin underneath.

Weird.

Shake out. Delete. Move on.

I fall into the phone box with relief, and ring Jenna's number. I imagine the phone ringing in her house, see the highly polished wood on the hall table, hear the cavernous sound it makes, as though it was in a castle. I imagine Jenna running down the curved stairs, as though I can make her be there.

'Pick up, pick up,' I chant – and suddenly, she does.

'Jenna!' I'm wickedly pleased to hear her voice.

'Hi.'

'Hey, Jenna!'

'Hal?'

'Yeah.'

Silence. Right, so she's not so thrilled to hear me.

'I've been to see Charley.' She says it quickly, like I'm checking up on her, or something.

'Yeah, Mum said you would. Rather you than me.'

'Ha ha, Hal, very funny.' She sounds indignant. Jenna's fun, even though I've hated her since I was five. Her and Sal and Charley have been friends forever. I know they miss her 'cos they're about her only friends who haven't stopped visiting.

'Jenna, I need to know about Charley.'

'What about Charley?' She sounds cagey suddenly, and my heart races. So there is something, then, and maybe Jenna knows what it is.

'Jenna, what happened last summer? What was Charley doing? Who might she have been on the beach with?'

'Hal, I can't— what makes you think that?'

'Your reaction, for one.'

'It's just girl stuff,' she says, 'nothing new, and nothing you need to know.'

'For Chrissake, Jenna, get real, my mum and dad are seriously thinking she might be better off dead. I need some help here, and Cornwall is total shit without Charley, just in case you're interested. And I . . . I . . . I think I've remembered something, I think that maybe there was someone on the beach with her, watching, you know, when she went under . . . so, please—'

'Like who?' she asks, and her voice is sharp and sudden.

'I don't know, that's the thing, Jen, I just don't think she was alone.'

There's a long silence. I wait. I wonder if she's crying.

'Jen?'

'She was – well, you know – she was crazy about that guy she was seeing, but that's just girl stuff, Hal, she was happy, you know, besotted.'

My heart drops, because I didn't know. I wonder if I could ever have told Charley about wanting to peel the skin off the girl's shoulders. Maybe there are just some things that can't be shared? Maybe there's a reason why Charley didn't chat any more.

'No, I didn't know – but why would he be there, and why wouldn't he get help, whoever he was?'

'Leave it, Hal,' is all she says. 'Just drop it, OK? I don't think Charley would want you to pry.'

'Oh, right, Jenna, which Charley's that? The one that you chat to every day in hospital, is it?'

There's a long silence, and I listen to her breathing at me.

'Hal, I'm—'

'JENNA,' I scream her name down the phone. 'If you tell me you're sorry, I'll . . . I'll . . .' But I can't think of anything very terrible that I'd actually do to Jen; I like her too much.

'JENNA, PLEASE. I'm BEGGING you. Look, I've got this feeling there's something she wants me to know, to remember – so just tell me why she felt unhappy if she was so stoked about this guy? What did Charley get into last summer?'

'No, Hal, just leave it.' She sounds scared. Jenna, scared? That's a new one – it takes some getting used to.

'Are you scared?'

'A bit.'

'Why, what happened?'

'Oh, it's not Charley, she was just doing normal stuff, it's – look – I don't know what happened, or if anything did. I don't think she had time to tell us.'

But I don't believe her, and Charley's right back in my

head, pushing me on, as though she wishes she could persuade Jenna for me.

'*Remember! Help me!*'

'You are scared, Jen. I can hear it. Why? What happened? Who are you scared of? Was someone with her on the beach? Who?'

'She asked me to keep a secret, Hal, and it's the last thing I can do for her.'

'She's as good as dead for Chrissake, it's a bit late for that!'

'Hal!'

'Does someone pay you to hope?' I screech at her. 'I'm the one trying to help her—'

'Be careful, Hal. Really, take care! And keep charged, I'll ring if I can.' And the line goes dead.

I stare at the phone. I stare at it in utter disbelief. I look at it as though it could still speak, as though Charley might whisper into it, even now, and all I have to do is wait, and she will tell me all about it. But all I can really hear is that dead noise a phone makes when there's no one there, when no one's listening.

'Shit!' I slam it against the glass.

'Oi!' some bloke yells at me, from the other side of the glass. 'Hooligan!' he shouts as I push past. 'We have to use that phone all year, you don't think of that, do you?'

'No!' I say, and I stare at him. I stare at him till he goes in and shuts the door. It makes me feel better, intimidating some poor old Cornish bloke. That's how sad I am.

Dad's waving at me from the terrace. He shakes his head, and points to me, and then the door of the house.

'Home!' he's saying.

I slog my way up to the house.

'I need a swim. Can you have Sara for a bit?'

He sounds as though he's right on the edge and about to dive over. I nod. I don't want to talk to him. I don't want to be with any of them – I want to work out what's going on with Charley – but even I know that he does all the swimming and rock-pooling and stuff on the beach with Sarz now; and that when he's truly fed up, nothing but a swim on his lonesome will work it off.

Inside the kitchen I can hear Mum bashing pans around as though she was killing snakes with them. Sara stands in the hallway, silently looking at the kitchen door, and then back at me and Dad, who's digging all the gear out of the boot cupboard.

'Rargh!' she roars, suddenly and loudly, making us both jump and then laugh.

'About right!' says Dad, and I don't have to wonder what the row's about this time.

What do we do about Charley?

We load up with buckets, spades, nets and towels, and clear out. It's hot. The sun bounces off the sand, turning it almost white in the glare, and the surf's a dim white whisper in the breezeless air. Sara trots behind us, silent, for once.

'First proper swim of the year!'

Dad's cheering up already at the thought, and for a moment I think that I'll go in too, yeah, and the sea will be all lovely-cold against my burning skin. I'll get that dizzy feeling afterwards, with the effort of climbing out of the water. Sweet. But I can't do it.

'Thanks, Hal.' Dad takes off into the waves, and me and Sara watch him go.

'Bye!' Sara shouts suddenly. 'Bye, Daddy!' And she waves frantically, worriedly, so that we have to wait for him to come up out of the water and wave back, just to make sure he's still there.

We wander away from the sea, along the beach.

'Will it hurt him, Hal?' she asks.

'What?'

'The sea,' she says.

'No, Sarz,' I tell her. 'He's a big boy!'

'Not as big as the sea,' she says, as she pulls me along.

'Where we goin'?' she asks, and I wonder myself, 'cos we seem to be struggling across the worst part of the beach, where mini-style cliffs rise up out of the sand in jagged, sharp ridges. I look down at Sarz as she struggles along, hanging on to her bucket and spade with one hand and me with the other.

'You tell me,' I laugh. 'You seem to be leading! Where are you taking me?'

'I don't know,' she says. 'I just know this is the right way, but I don't know where.'

'How?' I ask, curious. What does she mean, she knows this is the right way?

'When I go the wrong way I get a bad feeling!' she says simply.

'It's not VERY difficult,' she says, looking down at the rocks. I'm using a net pole to help me balance, and it's hard to hold on to her and everything else.

'I think it's difficult,' I tell her.

'Is it near now?' she asks me. She looks up, her face all red and sweaty under her hat, and it looks as though she really doesn't know where we are; but when I look up I realize, with a sense of shock, exactly where we're headed.

'I think we're already there,' I say. 'How did you know how to get here, Sarz?'

'I don't want to, Hal!' She's suddenly scared, the way she sometimes is. 'I don't know where! My tummy told me this way!'

I put my arm around her.

'Hey!' I say. 'It's cool, Sarz, it's the best place!' I promise her. And I try not to think of Charley bringing me here, of her making me close my eyes and swearing me to secrecy as she dragged me along, my feet hopping with the pain of the sharp rocks.

'Don't look, Hal,' she said. 'And then you can't give it away.'

I shake the memory off.

How did Sarz get us here? Just chance?

We press ourselves against the cliff-face, edging out along the ledge until the cliff turns back on itself, and we're there, in the tiny rocky cove full of sea-water.

The pool's just the way it's always been, surrounded by high rock on three sides, a great wobbly circle of water, with a huge flat rock right in the centre. Seaweed and ferns slide around on the surface, and under the water lichen turns the rocks pink and orange. Silvery fish dart about in shoals with flashes of electric blue. You can always find crabs here.

Sara stares at it all, wide-eyed. 'Is it magic?' she asks.

'Yeah,' I say, 'cos it is – real, sweet magic.

We swim out to the flat rock and sit on it, catching blennies in the sun. When it gets too hot I jump in, but Sara won't.

'Don't like the flowers!' she says, pointing to the blood-red anemones, so I splash her instead.

'Water spiders, you come 'ere!' she calls to the crabs, but when I actually catch one she screams and runs to the edge of the rock. I sit down and talk to the crab, and sure enough, she gets curious after a while. Soon she's over my shoulder, watching, and a little while after that she reaches out and strokes its belly with her finger.

'It's a shell!' she says, and we watch as the crab scuttles off the rock and sinks, finding a hole to hide in. We break off some limpets and chuck them in the net to catch the bigger fish with. Sara lies on her belly, her face inches above the water, and stares.

'Where's Charley, Hal?' she asks me suddenly, disconcertingly.

'In hospital, in Oxford,' I say quickly.

'Why is she stopped, Hal, did the sea do it?'

'I don't know, Sarz,' I tell her. 'The sea hurt her head and stopped her working properly.' The words are choking me as I speak, but I hold it all back, answering her questions, the way I wish someone could answer mine.

'Charley liked it here, didn't she?'

'Yeah, Sarz, she loved it.' The lump in my throat is as big as a rock, but Sarz suddenly smiles at me, a wide-open, sun-beaming Sara of a smile. 'Course she did!' she says and, just for a sec, I reckon I can see exactly what Mum gets filled with when she hugs her.

'Is Charley in there now?' she asks, still staring at the water. 'Her stopped bit?'

'No,' I tell her. 'Charley's in the hospital, Sarz, you know that.'

'Oh!' she says, and she gives me that freaky glance again, as though maybe I haven't quite got it.

We stare into the water. Sara can watch for a long time, much longer than me. It's so different to being here with Charley. With Charley it would be me lying on the rock . . . and I'd be closing my eyes and feeling the warmth of the sun melt my bones, feeling it search out each crevice of my face, and I'd be waiting for her to begin . . . I can hear her voice now . . .

'Guess what?' she's saying.

'What?' I ask, and I can almost hear my own voice, all drowsy and waiting, waiting for a Charley story.

'I was born here,' she says.

'You were born in Oxford, at the John Radcliffe Hospital,' I remind her, not quite ready, yet, to be taken in by the story.

'No I wasn't, Hal, listen: I was born here, only it wasn't summer, it was winter, and the waves were wild – wild and grey and crashing to the shore. And our house wasn't built yet, no houses were, 'cos this was my first life – the first one ever, when you're all new and shaky and a bit like you are . . .'

And as I give in, as I close my eyes and listen to her, I can feel the world she makes with her words rise up behind my eyelids, become more real than the sun on my face, or the rock beneath me, a world of seals and humans and changelings . . . and Charley. Sometimes I wondered if she ever really lived with us at all. How could she, when she had so many stories to disappear into, any time she wanted?

'And where was I born?' I ask her.

'Oh, you, on land, definitely. A first-timer and a human right from the start . . .'

'Hal! Hal! In the sand, Hal, quick!' The sound of Sarz's voice drags me back to the here and now.

'What, Sarz? Where?'

She points straight down. I can't see a thing.

'Geddit, Hal!' she says. 'Get that thing!' She's excited, but she keeps very still; whatever it is, she really wants to catch it. I reach for the net, and dig it quickly under the rippling sand and pull it up. Sand pours through.

'Oh, I missed it Sarz, I'm sorry,' but she just carries on staring at the trickling sand, waiting until it's nearly all gone, and then she points.

'There 'tis,' she says calmly, and she's right, because flopping about in the very last grains of sand is a flatfish, a tiny flatfish – so small I can almost see right through it, so beautiful and delicate, like something carved out of dried cuttlefish.

'I like it,' says Sarz. 'Can it be mine?'

Gently we lower it into the bucket, where it floats around the edges exploring its new territory, the water rippling across its wings. Two tiny black dots for eyes, and its movement, are the only things that really make it seem alive.

We stare at it.

How, I find myself wondering, how do we ever really know if something is truly alive or not? And as though Sarz can hear my thoughts, she asks:

'Where is she?'

'There, in the bucket, there, right under the seaweed,' I say, but that's not what she meant.

'No! Hal, I don't mean the fish, I mean Charley's stopped bit.'

I look at the flatfish. Is it alive, or is it just floating? I wonder what story Charley would tell for Sara, about where she is and why. I know that she would have a story, and I know that it would make Sarz feel better. All I have are questions.

'I don't know, Sarz,' I say.

'Sometimes,' she says, slowly, 'sometimes, Hal, I think she's in my tummy.'

She looks up at me, worried, and suddenly I do have a story – or at least a bit of it.

I smile.

'Well,' I say, 'maybe she is in you, Sarz, when you ask about her, and it makes you feel funny, and maybe she's in me when I remember her. Maybe that's where all her stopped bits are?'

Sarz doesn't answer, she squints at me in the sunlight, thinking – and then she picks up the bucket, or tries to.

'Let's show Daddy my fish!' she says.

We pack up, and search the beach until Sarz spots him. She runs up, water slopping out of the bucket.

'Look Daddy! We caught a fatfish, an' Hal trickled the sand all through.'

'Wow!' says Dad.

'Yep, Sarz spotted it, didn't you, Sarz?'

'It's mine an' I called it Flounder.'

'Shall we take him home and show Mummy?'

Sara nods. The sound of Mum's name seems to make her tired, and she stumbles over the rocks, clinging to Dad's hand, whilst I take the bucketful of water and the nets. Sara's muttering away to herself: 'Flounder says only Sara can find me in the sand where I hide an' Sarz looked an' looked an' she didn't find Charley in the sand, she found me, an' Flounder was happy an' said he is Sara's fish an' forever an' ever. Amen.'

She draws in a big breath – and so do I. Did Dad hear the Charley bit? No, he just thinks she's waiting for us to tell her that Flounder has to go back in the sea, like everything we catch does. We keep quiet. We're a long way from home yet. Dad grins at me, and I grin back. I'm tired, and that and the heat is easing the loneliness inside, just a little bit. Sara goes on muttering, waiting for us to disagree with her.

She sounds so normal, it's reassuring somehow.

It's late afternoon, and people are drifting off the beach. They always do about now, except the surfers, who just stay and stay – always hoping.

She'd be out there now, I think, and my heart leaps when a figure stands up by the rocks and waves. It's Jack, and my heart goes right on thudding, hoping she won't come over when Dad's around.

She doesn't hear the thought. She runs over.

'Hi!' she says to Sara. 'Can I see what you've got?' Sara grabs the bucket and shows her.

'His name's Flounder,' she says. 'He's mine.'

'He's gorgeous!' says Jackie. 'A baby flatfish, yeah?'

'I found him!' Sara looks at her, and we all stand around feeling a bit awkward until Jackie holds out her hand to Sara and says:

'My name's Jackie, what's yours?' Sara takes her hand and grins.

'I'm Sara and I'm five, this is Hal, he's fifteen, and that's Daddy, he's forty-three!' She says it so seriously. Me and Dad laugh, but Jackie just says:

'Hey, I'm fifteen too, thanks for showin' me your fish, Sara.'

'Nice to meet you, Jackie,' Dad manages, before giving me that annoying grin that means: talking to girls now, eh?

She smiles right through him, straight to me, and the smile goes in, right in, all the way down to wherever heaven is inside.

'We're all going for a swim, Hal, wanna come?' She's got guts.

'No thanks, gotta give Dad a hand with these.' I shake my full hands.

'Go on, Hal.' Dad begins grabbing the nets and armbands, dropping them in the sand.

Jackie grimaces at me. 'Sorry,' she mouths, and grins, and by the feel of my face, I reckon I'm grinning too.

'Here, let me give you a hand,' she says to Dad. 'I've always wanted to see the view from your terrace anyway.'

Dad really laughs then.

'You believe in shooting straight from the hip, don't you, young lady?'

I swear my toes curl up without any help at all from me, but Jack just settles the nets under her arm and shakes the hair out of her face.

She's incredible.

'D'you mind?' she asks, looking up at him with those

amazing eyes.

'Not at all,' says Dad. 'You're very welcome.' We all set off across the last stretch of the beach, Dad and Sara ahead, me and Jackie lagging behind.

'Hi,' I manage.

'Hi yourself,' she teases.

'Why'd you ask me to the barby?' I blurt, wondering all the time where the words are coming from.

'I wanted to,' she says, and the way she says it makes it sound so straightforward and simple. 'Anyway. You're a family with a history, aren't you? Everyone wants to know about you now.'

'True!' I say, and I sound so cool, but inside I'm thinking hard; right, is what I'm thinking, not interested in me then, merely in my family history. The warmth from her smile has gone, disappeared completely. Sara looks back, staring at us as Dad drags her along. Talk about being stopped. Charley's not the only one. You don't have to die or be in a coma, you can just have your feelings switched right off.

We hobble on, over the stones now, heads down, trying not to step on any sharp ones. I can see the faint golden hairs around Jackie's ankles as she steps along next to me. Her feet are long and burnt brown with scuffed-up toes. She has a thin gold chain around her left ankle. I suppose I feel angry with her. How can she make it all sound so easy? How can she talk about it all as though it's history, as if it was so long ago it doesn't matter to anyone any more? But I can't say all of that, so what comes out is this:

'That's the sign of a whore in Egypt.'

She stops walking and looks at me.

'What did you say?' She looks really angry and confused, and embarrassed! Her cheeks are flaming, flaming so much that her freckles nearly disappear.

Wow.

'That.' I point to the chain around her ankle. 'Didn't you know? If you wear it in Egypt it means you're a prostitute.'

'Well this is Cornwall, isn't it, Hal? And I'm not a whore.'

'Didn't say you were!' I shrug, but somewhere inside I'm smiling. 'It's just information,' I say, knowing it's anything but. It's a dig. A dig for being more interested in my past than in me.

Who's the angry one now, Jackie?

I imagine Charley smiling, and digging me in the ribs herself.

We're at the garden gate, which leads up from the beach; the grassy garden slope feels wet and cool on my feet, blissful after the hot sand and stones. Jackie storms up after Dad. I stand and smile at the sun for a bit.

'Well!' I hear him say as they get to the terrace. 'What do you think?' She looks out over to the camp site.

'It looks much nicer from up here than it does when you're actually in it,' I hear her say.

'Mmm.' Dad's being carefully noncommittal; he hates the camp site, has called it the only eyesore in this part of Cornwall for years.

'But we've got the best view, haven't we?' she says. 'We've got the cliff falling into the sea.'

'And us, of course,' grins Dad, but Jackie doesn't even bother to blush.

'My mum says she sometimes feels like she knows you all already,' she says.

'I'll bet!' Dad begins to pick up nets and stash them inside the door. The kitchen's silent now, and I wonder where Mum is.

'Drink, Jackie?' he asks.

'We've got real lemonade,' pipes up Sara.

'Hey, thanks, but no thanks. We've got our own stuff on the beach.'

'Bye, then. Thanks for your help.' Dad disappears inside the house, and Sara stands and stares at us, silently. I hang around in Jackie's path as she turns to leave, not sure if I'm still welcome.

'Oh, come on,' she snaps at me, and we set off back to the beach. When we get far enough away, she stops and sits on a rock.

'OK,' she says. 'I'll forgive you. After all, you're a boy with a tragic past, aren't you?'

'Forgive me for what?' I ask. 'You are a kind of whore, you know, Jackie.'

'And what are you?' she asks, her cheeks going that immediate, furious and fascinating red again.

'Not a whore, at least!' I smile. I'm enjoying myself; who does she think she is, picking me up just so she can hear all about it? Not into me, that's for sure.

'Take that back, Hal!'

'Nope. You are, you're an info whore. You only picked me up because you and your friends want to hear all about Charley, didn't you? I've met girls like you at school – 'poor little Hal lost his sister' – and when they've heard the story and got all the inside info, guess what? – suddenly not interested. I'm right, yeah? Why else would you be here?'

I watch her face racket about between disbelief and anger. She opens her mouth, but no words come out; her mouth just hangs there in surprise.

I wait for her to tell me to sod off. I wait to know if it's me or Charley she's into. She drops her head into her hands.

'God, that's a lot to think about,' she mutters through her fingers. I sit down next to her, unable to believe she hasn't told me where to get off.

'Are you really fifteen?' she asks, after a while.

'Yep. You?'

'Same.'

We look at each other. She looks sixteen going on seventeen, I look about fifteen.

'Unbelievable,' we say together, and laugh.

'I REALLY didn't,' she stutters. 'Look, I'm interested, everybody is, and the weird thing is – oh, never mind – anyway, you should meet my mum, she just likes people and I must have INHERITED it or something, it's not really nosy, it's just . . .'

She goes on in that lovely way she has, of just chucking up the odd word and then batting it right into your ears.

'Anyway, I AM sorry and I really didn't mean it like that, though I can see how it must've . . . oh GOD, I'm just so . . . although calling me a whore was a bit . . .'

It gets boring listening to her after a while.

'Thanks for not telling me to fuck off, anyway,' I say.

'Oh!' She finally stops. 'That's OK!' We laugh some more, and I wonder if maybe it'll get to be a habit.

'Coming for a swim?' she asks.

I shrug no, and she gets it straight away. She reaches out and touches my arm.

'Oh Hal, I'm REALLY sorry, what an idiot. Haven't you been in since Charley . . . ?' I shake my head.

'Shit!' We let the sun beat down on us for a bit. 'Why?' she asks.

'Just . . .' I shrug again, 'dunno really.' But of course I do, it's just not very cool telling a girl you've only just met (and already want to be with forever) that you can't go in the water because you made some dumb deal with God, a God you don't even happen to believe in any more, that if you give up the sea for ever, he'll one day bring Charley back. Stupid; how will not going in the sea help Charley? And actually, for the first time, I want to be in the sea. I want to know if my eyes still turn green in the water. I want to feel the water on my skin, and watch what it does to Jackie's eyelashes.

'Let's go!' I get up.

'No, no it's FINE, Hal, REALLY!'

'See ya, sucker!' and I race away to the waves, before I can stop myself.

'You bastard!' She isn't far behind me, her feet pounding on the sand. 'That's not funny, Hal. Hal! Not fair, you had a head start. Hal!'

The water's cold. Cold enough to make me gasp. The waves push at me and I push them back, diving through and out beyond the breakers, to where the sea is drifting. I drift too, and the water lifts and drops me on its back, lifts and drops me, and my eyes are closed, and it's almost like coming home until the thought of Charley suddenly runs right through my body. It's like she's inside the waves, holding on to me, and I hear her voice calling me again.

'Hal!'

I hear her breath, rising and falling.

Up. Down. Up. Down. Like the waves.

'Help me, Hal. Remember.'

Oh no, I think, not now. And then Jackie bursts up beside me, water pouring off her peeling shoulders, and I forget all about Charley.

The waves are really clean, rising in rows behind us, blocking out the sky as they break on our shoulders. They remind me of muscles flexing, and I lift my arm and flex back, challenging the sea. Jackie laughs, her eyes glinting in the sun, and then we steady ourselves, waiting for a big one. It's big enough. It hunches itself up over the sea, growing and curling, until it hovers over us, and we jump up, just before the white tip of it breaks and hurls us to shore, and we're beached and screaming and laughing for no reason at all, except that it was fun.

'Spit salt!' I yell at the retreating wave.

'Again?' yells Jack, reminding me of Sarz, and we play in the waves, just like I always used to, until I'm almost too tired to even stand. Then Jackie comes up with the idea of ice cream. It feels so easy to be holding hands, as we push against the sea, helping each other as it tries to pull us back into the waves. The cliffs tower above us, and the gulls scream across the rolling water.

I look up at our house, floating on the face of the cliff. I imagine it's dark and a light shines out suddenly, and then shuts off, like an eye blinking in the night. Then Mum comes and stands on the terrace, waving at me and driving the vision away.

The Haven caff's heaving with day trippers, all grabbing a last ice cream before heading home.

'What do you want?'

Jackie's already woven her way to the front of the queue. 'Chocolate, please,' she says.

'Make that two.' I collapse on the bench outside, but barely-breathless Jackie has other ideas.

'C'mon, let's eat on the cliff.'

'Can't move!' I mean it, my legs feel like jellyfish; my lungs have had every single ounce of breath knocked out of them by the sea.

'Course you can,' she says, and walks off. I practically

crawl up the cliff after her, muttering curses, following the drips of my rapidly melting chocolate ice cream.

'Help!' I yell to the passers-by. 'She's holding my ice cream hostage.' The oldies stare and smile. 'Somebody liberate the ice cream,' I try, but she just carries right on, waving it in the air, merciless. She doesn't stop until we're right at the top, then she cuts off the path and goes through some oak trees, until finally – mercifully – she sits down, right on the edge of the cliff.

'There, look at the view, isn't that worth it?'

'Mmmm.'

I can't answer, I can only grunt and lick what's left of my ice cream. Delicious. The late sun's slanting through the oak grove. I feel like closing my eyes and sleeping forever. I lie back and feel my lids begin to hover, light, like butterfly wings, across the balls of my eyes.

It feels so weird in the heat and light, like the trees around me are pulsing somehow. I'm so tired, but it's as if every time I close my eyes, the trees edge closer, threatening me . . . and I imagine that as soon as my eyes flick open, they retreat. It feels like they might jump me. I look at them closely, just to keep them in their place. Their bark is so deeply grooved, cut in curves that coil around the trunk reminding me of a snake, curling around a stick.

'Remember, Hal!'

And as soon as her whispered words enter my mind, I feel my head begin to throb, and my breath is knocked out from under me, taken over by the sound of her horrible breathing again, until the whole of my brain is lifting and dropping inside the casing of my skull, and breathing with her.

In. Out. In. Out.

The trees come closer . . .

'Where are you, Charley?'

What memories do the deep grooves of bark hold? I wonder what they could tell me?

And then I see her suddenly, I see her as though she was right here, below the trees, and a dark shadow hovers over her . . . a sudden breeze slips up over the cliff, and I shiver.

'Hey, Hal!' says Jack. 'There's something I should tell you . . .' but I can't hear her.

Charley: Hospital. Now.

'Where are you?' he says, and his voice wakes me from the deep-walled darkness.

Can he see me?

My mind's eye opens wide in the dark.

Hal's eyes are wide and green.

Green light . . . in the trees . . .

The trees . . . I can see them, unfolding, uncoiling, their whispered memories stretching out between us, until I can see him, lying below the green leaves, with the green and gold afternoon light cutting him into shape and shadow. He's looking at the trees. He's looking at the trees as though he knows they can remember me, and I watch as their coiled grooves slowly uncurl, spilling memories between us, each one as clean and clear and separate as raindrops . . .

I'm in the grove . . . me . . . and . . . I remember . . .

My fingers run through the ancient grooves bitten deep into the old trunks.

They are so deep and old. Words play in my mind.

Wise. Old. Twisted. Wizened. Wizards. I can feel the beginnings of a story rising, or maybe a poem . . .

That's it, that's what the trees are like – stunted old wizards, turned to solid oak.

'D'you think they were wizards once?'

I can hear my voice! Oh! My own voice, and it's working, it's talking to someone!

'Eh?' says the other voice, lazily. *Oh! His voice is so deep and warm and wonderful. It sounds . . . it sounds . . . like the sun. I want to spread myself out in it to dry. I can feel the sun falling on to my skin in patches of heat and shadow, and the other voice is beside me, breathing.*

Who is it? I can't remember. I can't remember. Who am I talking to?

'The trees, do you think they were wizards once?' I say.

He laughs, slow and lazy and heat-filled. He sounds so close; his face is coming closer, closer. So close, now, that I can feel the warm, sweet breath of his lips as he speaks.

Words dance inside me.

Summer. Breeze. Soft. Sweet. Expectation.

'Where do you get yourself from, Charley?' he asks.

And the breath of his words brushes against my skin.

Tingle. Delight. Turkish.

Uh? Turkish?

Keep coming, please . . . closer . . . closer . . . closer . . .

Ahh, so close now that I can smell him. We smell like we've been lying in the earth together for ever. We smell of leaves and moss, and each other.

'Why the smile?' he asks.

'You're as delicious as Turkish delight,' I hear myself whisper.

'No distracting, Charley.'

'Who are you?'

But there's no answer, just the whisper of the breeze in the trees above us, and the shortening of the air between us as his face gets closer and closer, and I can feel my heart beating so fast I think that it might break and pull me apart with the need to see his face, but my eyes are closed and lifted up, waiting for the touch of his lips. Closer . . . closer . . . closer . . .

'Who are you?'

But there is no answer, only the sun disappearing suddenly behind a shadow, and the heat is gone, and the trees are turning black . . . recoiling . . . the world is tipping into the ocean . . . where the waves lift and drop, lift and drop me in the shade of the shadow . . .

'Help me, Hal!'

The trees are closing, coiling shut, taking him and the memories away from me.

No!

'Hal!'

I'm falling, falling into the green, green sea, like glass.

'Help me, Hal!'

He can't see me any more, he's under the trees, in the green grove, with a girl with eyes as green as leaves.

'Look at me, Hal! Look at me!'

Who is he?

'Help me! Remember!'

Hal. Now.

'Help me!'

Her voice seems to cry right out of the old oaks, as though she is wrapped up tight inside them and crying to be let out. They shiver in the sunlight, and the leaves rustle, but there's no breeze.

Oh no. Not here, not now.

'No, Charley,' I whisper, but the air is vibrating with the memory of her, and the trees are closing in, closer and closer, whispering at me . . . talking to me . . . as though they know what I'm thinking, as though they can feel me longing for Jack's kiss, wanting to reach towards her . . . I jump up.

'Gotta go, Jack!'

She looks up.

'Thought you were knackered?'

'Help me!'

'Help you, Charley? Jesus, I can hardly help myself!'

'Never underestimate the power of the ice cream,' I say out loud.

'What's so important?' she asks.

'Nada, just remembered something.' I can barely speak for all the voices and feelings inside me; suddenly I'm Paddington station for psychics.

'Hal! Look at me!'

'Yeah right, one minute you're ready to drop off, the next you're action man. Something's up!' says Jack.

'Gotta go!'

'Right,' she says, disbelieving, 'a man's gotta do what a man's gotta do, eh?' She's angry again; sarcasm suits her. 'Sorry I got in your way, Hal – off you go then, if you don't want to play.'

'Look at me, Hal! Look at me!'

'No, Charley! I want to look at Jack!'

And I do.

She's sitting in the sunlight, with her hair all crusty from the sea and her cheeks burning red, squinting into the sunlight, and I know I can't go. More than that, I don't want to. I sit down again, torn.

'Sorry,' I say to Jack.

''S'all right,' she says. 'Listen, I just wanted to tell you, 'cos I think you ought to know . . . GOD, this is SO awkward . . .'

Her voice is fading in and out, the dizziness won't go, and I'm scared – scared that if I relax, even for a millisecond, I'll hear that horrible breathing again, and feel the trees beginning to move towards me, filling me with memories.

Her memories?

My imaginings?

'Hal, are you all right?' Jack's face is close to mine. Her eyes are wide, with huge black pupils that I can see myself reflected in, surrounded by a rim of beautiful deep green.

Wow!

'Yeah, just dizzy.'

'What is it, Hal? You look weird.'

'I FEEL friggin' weird.'

'No worries, I'll explain another time,' she says, and I begin to feel the warmth of her face slipping closer and closer to mine. Our eyes are wide, wide windows looking into each other, and then I feel mine begin to close in expectation; but somewhere behind the red and blue and black lights dancing under my lids, the sound of waves rushes up from far below on the beach, and as sure as night follows day, the breathing begins again.

In. Out. In. Out.

And I can hear Charley's voice, whispering at me, like she can read my mind.

'Tingle. Delight. Turkish.'

And there's the sound of laughter, somewhere in the trees, a deep, low rumble.

'Who are you?'

'Get away from me!' I hear my own voice scream, but it sounds high and strange, like a girl's voice.

'Hal! Hal!'

I can hear Jack's voice, whispering and urgent, calling me back to somewhere in the distance. She's somewhere behind the sun, and the sea, and the blackened silhouettes of the old oaks.

But Charley's voice is right up close.

'Hal!' she screams. *'Help me!'* and I'm up, and running through the grove to the edge of the world, where the cliff falls free all the way down to the sea, and the waves seem to lift themselves up on the air, on the ocean's own breath, only to drop again, far below.

She's down there!

For one wild moment I think I can see her body falling and landing, a fading outline, on one of the rocks; the way she was when I found her, with the waves reaching up all around, then running away as though they couldn't bear to come too close, and back again as if they couldn't bear to leave her.

'Charley!' I yell, as though I could change time, could make her hear me and stand up, get up.

'Get up!' I hear myself scream, because I can feel a shadow fall across her, cold and dark.

And I see the shadow under the street light. Is it that shadow coming?

'Charley!' I call again and again, across the empty echoing, glistening sea, but there's no answer, only the faintest echo of her words: *'Who's there? Help me, Hal . . .'*

'Hal! Hey, Hal!'

Who's that? Someone else is calling at me, and tugging on my arm. I try to shake them off.

'Shit, Hal, what the . . . ?'

'Green eyes, green as leaves.'

'Jackie?'

'Hal!'

I look at her in wonder. I look into her eyes and the whole world just seems to spin back into itself, to settle on its old and familiar axis. The trees are just trees. The air is still and golden, and the sea is back to washing the shore in the distance.

'Do you think they look like wizards?' I hear myself ask.

'Jesus, Hal!' she says, and her voice is all shaky. 'All I was gonna do was kiss you, and you totally freak out, and start muttering about trees.'

She tries to laugh. She's warm from the sun as she clings to my arm.

'Christ, I thought you were gonna jump, I really thought . . .' She runs out of words for once, and we sit together, shaking, watching the sun as it slowly shrinks from the sky, and loses its way across the waves.

'What the hell was that all about?' she asks after a while.

'I don't know.'

'Well you better try an' start knowing,' she says, making me smile.

So I make a start. I try to explain about hearing Charley, the voice and the breathing, but it's like trying to catch water with your bare hands, the feeling slips away, turns into something else. So I start with the real Charley, and how much I miss her. I tell Jack how we used to spend all summer together, on the beach, in the woods, climbing the old castle walls in Tintagel. I tell her how Charley told me stories, how it really pissed me off that she always had the lead part. I tell her about her old notebook full of poems, whole pages full of words, that slowly, page after page, became sentences, verses, poems. I tell her how I never look at them any more, because there was one about me, and it nearly got me, made me cry.

'How did it go?'

'What?'

'The poem about you?'

'Can't remember.'

But something flashes through my mind, words from the notebook, words I've heard, felt.

'Tingle. Delight. Turkish.'

'Mmm,' says Jack. 'Did she write about everything?'

I begin to tell her how Charley changed last year, wasn't around much, never really told me what she was up to any more. How it felt like she was hugging the best secret in the world, all to herself. How it drove me crazy, and how I hated her, for leaving me alone with Mum and Dad and Sara, and how I feel so bad inside, like the hate might have killed her somehow. What I don't tell her, can't tell her, is that I have two parents who really are considering putting Charley out of her misery. Isn't that enough of a shadow to have over you? I wonder if that's it? I wonder if Charley can somehow sense what they're thinking?

Right now anything feels possible.

Me and Jack don't look at each other; we look at the shrinking sun. I tell her about the graveyard and how I think I hear Charley calling me, like a child sometimes, lost and alone and all in the dark; like a warning at other times, or a call to remember. She lets me know how I'm doing with a touch here, a hug there, until I'm all finished, empty and silent.

'So you think it'll help to jump off a cliff?' she asks at long last.

'What?'

'Well, isn't that what you were doing?'

'No!'

'Well?'

'You don't get it. I hear her voice. I know it sounds mad. But I hear her voice calling me, and she wants me to help, to remember, to do something, I don't know. It's mad, maybe I'm mad.'

'I thought she was dead,' she says, after another while.

'She is, good as.'

'Not if she can do that to you, Hal. What does she want you to remember, d'you think?'

I look at her. I look at her eyes, darker now in the fading sun, at her golden lashes.

'Are you for real?' I ask.

'Why?'

'Why aren't you freaked out? Why don't you think I'm a loony tune?'

She smiles at me. It's another maddening girly poor-boy smile, and she says:

'You haven't met my mum, have you?'

'So?'

'She's had our whole HOUSE cleared of spirits. She says there was some poor boy up the chimney who kept crying, kept me awake for years, she says, but I can't remember it.'

'What happened?'

'A woman came round and spoke to him, or something, let him go, and I've slept like a baby ever since. So the story goes.'

'Do you believe it?'

'Mum does.'

I shiver.

'So why's this happening, Hal?' she says simply. 'And what made you nearly jump off a cliff?'

'I wasn't going to jump. I've told you! I just . . .'

'Yeah?'

I begin again.

'I just hear her voice, and I, I – look, I see things. Just now, it was as though she was in the trees – her voice, and her feelings – and then I thought she was in the sea . . . but it's just memories, Jack, that's all.'

'Right, and—?'

'And nothing.'

'And you were shit scared, Hal. You set off like a fox hearing hounds.'

126

She waits.

She reminds me of Dad, waiting, but it's a nice wait, as if she wants to give me time to put it all together and make sense of it somehow, to not be so scared.

And slowly an idea does begin to form. I try it out on her.

'There was a shadow, Jack, like a . . . shadow, on the beach, watching her,' I manage after a while. 'And I don't think, I don't think . . . she KNOWS who it was. That's the feeling I get, and maybe – it's not – maybe she wants me to find out who it is?'

When I look up Jack's face has changed; it's white with worry.

'What?' I say. 'What is it?' But she just shakes me off.

'Shadow of death!' she says, in a weird, horror-type voice, and I know this is kind of awful, but it just makes us both howl with laughter, until we're screeching like hyenas and holding on to each other for dear life, completely unable to stop.

'Stop, Hal!'

'Can't!'

We laugh until our eyes run out of tears. After a while, we wrap our arms around each other again, and we look out to sea, silent.

Far below us, the people on the beach have turned into shadows, black silhouettes whose voices drift and shiver on the wind, fading before they reach us. The sunlight has narrowed to a shining pathway across the waves, a pathway of light that looks as if it could take us straight up past the clouds, and on up to heaven, if only we were brave enough to try.

Jack leans against me and says my name.

'Hal.' I like the sound of it in her mouth.

'Jackie?' I reply, and I like the sound of that too.

'Yeah?'

'I was wondering . . .' I say, and I am, I'm wondering about what she said before: All I was gonna do was kiss you.

'Yeah?' she says.

'About that kiss?'

'Would that be this kiss?' she asks, and she leans towards me, slowly, and suddenly Charley's words aren't so weird any more.

'Tingle.' Like expectation.

'Delight. Turkish delight.' Like taste, the taste of chocolate and sea-salt.

We're kissing, we kiss until the sun drops right over the edge of the sea and we're hidden by the shadowy old oaks, and the evening. We kiss until the old oaks are black and silent in the glade. When I finally look away from her, the sun has gone, and I think, maybe desire is like a shadow, too, a shadow that covers up the whole world and makes it go away.

Is this what Charley's trying to tell me?

When we finally break apart it feels cold, as though the air wants to get between us and wrap us up in itself, take us back. In the deep blue dusk, there are only the fires far below on the beach to guide us back down the cliff, and we slip and cling and go on kissing.

'Come down to the beach,' she says. But I don't want to share her with anyone, ever. I want it to always be like this, just me and Jack in the dark, kissing and whispering, our hands discovering what our eyes can't see.

'OK, just for a bit,' I say. 'Just us.'

'OK,' she says. We're whispering, as though we might disappear if we spoke aloud.

The sand's still warm from the sun, and we dig holes, lie down in its softness.

'I wish we could stay here until the stars come out.'

'Why not?' Her voice is lazy.

I smile, then remember that she can't see me.

'Parents?' I say.

'But . . .' she starts, and then she stops herself, falling quiet.

'But what?'

'Nothing.' She holds my hand under the small of her back in the warm sand, but my radar's up.

'But what?' I ask her, and I sit up, and suddenly I wish it was daylight and that I could see into her eyes.

'Leave it, Hal. Not now.' Her voice is drowsy, dragging me back to the warm sand, to the dip where my own shape lies, just waiting for me to curl back into it, next to her.

'Leave what?' I need to know. I am surrounded by darkness and secrets.

'Remember!'

She sits up and flicks sand out of her hair, irritated. 'Leave it, Hal,' she warns, but I don't listen, can't listen, I need to know.

'Tell me what the "but" is, Jackie, just tell me.'

'OK, the "but" is this – how about all the time big sis Charley spent star-gazing, how come she managed it?'

'What? She what? What do you know about Charley?'

'She was around last year.'

'You knew her?'

She backs off, right off.

'Not really, she was just around . . . I know she used to be out all night sometimes with— I did try to tell you – earlier, up on the cliff . . . before you went all weird.'

'Thanks, Jack. I dunno how Charley stayed out, or where she was. I dunno what she was doing, but thanks for letting me know you knew her, thanks a lot, I owe you one.'

And all the time I'm talking, I'm thinking. I wonder how many nights Charley left us all in the house on the cliff. I turn to it, and it gleams white in the deep dusk.

'Ha, they're all in there. Sara's snug asleep, Mum and Dad doing whatever, and me, I'm out here, on the outside.'

Is that what she thought?

But the thrill doesn't last long for me, the difference being that I know exactly what Mum's doing; she's pacing, she's wondering where I am. And as though she can hear my very thoughts, I watch as the front door of the house slowly opens, and the light from inside floods the terrace.

'She worries,' I say.

'Yeah, right!' says Jack.

'See you tomorrow?' I ask. I hope.

'If your mum lets you out,' and then she's gone, before I can react to the words, before the shock of them settles. Whoa, that was a bit cruel. I touch the warm sand where her body was, and then I get up and walk out of the shadows, towards the light.

Charley: Hospital. Now.

'Charley!'

His voice echoes, disappears in all that air and sunshine, fades to nothing . . . and then he's gone, and all I can see are empty waves . . . and all I can hear are words . . .

Turkish. Tingle. Delight.

Words that make my skin rise and my breath catch . . .

'Who are you?' I ask, and something turns over inside me, a snag deep in my belly. I feel my lips fill with blood as they whisper a name . . .

'Pete!'

And I am caught in an Atlantic wave, rolling over and over, uncontrollably. The water's rushing through my nose, filling my ears and mouth. I can't breathe. There's no place on the earth to hold on to . . . I don't know which way is up . . . or down . . .

'Pete! Pete!

Who are you?'

And I feel the pull of a wave running over my body, as I dive straight through its centre.

Pete.

The memory picks me up in its arms and carries me away . . .
on the biggest, bluest, cleanest wave you ever saw . . .

Pete . . .

Charley. Then.

I'm in the waves . . .

God! He's gorgeous.

Gorgeous. Gorgeous. Gorgeous . . .

Pete.

'Fit or what?' I'm muttering to myself, and my whole body tingles inside my wet suit, as soon as he's within eye range.

Surf god!

Found one, Jenna, found one.

OMIGOD, he's TALKING to me, he's in the waves, he's coming closer.

'Hey, Charley,' he says. 'Try it like this.' And he reaches for the boogie, which looks suddenly small and controllable.

'Hold it sideways,' he says, or at least I think that's what he's saying. I can't quite tell, 'cos I'm watching his lips move, and I know it's words that are coming out, but somehow watching him is working way better than hearing him.

Before I can get myself together to reply, I feel his hands around my waist, they feel huge; they almost reach right round me. My heart falls right through my body as his hands touch me, connecting to parts of my anatomy I didn't even know I had!

Visceral? Explosive? Expletive?

Who knows?

Words fail me.

'Don't try to stand until it's worth it, rest on the waves,' he tells me. Stand? Stand? I can barely BREATHE, my knees are knocking together so hard beneath the waves.

'Just get the feel of the waves. Ready?' he asks, as though my world hasn't just stopped spinning, as though I'm not relaying every second in mental texts to Jen and Sal.

We're waiting in the water.

Up. Down. Up. Down.

The rhythm of the waves steadies me, like breathing.

I want the wave to hurry; I'm dying of embarrassment. I want the wave never to come at all.

'See the wave?' he asks. 'Watch it – watch it – one, two, go Charley!' He hurls me forward. The board races straight for shore, and it doesn't stop till I'm scraping sand in the shallows. By the time I turn and look back, he's already up on another one, he's winding and weaving, and practically singing the board up the wave to where it curls over, before dropping back to its deep blue base. His hands hang loose by his sides, and he just seems to step off the wave when he's finished. I could watch him forever.

Rhythm. Chant. Harmony.

He lands a few feet away. 'Come on!' He drops his board, and grabs my boogie before pulling me back through the waves, pushing the whole ocean aside, just to make way for me.

'Ever tried a double ride?' he asks, and I feel my heart stop, just skip a whole beat in pure wonder, at the thought of lying on his back and being carried through the waves with him.

'Best way to get the rhythm,' he says. I'm smirking, I can't help it, I know it's not cool and all, but rides, doubles, rhythms? I know I'm just a kid, really, and that he is definitely a seventeen-year-old surf god, but even he can't be that dumb. Can he?

He looks at me, and smirks back.

'When did you get to stop being about five?' he asks.

'When I was six?' I suggest. I am so pleased with myself, smart answer, quick.

He thinks so too, he must do, he's laughing.

I made him laugh!

If we were in a film, he'd be in slow motion now, and the sea-water would break up into a million rainbow droplets all around his golden head, and you would see my eyes grow as big as the sky in the effort to fit him all in; but we aren't in a film, so he just looks out to sea and says,

'Call a wave.'

'Number seven,' I say, and he smiles.

'Number seven it is, then.'

Stunning. Sexy. Sensual.

I almost believed, when that wave came in.

We're standing sideways in the water – well, he is, I'm just floating alongside him, weightless in the swell. I feel as though the only thing tying me to the earth, to what's real, is the feel of his body beneath my hands. They're cupped over the curve of his shoulder near his neck. My palms can feel the flex of his muscles as his head turns; the tips of my fingers graze across the long sweep of his collarbone. I lay my face against his wetsuited back and wonder what his skin feels like.

Hold on. Hold on. Drink every second.

'Face up, Charley!' he says. 'We're on our way!' and he turns and grins and I hold my face up to his in the suddenly too-bright sunlight, unable to look away. He's looking out to sea, and it's only the shadow of the wave across his face that makes me move.

'Now!' he yells, and we're up. He pushes off, and my whole body swings up with his, lying close as a shadow, clinging to him, taking up as little space as possible so that the waves are fooled into thinking that we're one.

The wave rushes forward to the sand. We're screaming, people parting before us, falling back. This low down, this close to the water, the speed is awesome. The spray's right in our faces and I hang on in one long screech of delight, pressing my body against his, hoping that this will be the wave that everyone mentions, that this will be the legendary one, the one that carries us straight into eternity, into a deep-blue non-stop, where we can scream and laugh and hang on to each other in one long, endless ride, forever.

But it isn't, and the wave runs out, and the board scrapes

to a halt against the sand. The water's warmer and gentler here, but the surf still runs over us, pulling us back to the sea. We're gasping for air, laughing, and wiping the salt out of our stinging eyes.

'Good ride!' And he pulls me up out of the sea, brushes the hair out of my face and stares at me for a moment, as though he's only just really seeing me. Suddenly the sea's gone; I can't feel the boogie against my ankle, or the salt sting in my eyes. His eyes are blue, really really blue. They don't take on the colour of anything else, they're just them-selves, and right now they're all that I can see.

'Wow, your eyes really are the colour of the sea,' he tells me.

'Only 'cos they're next to it,' I say, amazed to find that I can still do words.

'You mean they change?'

'Yep.' I blink them at him, just so's he gets the full effect. I'm thinking, where do I come from? What kind of idiot am I? I'm out of my depth here, struggling to stay afloat.

'Cool!' he says.

We think for a bit, and then we're awkward, standing in the surf, staring at each other. Suddenly it feels as though we're looking at us with everybody else's eyes, instead of our own.

Charley Ditton, your moment in paradise is now over.

'Do they go orange in the firelight, then?' he finally asks, after what seems like for ever.

'Dunno.' I'm finally tongue-tied, unable to do anything

other than stare like some miserable dumb animal at that lovely lush grass on the other side of the fence, that I could never possibly hope to reach out to, let alone eat.

'Why don't you come to the barby with me tonight, and find out?'

He's asking me? It's hard not to look over my shoulder. I search him all over, checking for the joke, the hook with the fly in it, the one that'll hurt if I dare to take the bait.

'Maybe,' I tell him, knowing that Mum'll say no, and then Dad'll say why not? And that both of them will want me back in by ten-thirty, which is just so embarrassing, when all the camp kids just seem to wander back home whenever.

'Surf's up. See you there, then.' And he's back in the water, diving through the waves and out to where the swell just lifts and drops. To where there's no real time at all, only the here, and the now, and the waiting for the next one.

Charley: Hospital. Now.

Pete.

Pete.

I whisper his name, hold it to me like scarlet ribbons, and wait.

'Who are you?'

But there is no more; there is only the sound of the clock in the room outside of me, endlessly ticking.

Tick, tock, tick, tock.

Somebody stop it, please stop it, it drives me crazy, but they can't hear me, and it goes on . . . and on . . . tick, tock . . .

Why am I trapped and unable to move?

Stuck, with the ticking clock, and the endless sound of something breathing . . .

In. Out. In. Out.

Up. Down. Up. Down.

Like the sea.

Dark.

'Mum!'

I miss her, miss her so suddenly and sharply, as though the very stitches that hold me together are being run through with an open scissor-blade, each strand slowly parting, as each stitch is severed.

'Don't leave me!'

Hal. Now.

By the time I get back from the beach, Mum's gone in, but she's left the door open. I can hear their voices, see their black shadows behind the curtains, sitting in the sun room, not knowing that I'm here, not hearing my footsteps, silent, on the night-drenched grass.

'Milly, I'm just asking you to think about it, that's all!' Dad sounds about as angry as he ever gets with her these days, but the anger's locked up tight behind his words, locked tight away, so that they come out sounding all odd and soft, but somehow hard-edged and dangerous as well.

'I am thinking about it,' Mum yells at him. 'I can't stop myself thinking about it!'

And then Dad's voice again, suddenly soft and truly sorry.

'I know, I know, Mill, but I need to know WHAT IT IS that you're thinking.'

'I can't . . . I can't say it . . .' Her words trail away in despair, and I watch as Dad's shadow holds an arm around her, and whispers something unheard to her shaking shoulders.

I feel cold and alone outside the window, the shiver-fist comes back, and then I hear her voice, Charley's voice, echoing through the star-filled sky.

'Mum!' she calls, and it's as though my own heart has suddenly been severed from my body, and I hear Mum's words loud and clear in her sob-ridden voice:

'But letting her go, Jon, how could I . . . I can't . . . even the thought is . . .'

And then my heart is back, back and pumping furious blood around my body, beating fast with fear and horror.

'Charley!' Her name's out before I can hold it in, and her reply is just as swift.

'Don't leave me!'

And then I see her, floating, alone and helpless in deepest, darkest space. I see that she is gravity-less and disappearing.

'Charley!'

'Hal?' Mum turns to the window and I leg it, I don't know why, I just don't want to be near them. I crouch behind the gate and watch as she sits on the wall, waiting. I watch as Dad comes out with a mug, and sits with her. I

139

hear Sara call. Dad disappears, but Mum sits on, and finally I realize that there's just no way past them, they're up till I get home, no matter how long it takes. I get up, my legs stiff, and try to stretch and look as if I haven't been hiding.

Mum's sitting in the dark on the low wall, waiting for me to get close enough for her to know that I'm not just some stranger, drifting up the wrong pathway. I don't call out, I don't help her. I can't.

'Hal?' She's anxious.

'Yeah, 's me.'

'I was looking for you.' She's apologetic, can't help herself. Neither can I.

'I know.'

'We just wondered where—?' I cut her off.

'I'm fine.'

'I wanted to tell you—'

'No problem.'

'Have you eaten?'

'Not hungry.'

'Hal, it's been a long day, and there are things we need to—'

'Night, Mum.'

'Hal!'

'See ya.'

'HAL!'

'WHAT?'

'How are you?'

I stop still on the stairs, so close to the bedroom, to

safety. I consider making a run for it, but can't. 'Fine, Ma, yeah, cool, and today I met a—'

'We rang the hospital today, just to check . . .'

'Right, yeah, and I met—'

'And we've arranged to talk to a consultant. One of the nurses thought there might be a change, but the doctors don't think so—'

Her eyes are all shiny bright with unshed tears, and before I know it the words are out of my mouth, they don't ask permission, and I can't take them back.

'Right, so nothing's happened at all then, Mum, yeah? So there's absolutely nothing to tell me, yeah? No change in Charley. Are you sure about that? Not some little thing on your mind that you might be forgetting to tell me, again?'

Where did that come from? Truth is, I'm angry, furious that she asks about my day only so's she can tell me absolutely nothing about Charley.

Dad's right there, right in my face before I know it. He comes out of nowhere and he's got me by the neck, and down the stairs, before I can even lift my fists to try and fight him off.

'You spoilt little bastard!' He's hissing low and hard, so that he doesn't wake Sara.

'You talkin' about me?' I ask, but the only reply I get is that he shakes me, hard.

'Put him down, Jon, NOW!' says Mum in her deadly-venom voice, and Dad drops me like I'm a piece of shit he's just flicked off his shoe.

'Go to bed, Hal. You've had a rough day.'

Mum's voice is gentle, but it sounds as though it's breaking apart at the seams, as though the only things holding it together are air and wishes, and I feel like a piece of shit myself, because I can't say sorry, and I should, because I know that she's trying to give up a wish, a hope, that Charley might be all right one day – and giving that up leaves her with nothing but air to live on.

When I wake up the room's grey, and outside the rain's falling, a fine rain that falls like wet air, making a grey mist that covers the sea and the hillside. I groan aloud. Was that really me, telling my girlfriend (Hey! Girlfriend, I like it!) that I have visions? Was that really me sticking a knife into my grief-stricken mother?

I turn over and hide my head under the pillow.

'It rainin', Hal!' I hear Sarz yelp from the next room, and then she's through the door like a cannon ball, bouncing all over the bed, and all over me. Being pummeled feels good. I deserve it.

'Hal, Hal, Flounder's in a bucket in the rain! He'll die!'

'Flounder's a fish, Sarz,' I tell her.

'Do fish like the rain?'

'Fish are partial to all forms of water.'

'They like it?'

'Yeah, Sarz, they like it.'

'Daddy says you gotta new friend.' She changes gear so quickly sometimes, it's freaky.

'Have I?'

'Yep, an' her name's Jackie.'

'That's right.'

'Hal?'

'Yeah?'

'What if the bucket all filled with water an' then Flounder FLOWED out of the bucket?'

'Then Flounder would definitely die.' I give it to her straight.

'Oh!' She thinks about it for about a millisecond, and then moves rapidly on. 'Is Jackie your girlfriend? Pingu the penguin's got a girlfriend, but he isn't nice. He eats fish.'

'Right.' My head's buzzing with it all, like the grey mist's inside my head and I can't see clearly.

'Will you eat swimmin' fish now?' Sarz asks.

'What?' God, she's so random.

'Now you got a girlfriend, like Pingu!'

'No! Never! I will only eat fish if they're dead and cooked!'

'Do fish eat people, Hal?'

'Yeah, big ones do, like sharks.'

'Oh.' She thinks for a bit.

'In our sea?' she asks after a while.

'No Sarz, not in our sea, our sea is safe.'

She shakes her head then, very slowly and seriously, as though she's thought about this a lot, as though she knows.

'It isn't, Hal.'

'Yep, it is. There are no eating fish in our sea, promise.'

'There are dangerous flower things that eat us!' She nods her head at me, and the thought of a group of vicious geraniums skulking beneath the waves makes me laugh and laugh, and somehow the day doesn't seem so bad after all.

'You are the funniest person on the planet!' I tell her, but for some reason she doesn't laugh, the way she usually does, she just stares at me as though I've finally let her down too, and then she stalks away by herself, head in the air.

'I'm goin' to save Flounder,' she tells me, and the way she says it sounds just like it might be me she's saving him from.

I punch the pillow. 'And I'm goin' down the garden to eat worms.'

It's what we say when we're so fed up we can't even stand ourselves. It's what I say when I finally get to play face-the-family in the kitchen.

'I'm goin' down the garden to eat worms.'

'Good idea,' says Dad. He doesn't look at me, he's still too angry. I know how he feels, I don't much like him either.

'Can I come?' Sarz asks.

'No,' I tell her, 'it's a thing you have to do alone.'

'Pleeze?' she says, and gives me the big eyes. I look at Mum.

'I suppose it is a solitary activity,' she says, and smiles, but it's like the life's gone out of her double time this morning, her smile's all in her mouth. Her eyes only come alive when they land on Sara, and then – well – then they're full of something I can only see, not imagine. Mum and Dad aren't together this morning, they're miles apart. Mum's grey and sad, Dad's angry and lonely. I can always tell.

'C'mon then, Sarz,' I say, 'this is no place for worm-eaters.'

'An' Flounder?' she says.

'Not Flounder, worms EAT fish.' I'm very firm. I am not dragging a bucket full of water around half of Cornwall.

'Wellies, not sandals, Sara,' Mum yells after her. 'And thanks, Hal.'

''S OK, Mum.'

She holds out her arm and squeezes my hand. 'We love you. You do know that, Hal, don't you?'

'Yeah!' I try to laugh. 'Mum, I'm sorry about – well – I didn't mean to—'

'It's yesterday, Hal,' she says, like I do, and she sighs as though the end of the week, and her visit to Charley, was forever away, and she's wondering if she can even make it to lunchtime.

'Missing her?' I ask. It isn't really a question, and only deserves the nod it gets.

'I might have to go up sooner, Hal, there's a lot I need to talk to the doctors about.'

I nod, not able to speak. I know what they're going to be talking about.

'We ALL miss her,' says Dad, and I try not to feel the anger come up inside, the fury at his stupid stupid dadness. Of course we all fuckin' miss her, I want to say, but Mum

145

more, an' more of the time, and it's NOT the same for all of us, however much you wish it was, and we can't share it. But I just nod and go to rescue Sara. Or maybe this time she's the one rescuing me.

Sarz sets off across the road, holding my hand, hard. She bends herself against the rain as we walk past the caff, empty and forlorn in the falling rain. Brooke and her mum, wave at us from behind the steamy windows, holding up cups of hot chocolate, but Sarz pulls me along, and I let her. I'm busy wondering what Mum and Dad are saying to each other right now, and wondering if there's anything I can say, or do – anything that will make them change their minds. Perhaps if me and Sarz could be happier they would feel better about Charley.

'She doesn't want to die yet,' I hear myself mutter.

'We're not goin' to the stream, are we?' Sarz looks up at me and gives me the speculation from beneath her lashes.

'You're the one making the decisions,' I tell her. 'Does your tummy have good feelings about going this way?'

'Yep,' she says, but she looks doubtful, as though she really isn't the one choosing where she goes.

'Are the feelings yours, Sarz?' I ask.

'They're inside me,' she says slowly.

I begin to lead her down a side path, away from the bridge and the stream and into the woods, but she tugs at my hand, hard.

'This way, Hal!' she says.

And once again, we're heading exactly where Sarz wants to take me, and I'm really not so sure that it's a good idea. I'm not so sure I want to be anywhere, near any place, that means anything to me and Charley right now, but somehow we're heading straight for the woods anyway.

'Charley likes the woods, I think,' Sarz says, as though she knows.

'Yeah,' I say, 'she did.'

I look at the sea; it's a steely blanket of grey, endlessly creeping up through the drizzle. There's something relentless about it today, relentless and ugly, like an army, intent on coming in to land.

'I'm not a big girl, Hal,' says Sarz out of the blue, and I'm filled with such an overwhelming sense of hopelessness, a feeling that I'll never really be able to get what she means, or how she means it.

I'll never be able to just 'be' with Sarz, the way I could with Charley.

'No, you're not big,' I say, 'but you can make it to the stream.'

The stream is deep in the valley, hidden in the woods. Once we're down the lane and over the bridge, the trees arch into a green alleyway. Water drips off the leaves into the mud. It's always quiet and empty in the woods; everyone comes to Brackinton for the beach, the woods are the forgotten place.

'Squelch, squerch,' mutters Sara as we slosh our way through the mud.

'Mmmm.' I'm not really listening to Sara; I'm remembering being here with Charley.

'We're goin' on a bear-hunt,' Sara sings, 'we're going to catch a big one, what a beautiful day, we're not scared.' She hangs off my hand, looking all around her, her eyes huge.

I remember coming along this path with Charley; it was raining then, too. This is where we always came when it rained. It's weird walking along the path without her. It doesn't seem real that she's not here. A sudden breeze catches the leaves and fills the air with the sound of falling water, and underneath it I can hear something else, something hiding within the wind, and calling out to me in her voice.

'Come on, Hal,' and then the wind fades and dies, but it leaves behind a silence and a space filled with memories, and before I can stop it, time's colliding, and the world skews and I'm not really here with Sara any more, I'm with Charley and it's our first time ever in this wood . . .

Charley/Hal. Then.
I am eleven.

Me and Charley are walking through the dripping trees, awed by the silence, by the sense of every single thing around us being bigger and older than us. Well, I am, anyway.

'If we follow the stream we can't get lost,' I say, I hope.

'That's what you think!' she laughs, and her eyes have

that wicked, dancing gleam running through them, like deep green moss holding on to dappled light. She throws her hands high in the air, like a conductor of cosmic power, and she shouts into the silence. 'This wood CONTROLS the stream, and it can bend the water any way it likes. It can take us HOME . . .' and then she creeps up close, and whispers, her breath still sweet with the smell of sherbet lemons, 'or it can take us deep into the heart of the wood, where there's nothing but time, and silence.'

'Oh, shut it, Charley,' I say. Truth is, she can really scare me sometimes. I pick up some stones and try to ignore her. I skim them; they bounce off the water and rocks and land on the other bank.

'Ha, seven, beat that!' I shout, but when I turn around, she's gone. The silence in the wood deepens somehow without her there, feels more threatening.

I pick up stones and skim and skim, and in between I try to spot her; and when I do spot her, I think, there's a big one coming her way. But none of the bushes move, or even whisper of her presence, the only sounds are the dripping trees and the stream, muted by the mossy banks and the dead still air. I can feel the panic rising up from my gut when she doesn't appear; it pushes up against my ribs, urging me to call her name, and it's only the thought of her scornful laughter that stops me.

'Hal!'

Her voice comes from nowhere. I turn and stumble, knocking stones everywhere, falling into the stream. She appears out of the trees on the opposite bank, pointing up into the air behind her.

'Look,' she calls. 'Can you see it?'

'Stop it, Charley!'

But she just grabs my arm and pulls me across the stream. 'Look, Hal, up in that tree, something red.'

She's right: high up, a glimpse of something, an impossible colour.

'Probably an old sock!' I say.

But she turns to me, her eyes wide with excitement. 'Let's find out!'

Let's not, I want to say. Let's just go home and have a cup of tea. But she's already pushing her way through the undergrowth and I don't want to be alone again, so I follow.

The bushes and brambles clear, and we're in a glade.

'That's it,' she says. Towards the end of the clearing there's a tree, its bark impossibly white, its leaves a golden limey green. Red flowers clamber all over it, climbing and hanging, and one flower has run all the way to the very top, before leaping out to hang in the air, as if by magic.

Charley looks up at it. We both do. How can it be there? Its stem is invisible; it looks as though it's floating in space.

'How can we reach it, Hal?' she asks, and I shake my head.

'We can't,' I say, and I watch her as she stares. Something flits through her eyes, a feeling I can't name, but which haunts me now, something she felt as she stared up at the

150

deep red, tightly-packed petals floating above us.

It's a beautiful place, but frightening after what Charley said about woods and streams and all that. It feels like the heart of somewhere old and forgotten, and waiting – waiting, perhaps, for two unsuspecting children to just happen to chance upon it. Charley turns away from the flower, and looks around.

'I think it's an old garden, Hal,' she says. 'I think someone used to live here.'

'Where's the house, then?' I ask.

'Let's see.'

It rises out of the woods slowly. I think we expected it to be either whole and shining or a pile of rubble, but it isn't either. It's like the wood's grown into its walls, hiding and protecting it. It's small, just a cottage really, and there's a little wooden gate, covered and bolted closed by ivy. We climb over it, too excited to speak. The old wooden door looks shut and locked, but the window frames are empty black holes. We're holding hands as we approach it. Together, we get closer and closer, our hands clasping tighter and tighter. What if someone jumps out and yells at us? Even worse, what if some totally scary unknown THING appears?

But nothing happens at all; the house just stands there, silently, letting us approach.

It's dark inside, too dark to really see.

'Give us a leg up, Hal, I'm going in.'

'Not without me.'

'OK, but me first.' I hold my hands together and lean against the wall. Her wellies are wet and gritty with dirt against my palm, as she slides through the glassless frame, slipping towards the floor. I feel my heart drop: it's like she's slipping into a black hole. I panic that she'll never come back, that I'll be left by the wall, waiting, for ever.

'Can you see anything?'

'Not yet, idiot!' All that's left of her is her voice, echoing through the black hole of the window.

'God, Hal, it's amazing, there's furniture and everything.' She reappears and hauls me up through the window.

It's as though someone's just wandered away one day and never returned. There's a newspaper by the fire, and the armchair still has a dip in the seat, as though some ghost might still be sitting there, watching us.

'Let's go!' I say, but Charley grabs my arm, and pulls me through the door to the kitchen. A big fireplace, tin plates covered in dry dust. As we touch and stare at everything the same thought comes slowly to both of us, and our footsteps falter on the stairs.

'D'you think there's a dead body up there?' I ask.

She nods, her eyes alight. 'Maybe!' She laughs. 'All dust and bones and cobwebs!'

'Shall we get Dad?'

She shakes her head. 'No, it won't be the same if Dad knows it's here.'

She's right, but I still wish for Dad, because if there was anything nasty he'd stay and fight it, and then I could get away. Charley can run faster than me.

'Ready?' she says, and I nod. The stairs are wooden, they creak and groan, grey fluff-balls float around our feet. I close my eyes and hold on to Charley's hand.

'Which door?' Her voice makes me jump, and we giggle. I open my eyes. Straight ahead of me is a wall; there are two doors, one on either side of us. I point to the one on her side; at least then she has to go first. She opens the door.

The room's almost empty. There's a big iron bed and a lumpy mattress that looks like a few mice might live in it. There's still a glass by the table, inside it a green dried-up ring, dust and dead insects in it.

'Amazing!' whispers Charley. The dust stirs and she sneezes. It sounds so loud it makes us giggle again.

'Let's go!'

Charley's coughing and sneezing, and laughing through the dust, but when we get out of the room she doesn't go down the stairs. She throws open the other bedroom door, and then she screams. She sits on the floor and screams, and I can't get past her, so I start screaming too.

'What? What is it?'

'It's in there!' I can't hear her properly, but nothing's coming out of the room, and I can't get past her to the stairs, so I go in. That shuts her up. The room's empty except for a cot underneath the window. I get there before I can think, and I yell at Charley.

'Shut up, Charley, it's a doll,' but even as I pick it up I'm scared, scared that when I turn it around, its eyes might blink, and its mouth begin to move. I throw it at Charley.

'Stupid doll, you scared me half to death,' she yells, and we go crazy with relief. We rip through the house, opening cupboards and pulling apart old clothes. Our faces and hands are black with the years of old soot and dust, and it's only Charley looking at her watch that stops us.

'Shit, we're late for lunch!' We don't put anything back, we just run through the woods for home, leaping through the stream, and throwing water over each other to get the dirt off.

'Well, looks like you two had a good time,' says Mum when we get home.

'Building dams,' we say together, and smile at each other. 'Sorry, Mum!'

'Get those clothes in the laundry, sandwiches are in the kitchen. Honestly, you two,' she grumbles – but she was happy then, happier than any of us knew. Happy that we'd had a good time, happy that we had each other.

Hal. Now.

I sit down on a log and try to breathe. I don't want to remember when we were a family. The pain is searing, like a blade that enters so silently and quickly, promising numbness, only to hurt even harder as the memories well up and finally spill over.

'Miss you, miss you, miss you.
Oh Charley, Charley, Charley.'

What is it with names? Why is it that just hearing the sound of a name, over and over again inside you, in whispers, can be almost like holding someone?

'Hal! Look!' Sara's tugging at my hand, pointing high up, her head craning up to the sky, but I don't have to look. I already know the exact bend in the stream, can see the permanent remains of old-built dams, have already spotted the broken pathway through the undergrowth.

'It's a flower,' I say, 'a flower in a tree.' And when I look up, it is – the exact same flower, still hanging impossibly high, from an improbable tree.

I can still see the look in Charley's eyes as she stared up at it.

'How can I reach it, Hal?' Her voice and eyes haunt me.

'You can't,' I say to her this time. *'You can't reach it, Charley, that's why it's so beautiful.'*

And looking back, I understand the look in her eyes now, as she stared up into the breezeless air where the flower hung, so still and silent and waiting; it's the longing for something you can't possibly ever have. It was in her eyes then, and it's in my guts now.

'Miss you, miss you, miss you.'

'I don't like that flower!' says Sara, and she folds herself against my leg, clinging.

'It's a sad flower, it's lonely,' I hear myself say. But the truth is, I'm the one who's lonely, even with Sara right next to me. I know that I'll always be the one looking after now, never the one lagging behind, and it's strange, because right now I miss it. I miss it all. I miss following Charley across the stream and into the empty house. I miss her stories and her plans. I miss her scaring me half to death, and I miss the way she makes things happen. I know there are some things that I'll never do now, just because she's not here to make me.

I get up and help Sara across the stream towards the house.

What am I doing, why am I going back? But I can't seem to help myself; I'm drawn across the stream, just the way Charley was then, towards the house and the flower – as though a long fine piece of invisible string is gently tugging at me, pulling me there.

'Oh look!' says Sarz. 'A house. Is it magic? Has it got a witch in it? Is there an oven in there, Hal?' And for some weird reason, I feel angry with her, angry that she can be so fearless and excited and curious . . . and just like Charley.

Charley: Hospital. Now.

Dark . . .

'Miss you, miss you, miss you.'

His voice wakes me, whispering of pain, of being in the dark and alone and lost, and he is staring . . . his eyes are so full of . . . something . . . a flower!

I can see it.

I watch as one of my hands slowly reaches up into the air, reaches up past this place where I am stuck and dying, and stretches itself out for the deep red flower. It is so high, so impossibly high and out of reach.

I want it.

My hand reaches into the air for it, I watch as it gets closer . . . and closer . . . until my hand is only a whisper away. I can feel a burning longing begin to spread right through my body, to possess me, so that every cell of each finger and toe is stretching, yearning, leaning out as far as it can go, until it's so nearly within my grasp, this thing of deep, red life, and beauty, and I can almost feel the petals brush my fingers . . . I am so nearly . . .

The pain arrives so solar-plexus sudden: his voice comes out of nowhere, out of the dead time, and the lost time, and the effort to remember.

'Miss you, miss you, miss you.'

'Hal!'

'Charley! Charley! Charley!'

He calls my name to life.

The flower has gone, and there is only the longing left; I am falling, falling away from the memory of the trees and the leaves and the woods, until only the longing to be alive remains . . . to be where he is . . .

'Where are you, Hal?'

Hal. Now.

I'm standing in front of the house with Sarz. I look down at her.

'I don't like it, Hal,' she says again. 'I don't like that red flower. Did it jump up there?'

'Let's get away from it, then,' I say, and my heart thumps.

'Let's go into the house.'

'Look at me, Charley.'

Charley: Hospital. Now.

'Look at me, Charley.'

His voice fills the dark . . . I can't see . . . I smell fire and danger . . .

Where are they? I don't know, I don't know, I only know this fear.

Fear, I can feel it in my fingers.

'Hal! No! Run!'

The feeling is where they are.

'Where are you, Hal, Sara?'

The darkness closes in, squeezing, until I am motionless, helpless, unmoving . . .

Until all I can do is hold on to his name in the darkness, like the sound of an unbreakable heartbeat . . .

'Hal . . . Hal . . . Hal . . . '

Hal. Now.

The house feels different. I can tell that straight away.

I smell it. Fire. Someone's had a fire. The kitchen fireplace is full of newspaper and twigs. Beer cans stand on the table. Someone's using the house, staying here.

'We should go,' I say to Sara, because suddenly my veins are humming with fear, but Sara's intrigued now; she's wandering around, curious.

'Who lives here?' she asks.

'Me and Charley used to come here,' I tell her. Her face falls again, and she looks around carefully, as though she's worried that Charley might suddenly appear.

I grab her hand. 'C'mon, let's go!'

She pulls away from me.

'You're hurting, Hal!'

'Sorry, Sarz, I—' How can I explain it to her, this urgency, this need to flee? 'I've got a bad feeling in my tummy!' I say. But she's already turned away from me, is bending over in the ashes of the hearth, making shapes with her fingers in the dust. I kneel down to help her up, and something catches my eye, something glittering in the dust. Without thinking I pick it up. At first it looks like just any old earring, but then I rub it clean against my hoodie, and my heart stops. It is an earring, but not just any old earring. It's Charley's earring. There's no mistaking it, the deep red ball of glass, with the green and gold foil swirling within it. It's one of a pair, and the other one is always in my own ear. It's the last thing I have of hers, I wear it all the time, just like she did, and I've always wondered what happened to the other one. I even used to look through flotsam and jetsam on the beach, hoping that one day the sea might give it back to me. And now I've found it.

What's it doing here?

I stare at it in my hand, I take mine out of my ear, just to check, but I'm right, they're a pair.

How did it get here?

I look around the house.

Why would Charley come here on her own? And then it hits me: she wouldn't, she was with someone.

And maybe that someone is still here; there's a sleeping bag near the fire. The humming fear begins to rise again.

Something's pulling at my arm.

'What's P for?' says Sarz.

'What?'

'Who is Puh?'

'What, Sarz?'

'Up there, Hal!' she says, pointing to the old oak lintel above my head.

I look up, and at first I can't believe it's really there, carved deep into the old wood.

Charley.

And Sarz is right, there's another name next to hers.

Pete.

Charley + Pete.

It's carved in the wood, names intertwined, beautifully carved, set so deep into the old wood of the fireplace that it's clear that someone wanted the world to know that they were here together.

And there's a date.

28/8/06.

My heart catches. I know exactly when that was, because the very next day was the day I found her. The air in the house is humming now, thrumming, as though the memories are about to catch up with us, and carry us away.

She brought someone else to our place in the woods.

The evidence is here, scratched deep into the old oak, and it's the name Pete. Who are you, Pete? What have you got to do with my sister? Are you the shadow that watches and waits?

And then I hear her voice calling to me . . .

'Hal! No! Run!' and the feelings, sharp as cold rain, full of fear and darkness.

'Pete.' I say the name aloud.

'Puh for Pete?' asks Sarz.

'And where the bloody hell are you at visiting time?' I hear myself shout at the name.

'Langwidge!' says Sara. I've forgotten all about her, but she's still right here.

'Hal . . . run . . . Hal . . . '

'Let's go, Sarz.'

'Is your tummy bad, Hal?'

'Yeah, very bad.'

I lift her up and push her through the window; she grabs hold of me as soon as I follow.

'Quick Hal, the flower's still up there.'

'Sara, it's a FLOWER, in a tree,' I snap. My head's still fizzing with fear, fear that I can't place, and I can't handle the house not being the way it should, and I'm scared of meeting Mr Pete, or whoever it is that's spending time in our house, because the fire's fresh and re-laid, and the LAST thing I'm worried about is a friggin' flower up a tree.

'Don't touch it, Charley!' Sarz suddenly shouts into the still, dead air.

The flower hangs beyond our reach, and for one weird, wild moment, I wish I could reach it. I wish I could tear it down and rip each petal off and throw them into the rushing stream. I want to stamp on it, until it lies squashed and meaningless in the mud.

'It's just a flower, Sarz,' I say, as we walk away.

'I don't like it, Hal,' she says, 'it gives me a bad feeling in my tummy.'

I'm sitting on the terrace, watching the cloud-shadows racing across the hillside, thinking. Will the barbecue happen? Will Jack be there? I don't know what to wear. I don't even know if Jack will still want me there.

The weather keeps changing, shifting itself across the sky. Great clumps of cumulonimbus bunch up and gather, like headless sheep, and the sun shines out from behind them, darkening their depths, lighting up their edges.

'Hal . . . Hal . . . Hal . . .' I can feel her clinging to me, holding my name hostage . . .

Who are you, Pete? Where are you? Did you look up here from the camp site, looking for Charley? Are you watching me now?

My mind feels as jumpy as the clouds.

The sun disappears completely for a moment, lost behind a cloud. I shiver.

Someone walking over my grave.

'Cuppa, Hal?' shouts Dad.

'No thanks.'

'Off out tonight?'

'Yeah, hope so.'

Mum appears with a tea towel over her shoulder. Her hair slips out of the clutches of her sunglasses and drifts around her face. She's burnt even browner by the sun, but somehow it doesn't help, just makes her eyes look even deeper and sadder. Her hair's curly, the way it always goes in the salt sea air, and her face is streaked with some kind of sauce.

'Are you eating with us, or are you barbying?' she asks.

'Barbying.' I don't know why I can't make it sound friendly, but I can't; it comes out so short and uninviting.

Daughter-killer.

Whoa!

'I'll get something for you to take – you can't go empty-handed. What do you think? Burgers, sausages, corn on the cob?'

I think.

'Fish, mermaid, octopus?' she goes on.

'Whatever!' I say in the end, and I hear her take a short sharp breath in, and stop herself saying anything.

The old Mum would have told me straight. 'Don't talk to me like that,' she would have said. 'I'm offering you something, young man. You say "thank you" when people offer you something, even parents, right?'

I miss her. I don't just miss Charley, I miss the old Mum who would put me right, and the old Dad who didn't get so angry so quickly. I miss having normal parents, parents who aren't right in the middle of thinking about whether or not to kill one of their kids.

'Hal?' Mum says.

'Yeah?'

'No swimming in the sea in the dark.'

'Whatever.'

'Not "whatever", Hal. No.'

'Got you.'

She nods and turns away.

The butterflies come back, dancing and flickering every time I think of Jack – although they're weirdly connected to my fear for Charley too – but the memory of Jack wins out. Of her warm skin in the dark, of how soft and lovely her lips are with the salt still clinging to them.

I get up and take a long bath, before deciding on a Salt Rock shorts and a long sleeve combo. My hair's a mess. The longer it gets, the more it curls at the edges. Going in the sea just makes it worse. I leave it.

My nose is burnt, my skin turning brown. With this tee on, my eyes have their blue tinge. They're definitely my best feature, I think, staring at the boy in the mirror. I look deep into them, and slowly watch as they change colour.

I laugh.

It's a game me and Charley used to play. We used to put on different things and look in the mirror to see if our eyes changed. We felt strange and special – and glad, I realize with a start, glad that we had each other. Because maybe without each other, it feels just plain weird to have eyes that can't settle.

I look at my eyes in the mirror, closer and closer, until they're all I can see. The butterflies swoop and glide inside me; do my eyes look the same to Jack? Who is the person she sees? Me? And what is it that Charley wants me to see? Slowly the room behind me fades away, until all that's left is a pair of deep green eyes, eyes the colour of a clean and clear-cut emerald, full of light.

But mine were blue, weren't they?

I know right then that the eyes staring back at me from the mirror aren't mine any more. There's a horrible, horrible moment, a split second when I'm nowhere at all, not in the mirror and not in the room.

And then I'm looking straight into Charley's eyes. They stare out at me, in just the same way as mine do, and they are asking the same questions.

'Who are you?'

'Who is Pete, and who is Jackie, and why do we love them? Do they love us? Do I look good enough?' The questions tumble through the eyes in the mirror. 'Hal . . . Hal . . . Hal . . .' The whisper goes on inside me, and then the eyes laugh and turn away.

'Am I edible?' Charley pouts. 'Simply edible?' And she flicks her head, turning so that she's looking over her shoulder, back at herself.

I step back and stumble. That's my reflection. Me doing that weird-looking sexy shake-ass pose over my shoulder? Shit.

The room spins around me, and then steadies itself, slowly taking shape again in the mirror, until finally my own body reappears, unfolding itself out of thin air and re-forming, until it's real and solid again, and staring, shocked, into the mirror.

It's like the mirror just confused us, noticed a connection, and gave out an old memory held somewhere deep within its mercury.

But now it's me standing there, definitely me looking bemused, me wondering if I'm worth kissing. My eyes are blue, not green, my lashes are dark. My eyes are my own, not Charley's.

What's going on?

And then I get it, 'cos it's obvious, isn't it? It's because it's me doing all the things that Charley did last summer. Didn't she fall in love with someone? Didn't she look in mirrors and wonder if she was edible? I know one thing for sure – she was. As for me, I think I could do with a bit of practice.

I look away.

Sometimes I hate the fact that my eyes remind me of Charley's.

I look down at her earrings, lying together again on the old oak dressing table. It feels as though she led me to the lost one, somehow; as though, if only I could find the right words, could only understand what it is that she wants me to remember, then the colours within the glass would unswirl, straighten out, and tell me what they saw in her last moments. They must know, she wore them all the time. I pick them up and let them roll across my palm, catching the light.

'Charley!' I whisper, and I put one back in my ear, and the other in my zip pocket, where I can feel it pressing against my hip, a little piece of Charley.

'Good luck,' I think I hear her whisper, and I feel ready, ready for the evening. Ready to remember.

'I'm with you, Charley,' I whisper, and I am – we're in the same place, we're both falling in love. Maybe that's all she did last summer, maybe that's all she wants me to remember?

'Hal . . . Hal . . . Hal . . .'

Outside, the early evening goes right on teasing. One minute, hot sultry sunshine appears from behind the deep clouds that float in from the sea, heading inland. The next minute, the sea whips up and falls flat, as though it can't make up its mind. I wait. I wait for Jack to appear down the old track from the camp site, to cross the bridge and look up, to call, to give me a sign. Just a glance, that's all I need.

But when it comes it's so much better than that.

She runs down the hill opposite, her long golden legs flashing in the sunlight; her shorts are tiny, sassy, surprising. Wicked.

She stands on the road below me looking up, her orangey-gold hair gleaming, held back with shades, her hand shielding her eyes from the sun, and from me.

'Hey, Hal! Coming?' she shouts up.

'On my way.' I try not to run too fast.

'Be cool,' I whisper to myself, but I don't feel cool. I feel like dancing and singing. I feel like whooping and spinning and falling at her feet and saying 'thank you' forever.

'Hi,' I manage.

'Hi, yourself. Where've you been?'

'Around.'

'Nowhere I could see you.'

'Looking, were you?'

'Don't kid yourself.'

'I won't!' I reach for her hand, but she hides it behind her back and smiles at me. Her face inches towards mine, her eyes smiling.

'Sure your mum's not watching?' she whispers against my face.

She looks like a cat, a cat with green, green eyes, and claws that hide behind soft padded paws. I lean back, away from her, and she laughs, grabbing my hand and running with me towards the beach.

'Why are you with me?' The question just arrives in the air between us. I didn't even hear it coming, but once it's out, I see it needs an answer. What is someone as out-and-out gorgeous as her doing with me?

We stare at each other for a bit. She looks me over, as if she's trying to work it out herself.

'Dunno really,' she says after a while, and it's funny, she's funny.

'Come and meet the guys,' she says, dragging me along

the beach.

'Cool,' I say, but it's not how I feel. My heart's beating fast, and I can already feel my pits beginning to prickle.

'Hey, Jack. Who's the kid?' He's big and hairy.

'Who's the Neanderthal?' I say, loud enough for him to hear. But she just shakes my arm as though to keep me quiet.

'Behave, Jake!' she says to the Neanderthal. 'He's called Hal.'

Jake-Neanderthal holds out his hand, as though he was human, and stupid me takes the bait. He pulls his hand back and pretends to be drinking a cup of tea with his little finger all crooked up.

'Oh, so nice to meet you, Henry!' he says in his crap version of a posh accent.

'Wish I could say the same,' I manage to squeeze out. I wish I could control my freakin' voice box, I sound like a hyena sometimes. And, of course, that's when I spot the gorgeous blonde standing by the rocks staring at me. I swallow. Must be the voice that attracted her. I smile at her, who is she? She just stares at me, right at me, but all the time it's as though she's seeing someone else.

'Handbags, boys,' says Jack, and I turn away. The other girls laugh.

Jake casually high-hands a nut, throws it in the air and just flicks his head back and opens his mouth. Clunk, it lands plum, and he smiles at everyone in that dumb endearing doggy way that some surf dudes have, nodding his head slowly and waiting for them all to laugh. And they duly do, because it's funny.

I'm surrounded by funny people. Hey! Maybe this is why Jack's with me, 'cos I went down on my knees outside a phone box, and made her laugh.

'I challenge you to a duel,' I hear myself say to Jake.

'Yeah, handbags at dawn,' yells some girl.

'I accept, dude,' says Jake, nodding slowly.

'Nuts at thirty paces?'

'You're on, man,' he says, and he's got it right away. Now he's smiling at me, dipping his hand into the bag of nuts and handing them over. Everyone's muttering around us, laughing, questioning, interested.

Jack seems pleased, happy that she's brought me over. I'm doing OK in her eyes, so that's good enough for me. She's having fun.

'OK, guys,' she shouts. 'Back-to-back.'

We stand back-to-back, and Jack counts out the paces. We turn, face each other, throw a nut high in the air and dance about like idiots underneath, trying to gauge it right. I get first blood, he misses.

He gets next go. I miss.

I get fancy and manage to catch it with a twist added.

'Penalty!' shouts a wisecracker.

'To you, man!' says Jake.

He scores with the crowd on a phenomenally high catch.

'No way that happened!' he laughs.

'Way!' I grin, and we're both laughing now, egging each

other on, helpless. He tries a double turn and lands on his back. I go down on my knees in sympathy.

'A draw?' Jack suggests, and suddenly it's like Jake's great, and everything feels fine. I'm here, and the people around me are asking questions. I look around for the small blonde stranger, but she's gone, vanished. For a strange second I even wonder if she was ever really here.

'Hey, Hal, where d'you live in real life?' someone asks, and it feels good. It feels like being part of something bigger, something different to home, wider. Perhaps, I think, perhaps this is how Charley felt last year, happy and included. I press the cold beer to my forehead to stop the thought. My life, I think, this is my life, not Charley's. And then I feel her earring press against my hip, as if to disagree with me. Jack gives me a hug, and it's just as I'm smiling right back at her, feeling grateful, that we hear a voice.

'Hey! Jack!' It breaks right in between us.

'Wotchit, Pete!' someone shouts as a dark, tall figure rips through the crowd, heading straight towards us.

Pete! My eyes and ears open right up.

I look up. He's huge, like a shadow. And then I see his face in the glow of the firelight. Something flickers, a memory, of falling, and then I recognize him – he's the guy I saw below our garden, the day we arrived.

Has he been watching us?

And then my heart sinks, because he's just the sort of guy that any girl would fall for – and he's heading straight for Jack. For a moment my heart starts pumping fear, he looks huge and dark with the firelight behind him, and I can't see me being able to do anything at all useful if it comes to a fight.

'Right. Where is it? Hand it over.' He thrusts his hand at Jack, standing over her, palm up, waiting. And it's obvious he knows her – knows her well.

Everyone's gone quiet. The fire flickers behind him, and my knees feel cold where he's blocked out the warmth.

Jack looks up at him, hugging her knees.

'Hand what over?' she says, and guess what – she obviously knows him too.

'Just give, OK?' He's angry with her, so angry that he doesn't give a toss about the rest of us staring, and he doesn't even seem to notice me.

'Give what, shit-head?' Jack's angry too, and you can see she hasn't got a clue what he's on about, but he just carries right on.

'You know,' he says. 'Not funny, Jack, not a funny thing to take at all.'

'Pete!' she shouts, and all the pieces fall into place. 'I haven't taken anything,' she yells back at him, and it's scary, the way they are both so completely and suddenly angry with each other. I hold her hand tight.

'The earring, hand it over,' he yells.

'How could I have it?' she screeches back. 'I'd have to rip it out of your fuckin' ear.' She's gripping my hand hard between us, hidden in the sand, but it's like the two of them are locked into a bubble, like they can't see that we're all here too.

'Oh, no!' says an older girl, pretty, with dark, bell-like hair. She sounds sorrowful, concerned. 'Not your earring, Pete, not the one that Charley gave you.'

So this is him. This is THE Pete, the one she was so busy falling in love with all last summer. It's him camping out in the house. It's him who dropped her earring in the dirt. But why does he think Jack's got it? And then the final piece clicks into place, and the anger kicks in, only I'm angry with both of them now.

I drop Jack's hand and stand up.

'Hang on, Pete,' I say. 'She hasn't got it, OK?'

And he sees me at last.

He steps back, almost stumbling into the fire. He looks like he's seen a ghost, and maybe he has? Maybe he sees Charley too, the faithless fucker. I hope she haunts him too. I feel cold, cold, cold, like ice, and the fist of fear inside is squeezing away at my guts so hard that I think I might throw up. I can hear her voice.

'Help me. Hal, why didn't you help me?'

I imagine Charley in the waves with him, see him bending over her helpless body and . . . stop it!

'Hi!' I say, and for once the voice box is doing just fine.

'Hey, sorry, didn't see you.' He holds up his palms in shock, as though he wants to ward me off somehow, but he's staring into my eyes, and I can feel his confusion. I know he's seeing Charley in me, that he is seeing a kind of ghost, only the ghost is me.

I feel my hand go into my pocket. He watches. He doesn't move. All around us I can hear people falling back into conversations. A slip, a stumble, a bro–sis flip-out, over and forgotten.

I can feel the hard stud of the earring in my pocket.

'*Give it back!*' comes the thought, in Charley's voice. I feel my hand begin to pull it out. I roll the warm ball of glass between my fingers.

'*No way, sis!*'

I hold my palm upwards, and it rolls in the hollow of my hand, the gold leaf glinting in the firelight.

'Are you looking for this?' I ask.

'How come . . ..?' he stutters.

'*Hal . . . Hal . . . Hal . . . remember . . .*'

'It's my sister's,' I say. 'Did she give you one?'

'You got it from Jack, right?' is all he says.

''Course not!' Jack's scornful. Pete can see we're telling the truth, but he can't see how I got hold of the earring. He doesn't know I've been to the house. He doesn't know I know he still stays there. So it's his beer on the table, his camping gear in the corner.

'How did you get it?' he asks, still angry, but it's straight away clear to me that all he really wants to do is to pick it up and have it back, and that he's looking at it with almost as much longing as Charley looked at that deep red flower, and for a moment I'm almost tempted to hand it over, but I don't. I tell him where I got my one from instead.

'I took it out of her ear when I found her.'

174

His reaction is so sudden, his face turns ashen and shocked, and he stares at me, wordless. Looks at me, as though he's got a head full of memories of his own – awful memories, none of which he can sort, none of which he wants to share.

He looks from me to Jack, and back again, and then he just backs off. He heads for the sea, picking up his board on the way.

I put the earring back in the zip pocket, where I can feel its hard lump safe against my hip, where I'll know immediately if it's gone.

'Shit, Hal!' says Jack. But I barely hear her, I'm too busy watching Pete on the waves in the fading light. Watching him wait, catch, and walk up the wall of water made of wind and swell, as easily as though he was a piece of driftwood held up by the sea – as though there are no worries in the world that could hold him – not even the thought of my half-dead sister Charley.

My heart fills with blood, a deep-red-rage blood. That should be Charley out there, I think, out on the waves, walking on water.

I turn to Jack.

'I did try to tell you, yesterday, on the cliffs. Remember? Just before you—' she says quickly, but I cut her short.

'He's your brother, isn't he?'

'Yeah,' she says, and her voice sounds so small in the deepening dark.

Small, and lonely, and scared.

PART THREE. Charley's story.

Charley: Hospital. Now.

I think I've been dreaming.

Dreaming about Pete.

I am walking on water . . . we're both surfing, skimming along the bottom of a glass green wave.

I look down.

There's no board there, nothing beneath my feet but water . . .

'Don't look down,' says Pete, 'you'll fall . . .' but I can't stop looking.

'What's down there?' I hear myself ask, and then I'm slipping, falling through his long and lovely fingers as he tries to hold on to me.

'Pete!'

I call and call his name. I can see the sunlight through the water . . . I can feel its cold . . . so cold . . . as it enters my chest . . . but there's no answer . . . only the echoing underwater silence . . . and the cold.

I open my eyes.

Dark.

Cupboard walls.

Why am I so scared?

I am full of dreams, like words I can't make out.

The endless breaths go on and on, outside of me, rising and falling.

'Hal . . . Hal . . . Hal . . . what's happening?'

I cling to the thought of him, and his eyes seem to answer me through the darkness, through a mirror, and behind them is our bedroom . . .

179

I am looking in the mirror and I'm scared . . . nervous . . . anxious . . . like balancing on your first wave.

My eyes are green, they stare back at me from the mirror, as I put my earrings in . . .

'What's happening?'

Charley. Then.

I'm looking in the mirror, listening to the heavenly Bob Marley:

'Oh please, don't you rock my boat . . .' thinking of the heavenly Pete.

Oh please will you rock my boat, more like! I'm laughing . . .

'Am I edible, simply edible?'

I strain to see from the back, and give that ass a little wriggle. Oh shit. Not looking so good.

I text Jen and Sal.

Help!

Past hlp! they send back, **txtul8r**.

I walk through the house, hoping Mum won't spot the extra eyeliner and mascara.

'See ya, Mum.' She looks up from her book, glasses slipping down her nose.

'Back at half-ten, Charley. OK?'

I manage not to answer.

'Bye, bro. Catch you later.'

He's sitting on the wall, his feet dangling over the steep drop to the street. He doesn't answer, just stares me out as though he's wishing me to hell and back.

The evening breeze feels so warm against my skin. I go slow, scared. Will he be there? How do I say hello? What if he's not there? I skirt the group on the beach, trying to look as if I'm heading off for a lonely enigmatic stroll, as if I'm not bothered.

'Hey! Charley!' Pete heads over, straight over, and he's shouting across the beach so that the whole world can hear him. 'Wrong direction!' he yells.

Cocky bastard.

'Maybe.' I stand still. 'Or maybe I wasn't on my way to see you? Maybe I was just out for a stroll?' I cheer at myself, and can almost feel Jenna clap me on the back.

'Were you?' he asks.

'No! I was looking for you!' I can't keep it up, I just don't have Jenna's cool.

'Come and meet the people!' he says.

'Right!' My heart sinks: not just the two of us, then. They'll hate me, I know they'll all hate me. We head over to the barbecue under the rocks. This is it, I'm thinking, stay cool, don't talk too much.

'Hey, Charley!' says a gorgeous green-eyed girl, younger than us.

'Hi.'

'Jack, my little sis,' says Pete.

Freckled. Funny. Feisty.

'We've seen you from the site,' she says. 'Where's the bro?' She looks about Hal's age, and she's friendly in the same way he is, too. She twists her hair around her finger and smiles.

'Not allowed out,' I say.

'Unkind.'

'Yeah.' I turn away. I don't want to think of Hal all alone on the terrace, listening to the music, wondering.

'Hey, Pete. Beer?' asks a tall guy, blond with a shy smile.

'Cool!' Pete cracks a can and offers it to me.

'Cool it is,' says a chubette, with mousy hair and a big grin. 'Straight from the cool bag.'

Chubby. Chinny. Cheery.

'Funny funny, Em.' Pete taps her on the shoulder, and my heart flips out; don't touch her, it thinks, touch me.

The names and people all begin to blur, but it doesn't really matter 'cos no one pays me much attention, they just nod and chat, and I listen. And then, after a while, just as I'm beginning to take it easy and relax, there's a voice that cuts like razor-shells, through all the friendly hum and buzz.

Em's just repeated her joke, 'Cool it is, straight from the bag,' and this new voice is cool too, cool and hard and tough as plastic.

'Nothing like you then, Em, eh?' it says.

'Hello to you, too, Am,' says the chubette, turning away.

'Loads of bag, Em, but sadly, very little cool!' says the voice, and a couple of girls giggle.

'Am,' says Pete, and his voice sounds as cold as hers. And suddenly, all around me, it's like everyone's ears just open right up. Like whatever else they're pretending to be doing, they're really just listening, and waiting for whatever it is that's going to happen next.

'Hi!' says the newcomer, straight at me. Then she turns to Pete. 'Who's the new playmate?' she asks.

Snaky. Sexy. Wild.

I manage to stop myself looking behind me, to see what the crowd are doing. I force myself to look at her instead, which it has to be said is no hardship. Her hair's like a soothed lion's, all tawny and long, and her body looks like it's just wasted in clothes. She's beautiful, beautiful, beautiful. Beautiful like an angry drug-fuelled angel who's just been thrown out of heaven, and is wild at the injustice of God. I can't stop staring at her. She pulses with something, just pulses, so that looking at her makes me feel like a kid. A skinny little kid, who likes playing in the big waves, but should maybe consider just rushing right back to the shallows, and leaving the big girls to play.

And she looks familiar too, but I can't work out how.

'Hi!' I manage. 'Love the skirt, is it Rip Curl?' It's so small it's practically crawling up her ass. My mind's racing. Why's everyone so interested all of a sudden? I can feel my back prickling with all attention it's getting.

'Thanks,' she says, and she smiles, but only with her mouth. Her eyes are too busy drifting all over me, marking me like punches. I feel like a hyena when the lion comes back for its share of the meat. Got my eyes up, and ready to run. She doesn't bother to answer me, just goes on looking me over, until her mate sniggers and chokes it. The kind of snigger you're meant to hear, the kind of choke-off that wants to be noticed.

What's going on? I'm out of my depth.

I look at Pete for help, and my heart sinks, 'cos it's clear that he can't see me any more, he's too busy staring at her. He looks like a cobra, head up and ready to strike – perfectly still, waiting for her to move or say something. She stares right back at him, and a weird, vibrating energy lights up the air between them. That's when I notice that her eyes are all soft and bruised-looking underneath, as though she doesn't sleep too well some nights.

She makes me shiver. I feel cold. Goose bumps.

Someone's walking over my grave.

Pete's eyes break away, as though he's finally sensed me shivering. He looks back at me, and the moment's over. I put the whole thing down to some serious imagining on my part. Like Mum says, if there were only half as many feelings in the world as I imagine, then it would probably explode!

And Pete smiles right at me, and my heart flips all the way over, and I can't see or hear anyone except him.

'Hungry?' he asks. For once I couldn't eat a thing, but I manage to nod, and without blushing!

'Here. Present!' says Am suddenly. She smiles at us as we turn back to her, a dazzling, unreal smile, and she chucks something. But before I can reach out, Pete's arm's already there, and a matchbox is resting in the palm of his hand.

'It's not for you,' she snarls at him. Then she turns to me again and laughs. 'Does he always make your mind up for you?' she asks.

Intriguing. Scary. Dangerous.

I don't have an answer for her. I'm too busy being thrilled by the idea that Pete might do ANYTHING for me, and that Am seems to think we're an item. Her eyes are stunning, unmissable; the irises are hard and beautiful, like cold blue water under arctic ice. But they look shattered too, somehow, as though she's still reeling from some long-ago blow, a blow that's left those deep dark shadows under her sleepless eyes.

Aquamarine. Glassy. Impenetrable.

I can't stop staring at them – it's like being hypnotized. Maybe that's all it was in Pete's eyes, this feeling of being hypnotized.

'Not funny, Am,' he says, breaking the spell. His fists are clenched by his side, with the little matchbox present inside them. They stare at each other. She's still smiling, he's still wary, and there's that flicker of something rising up again between them, something exciting and dangerous.

Fire. Backyard. Dirty.

'Play with kids too now, do you?' she whispers, and then she laughs in his face, but her eyes aren't laughing at all, they're full of a strange and frightening despair, or is it triumph? Whatever it is, it makes me want to hold her tight and safe. It makes me want to run as far away as possible, for ever.

Pete doesn't react, doesn't move, but his eyes trace her every move, and just for a moment, I think he's going to reach out and touch her, that he wants to lift her up. He could carry her so easily, she's so tiny-bird-thin. I imagine him picking her up and throwing her out to sea, where she splashes, screaming, into the waves. The picture makes me laugh, and then they both turn and remember that I'm here.

I blush.

Am stares. It's like it takes a long, slow while for her to get me exactly in focus, but then it's as though she's committing every detail of my face, every pore and freckle of it, to memory. Her eyes wash over me, taking me in, wiping me away.

Scary.

Pete gives his head a shake, as though he's just woken up.

'Whatever, Am,' he says, and he looks away. 'C'mon, Charley, let's watch waves.' I follow him away from the warm fire and the fascinated stares. A little shadow detaches itself from the fire and follows too.

'So that's the great I Am?' I say, and I try to smile, but I can't, I'm too busy shaking.

'Get lost, Jack!' says Pete without even looking.

'Get lost yourself!' But she disappears, and we're finally alone.

' "The great I Am", good one,' he says. 'But don't mess with her, Charley.'

'Who is she anyway?' I ask, as if I couldn't guess.

'Girlfriend, last summer, it's a mess, wants to hook up again.' He speaks in little jerks, like he can't be bothered with whole sentences, or maybe he's still locked away with her, somewhere inside.

I can't tell.

'And you?' I ask.

'Not really interested,' he says, and he reaches his arm back and throws the box way out into the waves, all-in-one-beautiful-easy-fluid-motion.

'Hey!' I say. 'That was mine. What was it?'

'Nothing you need,' he says. My head is fuming with him. My head says he's a first-class macho arsehole, but my body just doesn't agree. My heart leaps and connects with something behind my belly, digging deep into my insides so that I want to squeeze my knees together and groan – and Am's forgotten. He holds my hand. I try not to sweat too much, or grab too tight. The surf runs over my feet and I'm so grateful for it – it keeps me cool, grounded.

'You can make rainbows with it,' I say.

'What?'

'The sea, if you flick the water into the sunlight.'

'Cool,' he says, and finally smiles at me. My heart does that leaping thing, like it wants to reach up and rest against his smile.

I bring it down, try to control it. Stick my feet in the cold water.

'Haven't you ever done it?' I ask.

'Nah.'

'Oh.'

There's a silence whilst I feel my heart beating and ask it to please slow down, be quiet, don't give me away. The urge to cross my knees and squeeze is just total agony. Would it stop this feeling? I look up at him. He's looking out at the waves, and even now I can see him counting, watching, wondering which wave will rise high and clean enough to ride.

'View's better from the rocks,' I suggest, because I want to sit down next to him, want to lean against him and wipe out the picture of Am.

'Uh.' We head for the cliff.

People always gather on the beach when there's a clear evening. There's something about sunset that draws them; like the clouds, they drift and gather on the beach to watch. They stand, in knots or alone, watching and waiting for the day to stretch out across the sky, and reach for its end.

The clouds float across the sinking sun. They're beginning to turn rose and violet in long, graceful streaks across the darkening sky. The sun's last light gathers up behind them, turning their edges golden. The whole sky feels still and solitary, as though it, too, is waiting for the tide to turn, for the sun to drop, and for night-time to finally fall upon it.

We sit on the warm rocks and join in.

For the first time ever, I think how it's like the sun's dying.

Like someone's walking over my grave.

How maybe the reason we all come out to watch it go down is just in case it doesn't come back up again tomorrow.

I notice how hushed the beach is, that the only tune playing is the sound of the waves. The whole scene just fills me right up, and I lean against Pete and sigh.

'Good, eh?' he asks, and I nod, happy. He puts his arm around my waist, fits me into his shoulder.

Here comes my moment.

I close my eyes and take a big breath. He smells clean. Clean with just a hint of sea and sand and surf.

'Hey, I showered before coming out!' he laughs.

I look up.

Kiss me! I think. Oh, please, please kiss me!

His eyes are half closed, his lashes golden against the dying light, and his face drifts down towards mine. I feel my neck stretch up, my body lean in towards him. A voice that sounds just like Jen's comes from somewhere inside me and says, Where'd you learn that? His lips press down, and my own begin to open right back, but nothing doing. He's gone. A quick peck, an empty disappointment.

Whoa! Empty. Abandoned. Wasted.

'C'mon, let's eat,' he says, and he looks away from me, back to the rocks, back towards the barby and Am. I feel so stupid and alone. The sun's gone, the moment's been missed. All the way across the beach I wonder where I went wrong. I wonder how I could ever have thought I'd match up to that strange, vibrating feeling I sensed between Am and Pete, a feeling I can't place, a feeling that scares and excites me.

'What's cooking?' he asks the crowd. He eats like a surfer, but then so do I, especially when I'm sad and disappointed.

'More?' he asks, disbelieving, as the second burger goes down. 'Haven't you had enough yet?' He's laughing, joking with his mates, the girls are laughing too.

'Could do with some chocolate,' I say.

'Bet you can't manage a whole slice of Jane's cake,' says someone.

It's a huge home-made chocolate cake, looking almost as good as the ones from the Cabin.

'You're on!'

'I made it,' says one of the girls. I recognize her as the one who's been right up close and personal with Am all evening. As soon as I see her face I don't want it, I don't want to eat anything she's made, she's poison. I take an extra big slice, just in case she noticed the hesitation.

The cake's good, in fact it's fantastic. I sit back, beginning to feel part of the rhythm. The fire's warm, and people come and go, drop off the waves and eat a bit, change and swim, chat and eat. Everything feels smooth around me, as though we're all tied together somehow, with loose and easy bonds that will stretch but not break.

I let the thought of Am and Pete drift away.

I watch the crowd, and hold on to Pete's hand. I close

my eyes. I run my fingers over every bone in his fingers, feel each muscle as it flexes. My own hand feels lost in his, swallowed up completely.

'Hey,' he smiles at me. 'Just going to chat to Mark.' I nod, but it feels so sudden, so far away from where my own head is, him going off like that. I try not to gulp. 'It's cool, it's cool,' I mutter to myself. But it doesn't feel cool, it feels like being abandoned, like being left out, helpless and cold, on a mountainside.

'Hey!' says a tall dark girl, with hair like a black bell, that swings and falls back into place.

Classy. Elegant. Kind.

'Hi!' I say back.

'"The big I Am", I like it!' She laughs as she sits next to me. 'I'm Bella.'

Saved, saved. My mouth feels so dry.

'She's still crazy about Pete, I reckon, but who wouldn't be, eh? Lucky her, living here, and getting hold of Pete!'

Mine, I want him to be mine.

'Is she local?'

'Yeah, Dad's a farmer, I think, big place, at the top of the cliff.'

'Right – the big grey square house, with all the farm buildings?'

Tell me more, tell me more.

'Yeah, bit weird up there, don't you think? And windy that high up. Have you seen how the trees are all bent over, like they can't even grow straight? Shame the wind didn't 'get to Am too, she's lethal!'

'So what's with her and Pete?'

'Oh, she's history with him, I think. No worries there. But he did get inside that house. He said it was weird, like he could feel the no-mum in there . . . the big joke is that he went to the loo, and it took him two days to get out. We reckon Am locked him in, just in case he ever decided to end it!'

'He stayed there?' I could eat my head for letting that one out, but she just laughs.

'Yeah, lucky Am, eh?' she says. 'And lucky Pete – we're all dying to know what it's like in there!'

The cake just gets more and more delicious. I can't eat enough of it. I imagine Am high up on a windy cliff top, with a grey square building behind her, and in the picture Pete's running towards her with wide open arms, Heathcliff and Cathy style.

I begin to laugh.

'Tell?' says the bell-haired girl.

'Pete and Am, it's just the thought of them . . .' I trail off. Maybe not such a good idea to share this thought, says Jenna, in my head.

'Were they together long?' I ask instead.

'It's odd, isn't it,' she says, not really answering, 'how no one ever put them together? I mean, to be honest, before she got with Pete none of us really saw her, did we?' she asks. But I can't answer; I don't think I've ever seen Am before, but a sense of something familiar does hover about

192

the memory of her face.

Bella goes on. 'I mean, everyone thought Am was just sad – a weirdo local beach-child.' She looks away from me into the fire, and her face is kind of warm and troubled in the flames. 'You know, none of us actually ever noticed when she'd changed. She just went straight from being this gawky weirdo, to drop-dead gorgeous, from one summer to the next, and suddenly every guy on the beach thinks she's dynamite. And the only guy she's looking at is Pete, and the moment she's next to him it's just so obvious that they're both ... well ... dynamite. I mean – it's like – apart, nobody could really see that they'd changed, but put them together – well, you know, suddenly so equally gorgeous an' all that!' she finishes, and my heart feels totally stilettoed. And I know, just know, that however hard I try, I can't ever hope to match up to Am.

Arrowed. Archered. Agonized.

'Oops!' she says.

Bell-hair, belle-air, bel-air.

'Sorry! You should have stopped me, I honestly just forgot that you and Pete might ... I mean ... Pete is seriously better off without her, especially after ... shit ... and there's no way he ...'

'I didn't want to stop you!' I lie. 'I'm interested, she sounds amazing, she looks amazing. No wonder Pete fell for her.'

'Yeah,' she says, 's'pose. But you MUST remember her – she was always hanging around, climbing rocks and stuff, and she got rescued one year from up on Merlin's Hat.'

'That was Am?' I yelp, because everyone knows about the girl who swam out and climbed Merlin's rock, and had to be rescued – and everyone knows she looked nothing like Am.

'Yeah,' says Bella, laughing, 'that was Am. One and the same! No one saw her around for a bit after that stunt. I think Daddy kept her in, and if you knew Daddy you'd know that wasn't exactly a treat!'

And then she looks at me, and gives this wicked but friendly grin.

'D'you think Pete's developing a line in locked-away maidens?'

I blush. 'I've got an antisocial family,' I say, and I tell her about how it just never felt possible to walk over to the barby and chat.

She laughs. 'Yeah!' she says. 'It's a bit like a gang show, being on the camp site. I can see how anyone might find us all a bit much. Thank God for hormones, eh?' And she's smiling her wicked friendly smile.

'You mean otherwise you'd never mix?' I ask, and she nods, and then she touches my arm, just the same way that Jen does sometimes, when she wants me to really listen.

'Hey,' she says. 'Good luck. Pete could really do with some luck right now. Maybe you're it.'

'Thanks!' I say, and I mean it.

'Hey!' says a voice. 'Ask your brother to come next time.'

And Jack's beside me. 'We could be a bro–sis team!' she smiles.

I look up at the house, gleaming in the half-light. Hanging over the low wall is a faint shadow of greater darkness. It looks small from down here; it looks as though it could be Hal.

I turn away.

'Sure!' I say. She flicks the embers on the edge of the fire with a stick, and the sparks fly up and die.

'Great.' She looks at me intently, as though she's turning something over in her mind.

'Are you OK?' she asks suddenly.

'Why?'

'Just wondered, you know – all that stuff with Pete and Am, it can be a bit heavy.'

'What stuff?' I'm interested; I'm interested in every single thing about Pete.

'Well, you know the history, right?'

'No.'

'Guys!' she says, as though she had a shed-load of experience. She makes me smile. She budges up next to me and curls up with her head tipped sideways on her knees, making sure no one but me can hear her low voice.

'Well, you know Am's mum's gone, and she just lives with her dad?' I nod. I'm beginning to feel a bit sick – too much cake, maybe. 'Well he's weird too – lonely farmer type. I've never met him, worse luck, but we all know Am never invites anyone back – only Pete, once. And her dad, he, well . . . he used to come and drag her off the beach till just before last year!' She laughs, and I keep quiet, thinking my own dad might have been hauling me off the beach a few years ago.

'Yeah,' says Bella. 'Poor old Simon asked if she could stay till the barby finished, once, and his mum threatened to prosecute when she saw what Am's dad did to his ear. Didn't she, Si?'

Simon's short and fair; his face is big and innocent-looking in the firelight.

'I was lucky, I reckon,' he says. 'Round here they say he's unkind to the cattle.'

There's a laugh, and Em says, 'No wonder his daughter's a mad cow!'

The laughter stops. Just stops completely. The silence is suddenly awkward and embarrassed, like it gets when everyone knows the joke's gone too far – and I wonder what it is that they all know and I don't.

There's something.

Something to do with Pete and Am.

'Well she was definitely the first cow in line when the looks got handed out,' I manage. It's weak, but we all take the chance to laugh and move on.

'Listen, she really messed Pete up!' says Jack, indignant. 'So I'd just keep off the subject when you're with him, yeah? That's my advice.'

'What's the big deal, Jack? Why?' Perhaps she'll tell me what it's all about: the sudden silences, the interest, the feeling of fury and excitement that fires up the air between them.

'She's a first-class, Grade A bitch from hell! That's the deal!' she says.

'Oh!' I'm shocked at the venom in her voice. 'Why?'

'Don't play with fire!' she says, and flicks the embers high in the air, laughing at the shower of sparks against the rapidly darkening sky.

'Jackie!' barks Pete. 'Don't – you could get burnt.'

'Sorry, big bro!' and she's just a sarky little sis again. 'Have fun, you two,' she grins. 'And don't forget to bring me your own bro next time, yeah?'

Pete holds out his hand and pulls me up. The crowd around the fire begins to break up into couples who drift off, away into the warm shadows of the lonely rocks. I wonder what time it is. I wonder how to say I've got to be back by ten-thirty.

'What's Jack been saying?' he asks.

'Oh, just chitchat. Girl stuff.'

Why am I lying to him? Why does everything suddenly feel so secret?

'Right.'

Everything's right: the night's warm, the sound of the waves is soft enough to be lulling, the white surf has its late evening glow, Pete's hand's in mine. But the silence between us is horrible.

So what's up?

'Whassup?' The words tumble out without asking.

He doesn't answer for a bit, and we sit down against a

warm rock. I dig my toes deep into the sand for comfort, getting lost in the feel of it; the top's all warm and trickly, falling between my toes, the underneath is cold and solid. For a moment I really forget that I'm on a beach with this season's very own surf god. I forget so fully that when he speaks it makes me jump.

'Do you make me a kiddie snatcher?' he asks.

'Shit. Whew, you made me jump.'

We laugh, and I lean against the warm rock and try not to think about it; try not to feel too bad that he's sitting on the beach with me, but still thinking about Am – and what she said.

'You can't snatch someone who wants to come, can you?'

'Dunno really.'

'Has the big I Am got to you?'

'Yeah, a bit.'

'So, I'm a bit younger than you!' There, I've said it, and as soon as the words are out I start to laugh.

'Why are you laughing?'

'I just realized I thought it mattered.'

'What?'

'That I'm younger.'

'Am thinks it does.'

'Does she? What do you think, Pete?'

Why am I here, Pete? I want to know why, direct from him.

'Not sure, really.'

'So what's it all about, asking me here?'

'You don't feel younger . . .'

'Right, very articulate.'

'Big word, Charley.'

'You don't talk too much, do you?'

For the first time he looks up at me, really looks and grins at me.

'It puts people off.'

'Oh, are you meant to be thick?'

He nods.

'Well, I don't suppose it matters much, does it, if you're planning on being a surf god?'

He shakes his head at me, smiling, and then buries it in his hands.

'What?' I ask. I feel powerful. I feel like it's me he's got on his mind now, not Am.

'Just you,' he says.

'What about me?' Suddenly I'm worried I've blown it.

'Just stop a minute, Charley,' he says. 'You're hurting my head.'

We're silent. The firelight flickers orange in the deep dark of the beach. Someone starts playing a tune, picking out the notes so that they float into the air with the fire smoke. I shiver with delight; I can't stop, what's more, I don't want to.

'I can't believe I'm here.'

'What?'

I push him, but he doesn't move an inch, he's so solid

and thrilling.

'What can't you believe?' he asks again, and I wonder if he's for real. Surely he knows what a catch he is?

'That I'm here, you idiot. Me, Charley Ditton, sitting on the beach in the nearly-starlight, with you, Pete the surf god.'

It just bubbles out, before I can stop myself.

'Is that what it's about?' he says, and he doesn't sound too impressed.

Babbling idiot! I think. So uncool!

And actually, now I come to think of it, how do I know he didn't just invite me over for a chat, a friendly chat about his problems with Am? Shit! I think of the failed kiss on the rocks. Jesus, how embarrassing can this get? How many ways does he have to tell me that this isn't about pulling?

Blown it!

I think of Hal – boy, would he like to know about this one. I think of how we used to pretend to bale out when we cocked up. 'Mayday, Mayday!' we'd yell, arms out like dive-bombing planes.

Pete's still silent and unmoving, holding his head in his hands like some weirded-out statue. I wonder what's in his head; is he still lost somewhere – somewhere with Am and her bright, hard eyes and perfect body? I imagine their fingers touching, I imagine the air shattering into hard solid fragments between them. I can't bear it any more, don't want to know, can't wait around just to hear him say the words . . . 'Thing is, Charley, I need help thinking about Am . . .'

I start to bale out. 'Mayday, Mayday, Mayday,' I whisper, but when he begins his head-shaking again, I get louder and louder . . . until finally, I'm up and off, running across the beach, windmilling my arms in the warm darkness and feeling the soft sand give way beneath my feet.

At last, he's running after me!

'Charley, Charley!' The single picked-out notes of the guitar stop for a bit, and change to a rapid strum. Someone's singing Bob Marley into the warm air:

'O pirates yes they rob I . . .'

I pretend I'm on another beach, somewhere in the warm tropical night of Jamaica.

I hide behind a big rock.

'Charley!' He's silent except for his voice in the dark, no footsteps. I keep still, trying not to giggle, but the urge builds and builds, especially when I think of the confused look on his face almost every time I speak.

A snort.

A silence.

'Got you!' and he's beside me. 'Listen, Charley, I need to tell you something.'

'What?' I can tell he's deadly serious, but I still want to laugh, and this is scary.

'Charley, the chocolate cake that Jane made, did you eat any?'

'Loads, it was delicious.'

'Shit.'

'What?' I'm scared by the look on his face.

'It was loaded.'

'What?' But I know what he means straight off; it was literally loaded.

'I'm stoned!' I say, and the sound of my voice sounds so funny, as though it's far away in the distance and I'm listening to it. We both start to giggle again, and his arms are around me, and the dark night closes itself around us, wrapping us up in its deep velvet softness, where his head finally comes close to mine, and at long, long last, he kisses me.

Gotcha! No Am here now! I hear myself thinking, before my mind stops working completely. My text goes off just at the right time, just as we're lying deep in the sand, forgetting that we are on a beach, that I am fifteen and that he isn't, and that our hands don't really have lives of their own, it just feels like it.

'Leave it!' mutters Pete.

'Can't!'

'Need an out?' it says. **'Hope not!'**

I stand up and brush the sand off, try to rub the evidence off my face.

'Gotta go.'

'What! You're kidding, yeah?' he says, wrapping his warm palms around my ankle. Hey, let's stay, my ankle whispers to me, but I don't listen.

'Price you pay for being a kiddie-snatcher. I have to be home by ten-thirty, and it's nearly eleven.'

He grins.

'OK!'

'Because I'm worth it?' I ask.

'Definitely!' he grins.

'Was on my back, seeing stars!' I text, and their words fly all the way over the sea, straight to me.

'Lucky, lucky you!' they say.

Charley: Hospital. Now.

Lucky?

Why do I shiver, then, as though the wind is ruffling the surface of my skin . . . as though I'm waking . . . as though someone is walking over my grave? . . . I know who you are . . .

Pete.

Pete, and Am. I hold them, like pieces in my hand, wondering how to fit the edges together.

I don't remember being scared. I remember the firelight, and the beach, and the warm night, and Pete. I hold his memory to me in the dark, like a light. I wrap myself up in its warmth, and breathe in deep to smell the memory, the deep salt sea tang of him, but I can't keep a hold . . .

The dark keeps rising . . . the shadows rise up and cover me, like waves . . . until I'm adrift . . . and drowning in darkness . . .

'Hey!' *says a soft voice on the outside.* 'Hey, Charley! What's happenin' in the sleepy hood?'

Jenna!

'Oh, Charley!' *she says, and she sounds so worried.* 'What happened to you? What does Hal mean about somebody watching?' *she asks.* 'Why didn't you ring me that night, Charley? What was happening, and where was Pete when you were in the sea, eh? I thought you two were spending the night together.'

What?

'Because Hal's worried too,' *she's saying.* 'Was he with you, Charley? Should I tell someone?'

The blackness is suddenly thick and choking . . .

'No!' *I scream.* 'Don't tell!'

But the only answer is her silence.

'That clock would drive me mad if I was you,' I hear her say.

After a long while, I hear her move away from me, and then the ticking stops. She's taken the battery out of the clock!

Oh, thank you, thank you, thank you . . .

Her face leans over me . . . shutting out the sunlight.

I panic . . .

'Get away, get away.'

'Bye, Charley!'

She's gone. Only her smell, the smell of vanilla ice cream and roses, remains in the air, and a blessed silence, no ticking . . . only these four walls, and darkness . . .

I'm dreaming . . .

. . . I'm high above the beach with only the sea below me. I'm balancing on the rocks, and the waves crash and the air screams and I am high, high above it all, climbing higher and higher and higher until I reach the very top of the rock, and hold my arms out, right up to the sky, but when I look up there is no rope . . . no one is

coming to save me . . . the helicopter is flying away and someone waves at me as she swings up high on the rope ladder, laughing.

    It's Am . . .

    'Help me!'

Hal. Now.

'Help me!'

    And I know that she's desperate, lost and alone some-where, and that she's calling me. She's wishing she could see with my eyes, hear with my ears, wishing that she knew what this fear is: the fear that runs through us, a fear like the sea, much deeper than we can imagine – and filled with creatures we can only dream about. It's like she can't remember without me, and yet she's not here, is she? Only I'm here, only me, trying to make sense of it all.

    Whenever I think of Charley, it's like the crows are all gathering; landing on the power lines and waiting. What are they waiting for? What is it that makes them start and stop, and then finally decide to fly away? Where do all these feelings inside me come from? What do they want?

    I wish I knew.

    The crows are gathering around, like rain clouds. There's Mum and Dad and all the doctors, wondering if her life is worth it. There's the shadow I can see, watching her on the waves, and now there's Pete.

    Pete and Charley, and the whole different life she had going last summer.

Did she fall in love with Pete? So why do I get this feeling of fear when I think of them together . . .?

'*Remember!*'

I don't have to remember, I'm falling myself . . . only Charley's standing right in my way.

'*Remember,*' she whispers. But remember what? And the more I find out about Charley and Pete, the further I seem to be getting from Jackie.

'Tell me,' I say to her, as though she could remember for me. 'Tell me everything about them. What's Pete like?'

We're sitting high up on the cliffs, watching the gulls wheel through the air below us.

'Girls like him!' grunts Jack. She grins suddenly, and the breeze blows her hair across her face and into her eyes; she pushes it back behind her ears and wraps her arms around her knees. We look out to sea rather than at each other – and it's different between us, awkward, like the air between us just isn't ours to take over any more – it's too full of questions.

I can't really believe we ever kissed. I still want to, I just – it just – it feels like the thought of Charley's right there in between us, waiting.

'Was Charley happy?' I manage.

'Yeah, think so.' Jack's still staring at the waves, as though a mermaid might appear at any minute.

'Right.'

Looking down we can see both beaches from here. To the right is the kids' beach near our house, full of rock pools, and close enough to the camp site to have a barby. On the left, dipping down past the oak groves and fields, is the wider, wilder beach, with broader, bigger waves, and more sand. From up here the surfers look like seals: tiny black pinpoints, dancing in and out of the light.

'Can you tell which one he is?' I ask.

'The one who catches every wave,' she says without bothering to look. Her voice is flat and sad and not like Jack's at all. When I look at her, my heart does flick-flacks, and I wish – I wish – I could just lean over and pretend that I never had a sister called Charley, and that she never had a brother called Pete.

A piece of hair drifts over her eyes. Without thinking I lift it back and fix it behind her ear, the way I've been watching her do for the last hour.

And at long last she turns and smiles at me.

'Hello!' I say.

But she doesn't say hello back, just looks away again and says:

'Is that it, then?'

'What?'

'You and me?'

Her voice is tight and small, as though she has to squeeze very hard to get it out past her throat. I'm lost. What's she on about?

'What, Jack? Is what it?'

'Well, me not telling you I knew Charley, and Pete being my brother . . . although I did try to tell you . . . and you 'being so . . . so off with me.'

'ME being off?' I'm really surprised now. 'Hey, I'm not the one pretending you're not here.'

'Get lost, Hal, you can hardly look at me, an' you don't . . .' She trails off and looks away, but not before I've seen her face do its glow-red-and-fade sunset impression.

'Don't what, Jack? What don't I do?' And suddenly it's the most important thing in the world to me that she says it. I want to hear her say it; I want to know she's noticed for Chrissake, I want to know that she minds; but she's all scrunched up over her knees, staring at the sea as though it might make a sudden rush for the cliff, and drown her.

I reach out and try to turn her round.

'What, Jack? What don't I do?'

I need her to tell me that she's noticed that I can't touch her. I need to let her know that somehow, every time I reach out, Charley's already there, in the air between us, watching and waiting, and making me think of her and Pete together, not me and Jack.

'You KNOW,' she wails at me.

'Yeah, but I need you to—'

'You want me to say it, don't you, you—'

'Yes?'

She takes a big breath.

'You don't, you can't, you don't want to . . . to . . . come NEAR ME any more.'

And as soon as she's said it, I can do it, and we're hugging each other as though the wind only ever blew just to try and keep us apart.

'I hate you!' she says, as though she might like me.

'So do I. Hate me, I mean!' And it feels so good, so good to be in TOUCH again, but I can still feel Charley and all her questions inside me, waiting.

'It is a bit weird, that they were together, you know — our big brother and sister, and that you knew and you still—'

'I fancy you, idiot!' She smiles. 'And I liked – like –' she gives me a nervous glance, 'Charley too.'

'Remember!'

'And you don't think . . .' My turn to take a deep breath. 'You really don't think Pete was with her that morning, on the beach?'

She looks really confused.

'Pete, leave Charley in the sea? Are you nuts? Hal, didn't you hear me? He still loves her.'

'Yeah, yeah, I know, I know you think that – but Jackie, there was someone there, I know it. I can remember looking out of the window and there was this shadow under the street light and I just . . . I just don't know who she'd be with, if not Pete.'

She's looking at me, horrified.

'You think Pete would just leave her in the waves, if she hit her head?'

'I don't know him, Jack. It's not a crime to think about it.' But the look on her face makes it feel like one.

'Jesus, Hal! OK, so he's made mistakes, he's human – he's

got a temper – but he wouldn't just leave someone in danger. Anyway, I don't think we know the whole story. I don't care what anyone says, I know him best and there's no way, just no way that he really did what people— God, no wonder you couldn't bloody well face me, didn't want to touch me!' She's furious, and I begin to laugh. It's mad, I know, and it FEELS mad, laughing into the wind whilst Jack screams at me, but it's so funny. It's so funny. The minute we're OK together, or having fun, some dumb memory of Charley or Pete just seems to leap right in between us, and cut us apart.

'What now?' she's saying. 'Why the laughing?'

I calm down enough to tell her, and she smiles, sure enough, but she still looks pissed off.

'Sorry,' I mumble, but the shadow of that person watching won't leave me; it hovers behind every feeling. There's someone there, someone in the dim orange light of the street lamp: another shadow, curled up, hunched up in the darkness, watching Charley, intent on her in the waves, as though there was no sea, or sky, or growing horizon, only her. As though they were waiting for her. The thought makes me shiver . . .

Someone's walking on my grave.

I concentrate on the picture in my mind. The dark silhouette begins to take shape, to grow, stepping out of the shadow, and its shape feels familiar somehow, it's tall – could it be Pete?

'What are we going to DO?' moans Jack in frustration.

'We have to find out who was watching, whoever it was,' I say.

'How?'

'Ask Pete?' I suggest. 'See how he reacts?'

'Huh,' she laughs, 'enjoy opening oysters, do you?'

'Oh, come on, Jack. You're his sister.'

She looks at me as though I am seriously off the case.

'Hal, what d'you think I've been trying to do for the last year? The boy's a total tetra pack, he's not gonna open.'

'Mmm.' I'm not convinced. I wonder if she's scared of him, but I can't ask. Jack's already giving me the evils, as though she can sense what I'm thinking.

'Look Hal,' she says in her I'm-being-very-patient voice, 'when we got here this summer, he just stood and stared at your front door. No surfing. No mates, just hanging around pretending to read for Chrissake. I mean, "Pete", and "read", the two words just don't match. He's got this book Charley left somewhere, and he's actually READ it. He just stands there with *Wuthering Heights* in his hands, and looks at the door of your bloody house, up on the cliff.

'And he watches you all, and sometimes it's you who comes out, and sometimes it's your mum or your dad, and lots of times your little sis, and he waits. Are you with me?'

I nod; it's all I can do. Did you know that grief comes in waves? Did you know each one just washes all the words away? I can feel the tears beginning to build palaces behind my eyes. She's reading a roll call, a family register, only I know that Charley's not going to be on it.

'And Mum and Dad watch, and I watch, until the whole damn lot of us are just staring at your house: all waiting, and all pretending that we don't have a single clue what for.'

'I didn't know,' I whisper, appalled. But I feel angry too, so ANGRY that I didn't know, didn't notice I was being watched, couldn't see them watching me.

'And then?' I ask, taking a deep breath.

'And then,' she takes a deep breath too, 'and then we know, Hal, we know that Charley's not with you. And Pete turns around and goes into your house, and he . . . he stops watching. Stops living, he just surfs and surfs and some nights he's not home at all. Mum's tried and Dad's tried – when he's around, that is – and he just won't talk to us, Hal. Whatever's on his mind, why he hasn't ever asked to see Charley, I don't know. Hal, the police, they . . . they gave him a really hard time last year . . . and he'd already had some shit with them . . . anyway, Mum and Dad just wanted him to stay away . . . from you lot and the beach . . . and if Pete didn't tell the police or Mum, then he's not telling anyone. It's just not gonna happen.'

I nod and turn away, blinking.

'Hal?'

'Yeah.'

'That's why.'

'Why what?'

'You know you asked me that time, why am I with you?'

'Yeah.'

'That's why.'

'Uh?'

'I used to watch you up on the terrace, last year, when Charley was down on the beach. And watching you, this year, with Sara, seeing you up there with your mum, and then you were so funny, falling on your knees at the phone box.'

'Yeah?'

'Yeah! I've always wondered about you, Hal, up in the big house! I just wanted to know you.'

'Yeah.'

'Are you all right?'

'No.'

And she puts her arms around me and I bury my head in her shoulder until the tears don't show any more.

'Do you know where they went?' she asks after a while.

'What?'

'They used to disappear together,' she says suddenly into the silence.

'What?'

'Charley and Pete, they went somewhere. There were whole days when nobody saw them around.'

I see the old oak mantel in the house. I see their names wrapped around each other.

'Yeah,' I say, 'I think I do know.'

Charley: Hospital. Now.
Hal.

Sometimes, I think I can feel him thinking, like the tentacles of an octopus, floating deep below the sea . . . sometimes I can feel the tip of his thoughts tap me in the darkness . . . and I shiver at the thought of him holding us all close in the cold, dark, silent depths of the water, one of us in each long waving arm . . . as he stares at us . . . giving answers . . .

He's making the darkness rise . . .

Am.

Pete.

Me.

He's putting the pieces together . . . making the fear in me shiver and rise, higher . . . higher to where the ground begins to shrink and fail beneath my feet . . .

Stop, Hal! I'm so cold! . . . but his thoughts go on . . . he knows something . . .

Darkness . . .

Do not go into the house. Do not pass Go. Do not collect two hundred pounds.

What house?

Charley. Then.

I like lying awake in the night, listening to Hal breathing. I like knowing that the rest of the world is asleep, hearing our house breathing its night breath, creaking and stirring to its own rhythm, like a ship resting at anchor, timbers cracking and sighing. I like creeping through the dark, night-lit rooms.

Outside the stars glisten. The lights of all the other houses have gone off, and there's only the soft sigh of the sea out there, somewhere in the darkness, rising and falling. The breeze is warm and wonderful and I hold my arms up to it, unbutton, let my thoughts fall free, and they are all of Pete, of his hands and eyes, of his lips.

Cold. Salt. Stinging.

Of his body on the waves. Everyone else seems to fight the sea, but he gets up on his board and the wave all in one–swift–movement, like words without the need for any spaces in between.

Rhythm. Chant. Harmony.

I don't read any more, I don't text any more, I don't dream or write poetry any more; I just want to be with Pete.

'Hi.'

'Hi.'

We lie on the waves together.

'What happened to you last night?' he asks.

'I turned into a pumpkin.'

He laughs.

I made him laugh. Me – I made him laugh!

'But I've thought of a way round it.'

'You have?'

'Yeah!'

He pulls my board over to his, and we kiss with the salt sea on our lips and the waves beneath us.

'Don't want the parents to see,' I say.

'OK, let's go into Bude tonight, then.'

'Pete.' God, I love the sound of his name. 'I can't stay out past eleven on the beach, why d'you think they're going to let me go to Bude?'

'Right.' He's silent, and the boards beneath us lift and fall. We miss a good wave.

'Shit!' we both say, and laugh.

'Not concentrating, Pete,' someone calls.

'Oh, but I think he is,' shouts Bella.

'Be nice not to be in a crowd,' he says after a while. His eyelashes are wet, dark triangles; his eyes are so blue, like a summer sky blue, such a clear clear blue that I get a bit lost every time I look at them. We realize we're staring at each other. We realize we have no idea how long this has been happening.

We laugh.

'Missed another!' someone calls.

But their voices drift away on the wind, unheard.

'Yeah,' I say. 'Be nice not to be in a crowd.' And I tell him about meeting him at night, just him and me.

'Cool,' he says. 'Trouble is, it's still the beach – and, believe me, there are always couples on the beach, however late you make it.'

My heart sinks then, because it means he's done it before. Of course. And guess who with?

I float beside him, feeling the sun warm my back, and slowly an idea dawns.

'There isn't only the beach,' I say. 'I know where to take you.'

'You're taking me out?' he asks, smiling.

216

'Don't patronize me,' I tell him.

'I couldn't,' he says, laughing. 'I don't know what it means!'

'And bring a torch.'

I'm going to take him to the house, to our other house, far away in the woods.

Charley: Hospital. Now.

Not that house.

That house . . . it makes me shiver . . . I turn away . . . don't go there, Hal . . . not alone.

And you, Am, with your knowing smile that sweeps across his body, with lips that know, that curve upwards as though the memory of him was pulling them at the corners . . . tugging them, not gently, but just the right amount . . . I wanted to wash the memory of you away . . . like the sea over sandcastles . . .

Charley. Then.

I'm standing under the hot water, wishing I could wash the thought of Am away as easily as the sand, gathering in little heaps at my feet, through the steam I see my own body, golden and brown, apart from the white bikini marks; pale shadows, like signposts – here we are, Pete! I laugh, and that's when I get the idea.

'Keep still!' I tell him, and I spread the sun cream across my palm, holding it right over his heart. I can feel it beating under my hand. I hold it still, and kiss him to see if it races.

It does.

Wow.

I slide my other hand down across his stomach.

'I'm meant to be keeping still!' he says from behind closed lids, his voice all lazy and smiling.

'I know!' I laugh.

I do it every time we come out of the water after that, every time we lie in the sun, every morning that we're together. I lay my hand over his heart, with my head right next to it, and do everything I can to make it beat faster! And I whisper secret words right into his skin, words that he can't hear as we lie together in the sand.

'You are mine, all mine, Peter von Wunderkind,' I say aloud, in a manic, scary German accent, just to hide how real it feels, how much I mean it. If I could pick him up and put him in my pocket, I would. I think about him all the time, endlessly. I imagine living with him, I imagine us walking arm in arm on the way home ... choosing sofas ... eating Chinese in bed together ... changing light bulbs ... watching paint dry?

It feels like possession.

'You're mine!' I whisper to his skin, as though it could hold the words close to him when I'm gone, meld me to him forever, in his very pores. 'All mine!'

Possession.

'Mmm, I know some others who might have something to say about that,' and he smiles his lovely-lazy smile, and my heart goes straight from one hundred and ninety to zero. Does he mean Am? Does he know I think that I can never be as utterly enticing as Am? Does he agree with me?

What does he do between the hours of ten-thirty and midnight, or however late it has to be before I can sneak out and meet him?

I look at my hand lying on his chest; feel his heart beating beneath it.

I lift up my palm, and its pale shadow stays etched upon his golden skin, pulsing with each beat of his beautiful heart.

It's done.

I smile as I wipe the sun cream from my hand, and I know that I can't wait for Am to see it.

Am.

She never sits still, she's always moving, her body gliding to invisible music, like it's guiding the rhythm, taking control. She hops from rock to rock in the sand as she talks. She's sitting by the fire right now, her long fingers drumming across her thighs, her neck. They push her hair across her scalp and shake it out down her long back. The way she does that, it draws your eyes over every inch of her body. How does she do it? I wish I could hold her hands still, stop her.

Pete gets up close to the fire to flip over the burgers. He touches her head as he passes her – a small touch, a nothing touch, but the intimacy of it makes me gasp. She looks up through the smoke at him, staring, and her face goes the strangest colour, like dappled light falling on to a red forest floor. Her hands stop moving, her whole body stills beneath his touch, and her head turns towards me, and I can almost feel the air between us filling up with hate.

We both look up at Pete.

He's taken his tee off, the fire's hot. I laugh up at him, at his body, and I have to close my eyes for a minute – just a flutter – because suddenly I'm imagining how painful it might be if he wasn't mine any more. What if it was her hand across his heart, not mine? The thought makes me feel sick, but when I open my eyes, it's still there, right in front of me: the pale gold shadow of my hand, holding on tight to his heart.

'Hey, Pete?' says Bella. 'What's with the palm print?' Everybody looks up, and he grins at them all.

'Hey!' he says, looking down as though he's only just noticed it. 'Where'd that come from?'

'Go on, Charley, see if the hand fits,' smiles Bella, as though she knows it's just exactly what I want to do – 'bet you one of Jane's Very Special Brownies it does?'

'No!' I say suddenly, and the air feels cold. I shiver. I don't want to.

Someone's walking on my grave.

Pete moves away from the fire.

Am's staring, her whole body jiving, to some fast, impossible rhythm that no one else can hear. Her eyes linger over Pete's chest. She looks down at her dancing hands, and then back at my palm, melted on to Pete's skin. She stares at it, hard, as her own hands flutter and glide making it seem such a crude thing to do, to stop a hand moving forever and print it on a chest.

I wonder what possessed me? What mad thing made me think that pale imitation of a hand could ever mean that he belonged to me?

Am did. Pete did. They did.

'Go on, Charley,' says Mark, 'see if it fits!'

'Your prince is waiting, Cinders!' laughs Bella, and I look at Pete standing there, with his shirt hanging in his hands, waiting.

'No!' I say again, and Pete gives me that sideways grin, as though he doesn't really mind the idea.

'Ooohhh,' the crowd go, enjoying it all, revving up the tension that seems to be singing right through Am's body as she stands up, her feet still tapping.

'And I thought it was only farmers who branded their animals!' she says, staring at Pete. Her voice isn't even loud, but each word drives itself into the air. She's shaking, and I can't tell if she's angry, sad, or mad – I can only shiver, and go on feeling as though I've made some terrible, terrible mistake, a mistake I can't even see or hear, or ever hope to put right.

There's a heart-stopping silence, as everyone stares from her, to Pete, to me. The electrifying air is back and vibrating between them. Her body's still, now, but it's as though all that frantic movement is caught up in the air, as it shivers between them.

'Am!' he says, and he just sounds so totally gut-wrenched and horrified. Their eyes are locked on to each other, and his are so full of something like pain and horror that I can

221

hardly bear to look at them.

The crowd are staring and silent. I see them all through a strange haze, as though we're all drinking it in, all feeding off Am and Pete's horror and fear and excitement – and they're alone, trapped together, unable to get free – something holds them together, sticks them fast, what is it? What is it that makes him look as though he still wants to hold her in his arms for ever – and make her better?

And Am's anger – why is she so angry? Is it really pain – pain, and desire, and longing for what she's lost, for Pete?

'Well, you'd know, wouldn't you! Eh, Pete?' she says. 'You'd know all about making your mark!' She says it so quietly, but her eyes are blazing brighter than the bonfire.

'Am!' He gasps her name at her, as though she's stabbed the breath out of him.

The crowd almost sigh and sway; all except Bella, who is the only one besides me who doesn't seem completely caught up in it.

'Hey! Two sides, Am,' she says quietly.

'What's going on?' I hear my voice squeak, because they're all full of something, again, something I can't see. They're tight and together, the camp kids, and now it's only me on the outside.

Am doesn't take her eyes off Pete to listen to any of us; it's like her eyes are pushing him on, pushing him right to the edge of some cliff we're all balanced on – balanced and waiting.

Answer me, Pete, I'm thinking, tell me what's happening!

Turn to me, save us both from her. He doesn't. He can't. He's lost in her eyes, in her words, like he's still clinging to her, somehow, holding on and waiting to be understood.

'Am!' he says again, helpless, hopeless.

And I manage to stand up. I stand up and step into their circle – nothing happens, I don't explode, am not burnt up by the heat between them. I hold my hand up to the pale gold shadow upon his chest, beneath which I feel his heart beating so hard that it feels like a fish, a fish that's trapped in a net and gasping for air.

'What do you mean, Am?' I ask, and my own heart's going like a steam train, a train about to crash right through rib station.

And Pete's holding on tight, holding my hand.

'Ask Pete, why don't you?' she says, and then she steps back, and the connection's broken.

She smiles at us both, smiles as though nothing at all has happened, as if we are all the best of friends. Then she turns and disappears up the beach, leaping over the rocks as easily as if each one was a personal friend, and laughing.

'No worries, Pete!' says Mark. 'She was always a bitch-in-waiting.'

But Pete doesn't answer.

What, I hear myself wonder, what will they say about me, if it all falls apart one day, and I'm history?

'C'mon,' says Pete, and we disappear, away from the excited whispering and re-living. I want to stay, I want to hear what they're saying – but Pete pulls me along until we're sitting behind our favourite rock.

'What did Am mean?' I ask him over and over. 'What a sick thing to say, I wasn't branding you like an animal! Was I?'

'She sees things differently, Charley, forget it!'

'What is it with you two, Pete? Just tell me.'

'I can't, look, you need to forget her . . .'

'What is it? I feel like everyone else knows something and I don't.'

'Listen, Charley!' he says, and his voice sounds so earnest, so serious and true. 'They only think they know! OK?'

'So I have to trust you, is that it?' I ask.

'That's about it!' he shrugs, as though there are no second options.

'But I know something's wrong!' I wail.

'And I know you're not part of it!' he snaps back.

And I start to laugh, and once I've started I can't stop. 'Not part of it! God, Pete, I'm up to my ears in you! And you and her; have you ever stopped to feel how hot the air is between you? What am I meant to think about that?'

He's staring at me now, and I know I should stop – stop right now! But I can't.

'But it's all OK, because all I have to do is trust you? Jesus, look, I know there's no way the earth can move for you with me the way it does with her . . .'

Oh, disagree with me, Pete, stop me.

'How would you know that?' he asks, and his sigh sounds so old, older than seventeen, older than forever.

'I don't, but I know you all know something, Pete. It's only me who doesn't know anything – and you want it that way!' I'm shaking with anger myself now. 'She's crazy, isn't she?' I say. 'Am, she's mad!'

'She is, a bit!' he says in his slow, surf-dude way, and he makes it sound so safe and normal and far away, as though it's nothing to do with us at all really, and he holds me close and he whispers my name.

'Oh, Charley,' he says, so sadly and softly into my hair. 'Trust me?'

And it's awful, just awful the way my heart melts beneath his hands, and I'll do anything, anything, to make the world all right for us, for me.

'More girl-fiend than girlfriend' I try to laugh.

'I guess,' he says, sadly, 'but, Charley, leave her alone, eh?'

And my heart twists at knowing that he still cares so much about what she feels.

'I will,' I promise, 'but can we stop talking about her now?'

'What d'you wanna talk about?'

'Nothing,' I tell him, 'I don't want to talk.'

So we stop talking, and maybe it's not what we're best at anyway.

Hal. Now.

We're back on the cliffs We practically live here now, as though if we stay up here for long enough our lives might become as clear and spread-out as the beaches below us.

'So if it wasn't Pete on that beach, watching, who was it?' I ask for the millionth, trillionth time.

'Well, I wasn't there – was I?' she snaps back at me. 'So how would I know?' She strips the bark off a piece of willow as though she wishes it was me she could strip down and clean up.

'I know that! But you've got to be able to come up with something, Jack. You were there – I wasn't!'

'Hal?' she asks.

'Yeah?'

'What about you? I mean, you remember seeing her on the waves, right?'

'Yeah,' I say slowly, 'cos somehow I don't like the sound of this. I don't like the look in her eyes much, either.

'And the next thing you remember, you found her on the big rock?'

'Yeah?'

She's watching me like a hawk, and she's speaking slowly and clearly, as though she's only just thinking it out for herself. 'Well, where were you in between seeing her and finding her? I mean, did you just go back to sleep, or what?'

I can feel the panic rise inside me as Jack stares, holding me with her eyes. How can she tell that this is the question that haunts me in the middle of the night?

'I don't know,' I say. 'I don't know where I was in between.'

'So in a way,' she goes on, 'you were the last person to see her,' and the wind blows her hair across her face, but

226

neither of us move to fix it.

'What are you saying?' I ask.

'I'm not saying anything . . . I'm just asking you, Hal.
Where were you?'

'I don't know,' I say again, and I feel my mouth fill with
spit and fear. 'The shadow was the last person to see her!'

'But maybe . . . I mean . . . maybe . . .' She tails off.

'Maybe I'm the shadow, is that what you think?' She
shrugs, and inside me the picture of the shadow grows. I
watched Charley too, last summer. I wished I was doing
what she did. I was angry with her for disappearing, for
leaving me alone in the house on the cliff, kicking my heels
over the low wall with nothing to do but watch and listen.

Was it me, hunched up in the street light?

'I mean, you having all these feelings of hers inside you
now, d'you think it's just guilt? Guilt that you couldn't save
her?' asks Jack.

'I did watch her,' I say. 'She was different, she had something on her mind, not just the crazy-in-love stuff,
something different . . . something not so nice . . .
something worrying, and I was angry that she wouldn't tell
me, talk to me, but I wouldn't . . . I wouldn't . . .'

And as I'm talking I realize something – something
wonderful. I realize that even if it WAS me on the beach,
watching, I wouldn't actually hurt Charley, not ever.

'I didn't hurt her,' I say. 'Even if the shadow was me, I
didn't hurt her!'

'No?' asks Jack, and her eyes don't move from mine. 'And

what do you think was getting to her, Hal?' And for the briefest moment, I wonder if it wasn't me, then who does Jack think hurt her – but the thought disappears.

'I dunno,' I say, 'but she wasn't . . . she wasn't . . . easy . . .' is all I can manage.

'Know what?' she says suddenly, as though she's made a decision. 'I watched her too, and she was unhappy. We were all a bit wired that summer, the whole group, but Charley didn't know why, and none of us felt we could say, 'cos . . . anyway, I think she was unhappy 'cos of Am.'

'Who?' I'm so relieved the shadow's not me any more that I can hardly hear her.

'Oh, come on, Hal, even you can't have missed Am.'

'What's she look like?'

'She was around when you and Jake were duelling, kind of Kate Moss-ish, only better hair.'

'Omigod! You're telling me that's Am, as in Am-the-crazy-beach-girl?'

She laughs. 'I know . . . hard to remember she was ever such an ugly duckling.'

I try to remember Am. I mean, she's been part of the beach as long as us, much longer if you count being local. At first, trying to spot her was like trying to spot fish in the rock pools. I mean, you'd see her, maybe looking down at you from a rock – sense her there, reflected in the water – and then, when you turned, she was gone, and you wondered what had happened. Mum and Dad thought we made her up at first. Hell, we thought we made her up, but then she got older, was around more often. She used to freak the parents right out, and when she was about eleven, she used to climb anything – everything – the higher the better. There was even a rumour she climbed over the pub roof and up the church spire. 'If I ever catch you doing that . . .' said Mum.

And then she wasn't climbing and catching crabs and waving them in girls' faces any more. She wasn't having fun and scaring us all, she was just sitting on rocks, smoking, alone . . . and the kids all made sure she got it back . . . they threw limpets at her . . . called her names . . . but she just sat there smoking, and now Jack's here telling me she's turned into Am–super–model . . . ?

'And the weird thing is,' she says, 'Pete became gorgeous about the same time, and that's how they ended up together – I s'pose neither of them could believe the other one was interested!' She sighs and strips more bark, curls it round her fingers. 'I wish they'd never met!' she says as she throws the soft white curl out to sea. It floats on the wind, dancing, refusing to fall, and she laughs.

'I wish I could do that! Do you wish you could fly, Hal?'

And in that moment I do. I wish I could stretch out my arms and fly far, far away, to another place, where there was only me and Jack, and endless sunshine.

'Yeah,' I say. 'So why do you wish that?'

'What, that I could fly?'

'No, that they'd never met – and what's it got to do with

Charley?'

She sighs, and strips another piece off the bark. It's almost white now, white as bone.

'You thought you were the shadow, back then, didn't you?' she asks.

'Yeah.'

'So it could've been you, yeah, Hal? It could've been you on that beach, watching?'

'OK, Jack, it could've been me!'

'Just remember, Hal, what that feels like, and that you KNOW – you know for SURE – that you wouldn't hurt Charley, right?'

'Yes, OK! Get on with it!' For just a second, I feel like taking a strand of her lovely hair and throttling her with it.

'And I KNOW Pete wouldn't hurt her, OK? So we're quits, right?'

'Right!' I yell at her, but I don't mean it. I mean, she's not Pete, is she, so how COULD she know? 'Just tell me what any of this has got to do with Charley and Pete!'

'Well, last year, when Charley and Pete were together, we were all so stoked for him, 'cos he was having a really hard time, Hal, and . . .'

'Yeah?'

'Well . . . we all wanted it to go right for him, he liked her so much, and it felt right him being with her, especially after Am . . . and . . . we just . . . I mean, maybe we should have told her. I did suggest it to Pete, but I think he thought . . .'

She stops and looks at me, looks at me as though she wishes she was already five minutes ahead of herself, and knew already how I was going to exactly react – and then she finally goes on.

'I think he thought he might lose her if he did . . . tell her, I mean . . . I think—'

'Jack! For Chrissake, you've lost me already! Just tell me what you're on about!' But my heart's already screaming at me, don't listen, you don't wanna hear this, Hal, stop her! But it's too late, she's already talking.

'Last year . . .' she's saying, and her eyes drift into the distance, as though she's seeing it all in her mind's eye. Her hands finally fall still, and the stick lies across her knees, stripped bare.

'Charley was like, oh, I don't know, Hal, she was just like fresh air after Am, and she was fun. First time she came down to the barby she ate loads of Jane's cake, had no idea it was loaded . . . I saw her running across the beach, yelling "Mayday", and we all just wanted to keep it that way. I dunno if it was right . . . I was worried about it. So was Bella . . . but we didn't think . . . they just looked so good and happy together, it was like if you touched it, it might all fall apart, it was so perfect . . .'

Can't Jack hear my heart thumping? Doesn't she know how much I need her to say whatever it is that is haunting her?

'Well, they're not together now, Jack, and he doesn't even visit . . . so . . .'

'Pete was in trouble that year, Hal, real trouble, with the police,' she says at last.

I can't speak, I can't say anything, I can only stare and wait for her to go on . . . hoping she might be able to explain why I feel so sick, why I'm seeing my sister and her hunky, gorgeous boyfriend disappearing into the woods, alone together.

'What for?' I manage to ask into the silence between us.

'He was being questioned,' she says, and her own voice is slow and disbelieving. 'He was suspected of grievous bodily harm.'

I hear myself make a noise, a strange indescribable noise, and Jack is staring at me, silent and waiting, but I don't have anything to say to her. All I can see are two people – Charley and Pete – and they're heading into the woods alone, and only one of them comes back.

'He didn't do anything, Hal,' she says. 'He didn't hurt her.'

'Didn't he, Jack?' I ask, and I pick the dead stick up off her knees and hurl it, watching it as it flies out over the cliff, spinning up and up, high into the air, where it seems to stop for a long second before tumbling into the sea.

Charley: Hospital. Now.

And we leave them behind . . . Am . . . the gang . . . the whole lot of them. We go away, far away. To a place where we can believe that there is only us . . . like being on a wave . . . no past, no present, no future . . . just now . . . and that's what I want. Just memories, me and Pete. No Am, no house, no Jenna, no questions

. . . yeah, just leave us alone, Hal, stop tapping at us with your tentacles that want to know . . . stop looking at us with eyes that want to see. There are some things, Hal, that are not for you to see . . . Me and Pete, our way to the house in the woods.

It's fun in the twilight, whispering under the dark alleyways of trees, tasting each other's lips and forgetting that we're on our way anywhere. He's never been in the woods before.

Charley. Then.

'You're gonna leave me here, aren't you?' he says.

'Yep!' I say. 'I'm going to lead you to the heart of the wood, and abandon you, so you'd better just leave a trail of olive stones behind you, so you can find your way out.'

'Olives?' We laugh. 'Jeez, where do you go to school?' he asks.

The stream sounds loud in the darkened woods. We hold hands. We wander along.

'I might leave YOU in the woods,' he says, laughing, 'for the Red Indians.'

'You've forgotten I speak Apache,' I tell him. 'I'll send them right back at you!'

'Oh yeah? And what kind of school teaches Apache?' he asks.

'All-girls' school,' I tell him, and watch as his eyes light up, the way guys' eyes always do.

Sad.

'Wow, can I visit?' he asks.

'Nope, too much competition,' I tell him.

'Seriously, no boys at all?'

'Not a single sausage,' I say, and we fall about, and kiss, and I ask about him. He hates school, he's always being suspended.

'Why?' I can't imagine it, he's so chilled and gorgeous, how can he ever work up enough sweat to get suspended?

'That's 'cos I'm here, it's different on the beach,' he tries to explain. 'I can't stand school, I just get so . . .' He trails off, and I drop it, not wanting to spoil the mood, not liking the dark shadow that sometimes crosses his golden face.

His dad's a tenant on a farm.

'A farm, that is SO cool.'

'Not really,' he says, but I can see it already: the trees in the hazy morning light, the peace at night.

I'm there.

'The sea's near. That's why I'll stay, I guess,' is all he says. We walk on, growing used to the quiet, enjoying the sound of our voices loud in the woods, enjoying the fact that we can stop and kiss whenever we like, with no one else to see.

'Where IS this place?' he says after a while, and I notice that the rucksack dangles from his hand as though it weighs nothing at all.

'There,' I say, and it's in front of us through the trees: a dark and empty shadow of a house.

'You have to climb through the window,' I say, and we climb up, and the house is just as it's always been: empty, quiet, deserted – alone.

'Wow!' He stands and looks for a while, nodding his head.

'You said you wanted to be alone,' I say.

'Except for you,' he says, and he turns away. 'Whoa, a fire. Does it work?' And he's back through the window, collecting logs, and I'm outing the tea lights and dreaming that we live here.

I remember.

Oh, Pete.

We sit and talk and kiss in the firelight. I tell him about Jenna and Sally, and how I hate being the oldest, and how Mum and Dad are so completely freaked by the idea of me being with anyone let alone him.

He tells me about David, his older brother, who took off as soon as he was sixteen, and his mate Martin. How his mum says Pete has a terrible temper, but a slow fuse, and how this summer is so good – mainly, he says, because he's not with Am.

I try to just take it all in, to keep quiet, to listen and smile, but it's not happening.

'How can you say that?' I ask. 'I mean, she's so . . . amazing looking! How did marine girl end up looking like a supermodel? Tell me, Pete. I want the potion!'

He just stares at me like I've crept out from under a rock.

'She's Am!' he says.

'And who is she, then – marine girl or supermodel?' I ask. 'Tell me.'

He hesitates, and then he tries.

'Well, she is gorgeous, I mean, like so gorgeous you can't see anything else sometimes, but . . .

OK, enough!

'Oh, I dunno, Charley, she's just Am, isn't she? And we're not together now, and I really don't want to think about it . . . it's a total downer . . .'

'Why not?' I ask, 'cos here it is again, the thing he's not telling me. It's so obvious; he's just not a good liar. Or is he?

'It's – she's – she can really drive you to—' the firelight flickers across his face, and in the shadow of his frown he looks troubled. I reach up and try to wipe it away.

'What is it?' I ask. 'There's something, Pete, isn't there?' And I feel a cold dread, an icy chill in my heart.

What if he still loves her?

'Just leave her alone, Charley!' he says suddenly. 'Don't talk to her!'

It's as though I've touched a raw nerve; as though he can sense how much I'd like to wipe her off the face of the planet, to wipe out that high-voltage, supercharged buzz between them.

A sudden breeze whistles through the window, rattling the tin cups. It feels so cold, and for a moment I wonder what I'm doing here, in a damp old house, with a surf god. The thought makes me laugh, but the laugh comes out all wrong, and I think I hear a rustle somewhere outside, a sudden loud snap of tree bark.

Pete's up and at the window before I can speak.

'Nothing. Wind,' he says, and wraps me up so tight in his arms that however much I try to turn, I can't quite see out of the window, to where the noise came from.

His eyes shine in the firelight and I lose myself in them. How can we spend so long just staring at each other? We run out of words, and kiss and kiss until our mouths aren't enough any more, and our hands take over, spreading the feeling from our mouths across our bodies, searching for more skin, more tingling. My T's off, and his is hanging off one arm. God, he's so gorgeous, I can't stop touching him. Feeling the difference between his cool, cool skin and the heat of his lips. He pushes against me, I push back. We begin to giggle. He pushes harder, so do I, and then suddenly it's like he disappears, and I'm crushed up under him. The whole weight of him is pressed right up against me, and my voice is muffled, my mouth squashed up against his skin.

I dig my nails in to get him off, and sit up.

'That's not funny, Pete, I couldn't breathe.' I'm gasping for air.

'Uhh!' He can't speak for a bit, either. 'Sorry, what did I do?'

'I couldn't breathe, you were squashing me!'

'It was a GAME, Charley. Jesus.' He sounds irritated.

'Play that one with Am, did you?' I picture her burning eyes, gazing at him, pushing back at him, harder than me.

More fun?

Where did that come from?

'Look Charley, I don't want to talk about her,' he says, and he's smoothing my hair back over my scalp, and leaning over me, face to face, so that all I can see are his eyes.

'I'm not looking!' I laugh and close my eyes, but it's no good, I can still feel his lips, soft against mine. I can feel my head, weightless in the palm of his hand where he holds it. I can feel my eyes opening up into his, and it's just so hopeless to think that I won't get lost in them again.

We're skin to skin, and it's better than dreams, chest to chest, my legs curl up around him. It's like my body has been hiding for years, and has only chosen now to let me know I was never in control anyway. Now it's me pushing him. And then I hear it again, clear and definite: the sound of a gasp, or is it the wind, somewhere outside?

'Stop!' I can't believe that the voice is mine, but it is. 'Stop a minute.'

He does, breathing hard, like he's been punched – but he's laughing.

'I need to stop a minute.'

My voice is shaky. I feel sick. Is there somebody out there, watching? Jack?

'Charley, are you all right?' He sounds worried now; did he hear something too? His head's up, alert.

'I thought I heard something,' I say.

'Sure.' He puts his T-shirt on quickly and hands me mine. Gets up and looks out of the window.

'Can't see anything,' he says.

'Sorry,' I say, 'cos it suddenly sounds like such a feeble excuse for losing my nerve.

'No worries!' He comes back, hugs me tight. ''s OK,' he laughs, 'probably good timing!' But he's still looking around.

'Why?' I ask. 'Why was it good timing? Don't you want to . . . to . . . ?'

'Do you?' he asks.

'Sometimes! Like just then!' I say.

He's silent. The fire's burnt down and we both know I've got to head home. He doesn't answer.

'You've done this before, haven't you?' I ask after a while.

'Yeah.'

'With Am?'

'Look, Charley, please, leave Am out of this, she's—'

'In a different league?'

'Christ!' He's angry, suddenly and completely angry. 'You don't know anything about her, or her life, and you need to leave it, OK?'

I'm angry back.

'Is that some way of trying not to tell me you've slept with her, or what?'

'No, it isn't, and yes, I have!'

'Oh!' The words sound so small and silly, and I FEEL small and silly. I can see Am's eyes, taunting and teasing, older and wiser, knowing something I don't know. Something they both know. Something I don't.

I'm too young. He'll ditch me.

'I want to too, Pete,' I whisper, desperate not to lose him, not to be on the outside. To be where they are, Pete and Am, knowing each other, inside that strange buzz . . . oh, shit! How do you do this, I'm thinking? How do you say, I want to, really want to, let that feeling just carry me all the way down the river? How do you say, but I'm scared, and I know I'll never be as sexy as she is? And what if I'm crap at it?

'Maybe *I* don't want to, Charley!' I hear Pete say, slowly.

I can't believe it, I'm stilettoed, what've I done? Is it over? Has it really been that bad?

'Is that it, then?'

I might as well know; I can't possibly feel any stupider.

'Is what it?' He looks down at me.

'Us.'

'Is it for you?' he asks.

'NO!'

'Well then,' he says, and we're kissing again, gentle kisses going nowhere.

'You won't be fifteen forever,' he says as we get up.

'Why should that matter?' I ask him, but I can already hear the answer.

Playing with kids now, eh, Pete? says a voice in my head. A voice called Am.

He holds my hand all the way home, making me laugh, making me feel so safe and held. Somewhere out in the woods behind us, a twig snaps, or a bough breaks. I feel followed, and I try to turn back, to look behind us, but somehow Pete's always in between me and the noise, always there, with a kiss, a joke, a laugh.

'Don't be scared!' he whispers. 'I'm here.'

But I am scared.

'I feel as though we're being followed,' I whisper, and I try to laugh too.

'Must be your conscience.' He smiles, and then he leans over me, looking deep into my eyes. 'No,' he says, with a smile, 'as clear as the stream.'

And we laugh.

'Not forever, I hope!'

'Second that!' he says.

But when, I think, and why not now?

And in my mind it's like the answer, written clear in the air, in that vibrating, buzzing air between him and her – Am.

I feel so wild when I get home. And I'm scared: scared by how badly I want Pete, scared that he doesn't want me back, scared I might dive headfirst right off the cliff, without even knowing how deep the water is . . . but that's not all.

I can't shake this feeling of being followed.

'The wind's caught you,' Mum says. 'You're wind-wild, child!' and it feels just like that, as though the power of the wind's rushing right through my body, as though the sea's caught me, and thrown me high in the air, where I'm danc-ing on clouds.

'Hey Hal, c'mon.' I grab him and try to dance across the kitchen.

'Get off!' he says.

'Father, may I?' Dad's a hopeless dancer, but he tries. I can't sit still. I dance, I sing, I drive everyone except Sarz completely mad.

''gain!' she says, and I do it again, lifting her up, throwing her just like I remember Dad throwing me, high in the air, where I stayed for a moveless moment, for a still split second, with all the world spread out beneath me and waiting for me to fall. That's just how it feels to be with Pete.

'Got ya!' I say to Sarz.

''gain!' she shouts, and so me and Sarz play, and Mum laughs, and Dad says, 'Nice to have you back, love,' but Hal just stares at me, like he knows I'm not back. Like he knows I'm somewhere else completely, somewhere not in my right mind, somewhere far away, and wondering if I can ever return.

'Easy!' he says, and we glance at each other for a moment, so close together, like he can see my feelings with his deep grey eyes, and yet we're so far apart. I could never explain in a million years what it is, this sudden fear, so that every time I'm with Pete I hear the trees rustle and the boughs crack. Every time we lie in the lonely late-night shadow of a rock, I find myself imagining someone creeping up on us.

I feel like we might turn the corner one evening, all happy and laughing, only to be caught in the beam of a torch, like rabbits, stunned by the glare, paralysed, and unable to move.

And sometimes, for no reason at all, I find myself thinking: Mum, help me . . .

Charley: Hospital. Now.

'*Mum!*'

'*Help me!' And suddenly, wonderfully, she's here. I can't believe it, but it's her, her voice beside me.*

'Hello, Charley. Oh, darling! It is so good just to see you, even in all that horrible hospital gear. My good God, girl, you look like a red-haired Wendy in that gown!' *She turns to the nurse, and her voice is so wonderful, wonderful, and angry, as angry and sharp-edged as a clam shell.*

'What's she doing in that gown? I thought we asked for her to be dressed each day? Oh, Charley!' she says, 'you can't believe how much I've missed you, and I mean you, just as you are, in that joyless bed.'

Mum!

Her voice. Warm.

Warm like summer rain all over me.

She opens the window, and the sweet air rushes over me, she smells of the sea!

There, that's better!

Silence.

Someone must have put a new battery in the clock, because its tick sounds unnaturally loud, like a new heart in an old body.

'Well, we hardly ever see Hal, would you believe it, I think he might be with a girl, but he's as difficult as you were, and as secretive. What a pair!'

Her words tingle on my skin, like goose bumps.

She strokes my cheeks. Is silent.

'Where are you, my love?' *she asks, quietly.* 'And what shall we do with you?'

'Here!' I say. 'I'm here, Mum!'

She can't hear me, but she kisses me anyway, her lips as soft as wings against my cheek.

'Ah! Mrs Ditton! Nice to see you!'

I shiver.

Someone's walking on my grave.

'Well, as you can see,' *the voice goes on,* 'no change, I'm afraid, and I think you and your husband are very wise to be considering the situation so carefully.'

'Hello, could we discuss this elsewhere?' *says Mum firmly.* 'I'd rather not involve my daughter.'

What? What are they discussing? Me?

'I'm so sorry, Charley!' *she says, and the helpless, hopeless sound in her voice scares me . . . then I hear the door swing as she leaves. I feel the frail new stitches that barely hold me together beginning to split . . .*

'Mum!'

She doesn't answer, but a hot, salt tear still lies burning and liquid on my forehead. At its touch I begin to come undone; all the bits of my body separate and fly away from each other. Arms are floating, grabbing at legs, and my head is spinning around, bodyless, staring, and unable to co-ordinate any of the bits.

'Mum!'

But there is no answer, only the cold and silent dark that lies

*between my hands and arms and face and legs, as I hang in bits,
unmoving.*

'Somebody! Help me!'

'Hal . . . Hal . . . Hal . . .'

I call and call . . . but this time, there's no answer . . .

Hal. Now.

'Help me! Hal . . . Hal . . . Hal . . .'

She's calling, and my head aches with the effort of trying to shut her out. I've tried helping, Charley, but all it
does is get between me and Jack. The centre of my forehead burns, as though a drop of pure acid is burning itself
all the way through to my brain.

Stop it! I tell myself.

But how? That's what I want to know. How do you stop
loving somebody just because they're half dead?

'Be here, Hal,' I whisper to myself. 'That's how.'

Be right here, right now, not in the hospital, not tied up
in last year, trying to work it all out. Not imagining shadows.

I look around me; I'm here on the beach with Jack.
What could be more normal than me and Jack on the
beach? Only it isn't, is it? Trouble is, everyone knows about
Charley and Pete, and everyone's always watching to see
how we measure up. At least, that's how it feels.

There are one or two girls with hand prints on their
bodies, pale shadows of hands that drift across their
midriffs. One girl has a hand print that looks like it's

crawling all the way down her back. Funny how I'd never noticed them before; horrible how every time I see one now my heart lurches, and I see Charley. Charley, who would've been so thrilled to have started a craze that's still around, lying in her hospital bed, barely breathing.

Switch it off, Hal. Delete.

'Hey, Hal!' yells Jack, and she's on my back, whispering in my ear. 'C'mon, lover-boy, roll me over in the sand, kiss me.'

And I do, and it's fun. Sometimes there are whole afternoons when I'm not just pretending to have fun, I really am. Me and Jack in the waves, on the sand, under the oaks, behind the rocks. Sometimes we don't think about anything but each other, and those are the good times.

'Do you think they did it?' she asks one day. She's got her lazy cat's eyes in. We're full of the sun and each other, and I'm beginning to wish the summer could go on forever. To wonder how I can ever bear to leave her. To believe that maybe, just maybe, I could get over Charley.

'No,' I say, not really listening. Did what?

'Oh, I do.' She says, and then I get it: did IT, she means, as in, did Pete and Charley do IT?

'Oh, I dunno, don't wanna think about it.' And I don't. To even go there makes me hate Pete. Don't know why, don't even want to know why.

'I hope they did,' she says suddenly and passionately. 'I hope she did, before she . . .'

We stare at each other, and Charley and Pete are right

back there in between us, as they always are these days, whether we choose to notice it or not.

'*Help me. Oh, Hal, please.*' It's Charley's voice, and I try to resist her, but it's like she's in little bits and begging me to piece her together. But we're all in bits, Charley, just cut to pieces by losing you without ever really being able to say goodbye – or to know why. I never knew what it meant before, being in bits. I do now. It's like being paralysed without even knowing it, like waiting and hoping that one day all the pieces will just fall into place, and the world will begin to make sense again – and knowing it never will.

'I don't wanna go there, Jack.' I try to say it kindly, gently, but it comes out like desperation, and I wonder how much time we've got left, me and Jack, how long I can hold on to her, knowing all the time that her brother might have hurt Charley.

'I just hate them both, sometimes!' she whispers.

'Yeah, just for existing,' I answer. And we get up off the warm sand, and drift off the beach holding hands. We sit deep in the shadow of the trees, off the path, where it's cool and quiet, and we kiss, and slowly the world begins to fade away. Slowly, it really is just me and Jack, and the whisper of the trees, and our breath, sweet and close and tangling.

And that's when we hear voices on the path, and Jack sits up and pulls away, before I've realized what we're hearing. It's Am. Am and Pete.

'No!' Am's saying. 'No, no, no, no! I won't!'

'Look, Am, it's in the past, isn't it, whether Charley's in

hospital or not – she's not going anywhere, not talking to anyone, is she?'

'I thought she . . . I thought she died, it said in the paper that she was in a coma, unlikely to survive . . . that's what you said . . . that's why I . . .'

'Listen, Am,' Pete cuts in. 'None of that matters now; what matters now is getting you out of here . . . that hasn't changed, it's the only way any of this can make sense. What happened to Charley can't matter now, Am, and if we don't . . .'

'Oh, Charley, Charley, Charley . . .' chants Am, and at the sound of her name in Am's mouth I rock back, reeling.

Jack's face, when I turn, is white and staring, her mouth open, no words coming out.

'Stop it, Am!' Pete's voice is stretched thin. 'We've got to think . . . we've got to . . .'

'What? Think about what?' she shouts at him. 'There's nothing to think about! Nothing happened . . . it's like everyone says, exactly like everyone says – she went in the waves and never came out.' And then her voice changes, goes all strange and silky smooth, and she stares up at Pete. 'And that's what I'll say, Pete, you know that – so why do you keep going on about it? Why do you worry about it? I won't tell, I promise.'

I start up, but Jack grabs my hand, hard, and pulls me back into the shade of the trees as they pass. She holds her hand to her mouth, and her face is deadly white now, as white as the skinned sticks she strips of their bark.

'You know what happened, Am,' Pete says quietly, and I wonder if I've imagined the sound of menace in his voice, as it fades away, 'and you need to leave here – to get away!'

I turn to Jack, furious.

'Didn't hurt her, eh?'

'Shhh, Hal, we need to follow—' She starts up after them, but I pull away, and then I run, run as far away as I can get from all of them.

I head deep into the woods, into the soft safe shadow of the oaks. When I stop I'm lost, deep in the wood, and the light is a strange green. The shadows of the trees stretch out in it, and the lichened tree-bark seems to glow in the dappled light. The wood breaks out into a sudden glade of twisted trunks, surrounding a strange, lumpy, moss-filled clearing. I stop. I can hear Jack, somewhere behind me, cursing and stumbling over branches, cracking twigs, and calling my name.

'Hal! Hal!'

I don't answer. I listen to the voice inside me, the voice I've been trying so hard to silence, Charley's voice. I can feel it all around me, whispering; it's in the air and the trees as though they're holding her memories tight, and waiting, just waiting for me to collect them. A cry rises from my gut, it's her name, and I stop holding her back, I let myself feel the hot, burning drop on my forehead, and I follow its searing acid pain, deep inside the curls of my brain. I let my head go, let it fill with the dizzying pain of emptying, of being me, and when the pain hits my heart, that's where I stop . . . where I stop . . . and Charley begins.

I hear her voice: *'Hal, Hal, Hal, Hal . . . help me!'*

'Charley!'

Charley: Hospital. Now.

'Charley!'

Hal! He's back. Thank God . . . his voice rolls through me like my own heartbeat, and slowly the abandoned pieces of my body gather, like dust in sunlight . . . and I become whole again . . .

'Where are you?'

Hal. Now.

'Where are you?'

She calls, and I look around me. I'm in a glade, the moss is dried-out and springy, it spreads through the clearing in strange curved shapes. As I watch, the shapes seem to move, to bend and sway and shift over the ground, as they come towards me . . . I hold on to the trunk of a shrunken oak. The ground is moving, waving beneath my feet, and slowly, as I watch, shapes form in the wild moss: shapes of bodies, pressing the soft fronds down, leaning into them and lending them their weight, rolling over them and sighing, laughing, as they come towards me.

'No! No!' I hold my ears, but I can still hear the voices – not Am and Pete, but Charley, Charley and Pete, laughing and lying together in the glade, and then I hear his voice, cold and sharp as rain.

'Fuck off, Am.'

And the next thing I know, Jack's right beside me.

'Hal, what are you doing?'

I turn to her, shaking. 'ME? What am I doing?' I scream at her. 'What about your perfect bro? What's he doing? Oh he's so in love with Charley ... he stares up at your house, he just can't live without her, there's no way he'd hurt her ...'

Her hand comes out of nowhere, and suddenly my face is zinging with the pain, just zinging, like a thousand small needles are all dancing on my cheek.

'Oh, Hal, sorry, sorry, sorry – I just—'

Her face looks so pale and contrite in the green light, and she sits down suddenly, like she's collapsed from the inside ... like whatever it used to be that made standing up worthwhile has just been pulled right out from inside her. And I stop too, because I know that feeling, it's what it feels like not to have Charley.

She's sobbing. I've never seen her sob before. The tears just fall through her fingers, and her whole body's shaking up and down with her ragged breathing, but she doesn't make a sound.

'Jack!' I sit down on the soft moss next to her, and we shake together. 'Pete!' she says in an agonized, strangled whisper. 'Pete.' She says his name over and over again, like she's lost him. Her idea of Pete is shattered, dead and blown to pieces in a few sentences, and she's chanting his name, just like we all chant Charley's name, over and over in disbelief, as though just the sound of it will bring her back.

'But I don't get it, Hal,' she sobs.

'What's to get?' I ask.

'It was Am!'

'Yeah,' I agree. 'Am and Pete, definitely. Together.'

And she turns to look at me in puzzlement.

'But it was Am who was charging him,' she says.

'What?'

'It was Am who he was meant to have hit – and, Hal, somebody did, because her face was a mess, and it was just after they finished, and . . .' She can't go on, she looks like she might be about to throw up – I step back a bit, out of range.

'What?' I say again.

'It was her . . . it was Am who he's meant to have beaten up,' she says.

'And you all knew?' I yell. 'And you didn't warn Charley? What kind of a person are you, Jack?'

But she doesn't answer, just goes on: '. . . and Pete was all for admitting it, as long as Am didn't press charges, I think that's right, but there's something that doesn't make sense . . .'

'Too right, Jack, it doesn't make any sense that nobody told Charley!'

'He didn't do it, Hal!'

And we're on opposite teams again.

I can't speak. Suddenly, Pete, and Jack, and Am, and the camp site, none of it appeals any more. It's all frightening and grubby and dirty, just the way everyone says it is.

Why am I nodding at her?

'He didn't do it, Hal!' Jack says again, and her eyes hold mine, determined, definite, against me.

I want to get up and go home, I want to be with Dad when Mum gets back from visiting Charley, I want to hear how the real Charley is, I want the whole thing to stop right now, and that includes Jack.

I can't look at her.

'He can really lose it sometimes, Hal, but he would never, ever hit a girl.'

'Well that would make it all right then, eh, Jack? I mean, the use of violence in general?' But I don't really need to say it, she can tell how I feel just by looking at me.

'I don't think it was him, that's what I'm saying.' She grabs my hand. 'Listen to me, Hal . . . I think it might be her dad that's doing the hurting . . . it's the only way it makes any sense.'

'Not to me, Jack.' And I pull my hand away.

'Why don't you believe me?' she shouts, into the dead air under the branches, but there's no answer, not from me; there's only the creaking of the trees, sudden and loud in the silent glade.

I stand up and walk away, and this time, she doesn't follow.

Charley: Hospital. Now.

The glade glimmers, so clear in my mind, beckoning with memories, soft fronds of moss glowing in the green half-light . . .

Charley. Then.

It's such a long walk back over the cliffs, and we always stop just above the beach, deep amongst the trees, in the glade. We stop for the cool and the shade, and because it's way too far to walk all the way home without kissing.

'How do you know all these places?' I ask him.

'How do you know the woods?' he says right back.

We sit on our boards under the oaks, but as soon as I sit down it comes again, the feeling of someone watching. Maybe it's the trees, or the woods themselves holding us to them ... imprinting us, like memories. On the other hand ...

'Where's Jack?' I ask. She can be a little shadow sometimes, Jack.

'Surf school in Bude.'

'Right.' He begins looking at me, and my eyes just get pulled right in, but it's like there are eyes somewhere behind me too, and it makes me want to wriggle.

'What's up?'

'Ants in my pants.' I'm sure I hear a snort, can't he hear it? Am I going mad? 'What was that?'

'People on the path?' he suggests, smiling.

'Oh, yeah.' I feel so stupid, but it's easy to forget the path's not really that far away. It feels miles away from anywhere in here, on the soft moss, amongst the old oaks.

'I'll protect you from the zombies!' he laughs, and his arms are all the way around me, and the soft, soft moss holds me up from underneath, and I'm lost, because it feels so safe and warm and lovely, as well as dangerous and crazy and difficult.

'I really, really want to . . . with you,' I say, but he just looks away, and a quick sharp shadow flits across his face.

'I can tell!' He laughs, but he doesn't say that he wants it too, doesn't explain why not – or why it's always him that stops us, that holds me back and smiles. Why, I want to say, why aren't I good enough, not as good as Am?

'I hate the thought of you and Am. You know, together.'

'Great reason!' He looks angry. 'Really, Charley, great!'

There's a sound, a sudden crack from somewhere in the trees, and I jump.

'Old oaks,' he says; does he say it a bit too quickly? I get up. I'm gonna find Jack this time, and let her know it's not funny.

'Come out! Come out! Wherever you are!' I call, but the only answer is the sound of the faraway waves, and the slight rustle of the breeze through the leaves. I feel Pete's dappled shadow fall across me, as he turns me around, away from the blank stare of the trees, back towards him; but his look over my shoulder feels sharp and suspicious – as though maybe he's wondering, too.

'Getting back to us . . .' he says, and his voice is so soft and hazy . . . inviting . . . I shrug him off a bit.

'But about Am?' I ask.

'What – about – Am?' He's barely patient, and it makes it difficult to think.

'There's something—' I try, but I can't find the words.

What I want to say is: there's something between you, and I don't know what it is, all I know for sure is that you wanted to, with her, and you don't with me . . . and I can see her eyes, staring and laughing at me, her bruised blue eyes. And I wonder, what does she know, and I wonder why it feels so exciting, and frightening, and what it's got to do with Pete.

'OK. So maybe there is something,' he says, before I can get any more words out, 'and maybe it's none of your business! And anyway, that's a shit reason for doing it!' He looks so angry and hurt; the power of it shocks me. He's always so laid back, so chilled and surf-cool; seeing his face turned away like that, so cold and angry, it does something to me, gives me power!

'It's not the only reason,' I shout back at him.

'Right!' He doesn't turn, doesn't look at me, so I look at him instead. He is truly, truly gorgeous. I cannot, simply cannot, believe that he is with me, but maybe that's part of the thrill for him, that I am so sickeningly grateful.

'It's not just Am!' I say, although it partly is. 'There's this,' I say, and I sweep my fingers across his warm, sandy stomach. 'Hey! Surfboard Sixpack!'

No answer.

'And these?' I pick up his hands. 'Amazing what they can do. I want to know more! And these.' I touch his lips with the tips of my fingers.

He begins to smile. I can tell he doesn't really want to, but he can't help himself. His lips begin to twitch at the corners, and he turns his head to mine.

Got him.

'What about me?' I ask. 'What is it about me?'

'Everything!' he says and then he sighs. 'The whole Charley package, but first off, it was the way you fell off your board!'

'Bastard!'

'You even looked good doing that!' he says, fighting me off, and then we're looking at each other again, deep into each other's eyes, and after that it doesn't really matter if the trees rustle, or the boughs break, or even if a whole oak pulls up its roots and decides to land right beside us, because we're lost. We're nothing but hands and eyes, and touch, and wordless noises. I can feel the soft, soft moss give beneath us. At times I can't tell which bits of body are his and which bits are mine.

We fall asleep under the trees.

'Wake up!' I say. The shadows are growing longer and the glade suddenly feels green and alien. It's late afternoon, I'm thirsty and hungry, swollen. I need water. God! He looks so gorgeous asleep, like I should be kissing him awake after a hundred years. I imagine waking up with him, day after day, and I imagine how we might be together at night, in the afternoon, in the morning, whenever. And then I'm wondering, what do people actually do – and how? I mean, it can't all be like in films, can it? The world doesn't really go all soft-focus just to help you get past the embarrassing bits. I wonder if he can really feel this way about me. Could he really spend hours looking at skinny, red-haired Charley Ditton, the way I look at him? I pinch him, just to make sure he's real.

'Fuck!' he says and turns over, groaning. I laugh and do it again.

'Fuck off, Am!' he says, and it's like he's slit open my heart; really, the pain is so sudden and startling. I turn away, the tears already gathering. He sits up.

'Charley!' He's dazed with sleep as he reaches for me. 'Sorry, I thought you were— oh, Charley, don't!' He lifts a hand to wipe away the tears.

'I was pinching you to see if you were real,' I say.

'Sorry, it's the kind of thing Am did, only she did it . . . well, she did it to hurt.'

'Careful, Pete, you might actually tell me something about her.' I stick on a smile. 'Let's go.'

After the woods and the shadowy glade, the late sun feels hot, like the ground has had all the heat it can take, and it throws it back out at us, up into the air. I drag my board along.

'Don't!' says Pete. 'It's a nice board!'

I don't answer.

Am, Am, Am. Her name runs through my head, and I can see them together, both looking so perfect, Yin and Yang, like they fit. I see his hand, over and over, dropping on to her head, so softly, so gently, like she was made of clouds, and I know how his hands feel – like the sound of leaves, like the lift of a wave – and then sometimes sudden, like a gasp.

And then it comes to me, a picture so clear and sharp, it's almost like it's traced in outlines on the shimmering air. I see her head in his palms, and his thumbs are stroking the deep blue bruises under her eyes, barely touching them, and yet somehow managing to wipe them away.

I stop walking.

'Don't stop, we're nearly there.' He takes my arm and bends over, kisses the top of my head.

'Sorry,' he says, 'super, super sorry.'

Our shadows are long and thin and spread out ahead of us. He's a whole head and shoulders bigger than me, and a completely different shape. When I stand in front of him his shadow swallows me up completely.

'Swim?' he asks when we finally get down the cliff, and he smiles, like 'sorry'. 'Make you feel better!' he says. I know what he means, but I just want to be home, for once, where it feels safe and easy, and Mum and Dad are waving at me from their world, up there on the terrace, and I'm just so sick of being watched the whole time by everyone, when really all I want to do is be in the surf, with Pete alone, or maybe in a bed – yeah, that would be nice. To be legit. To not have to hide in moss and sand and woods.

'See ya,' I say.

'Come down to the barby,' he says. 'Come on, Charley, we haven't hung out with the others for ages.'

'Sure!'

I walk away. I don't want to go; Am will be there.

Am, Am, Am, with her sea-perfect skin and her go-anywhere stare; with her knowing gaze that skims over his body, seems to read it like a book, a book that's so well read she only has to glance at it to know EXACTLY what word's coming next.

But I go to the barby, of course I do. Pete's there. And later we drift away to our favourite spot, behind a warm rock.

'Race you to the sea,' he says.

'Don't want wet jeans.'

'Take 'em off, then?' he suggests, smiling his wicked smile, and I stand up.

'After you!' I laugh. He stands up too; we start to giggle, falling over in the sand, trying to get our legs out.

We never make it to the sea.

'That was a very cunning plan, Peter Piper,' I whisper, later.

'Mmm, backfired a bit.'

'Elmer the elephant on your boxers!' I get the giggles again. 'Such a hunk, eh, with multi-coloured elephants covering your trunk!'

'Yeah, yeah, all right, they were in the Christmas stocking, don't tell me you're always in Calvins.'

'Only for you!'

And then, without warning, the feeling comes again, the feeling of somebody just out of sight and watching . . . watching and waiting.

It must be Jack; she followed us all the time when we were first together, she's almost as crazy about Pete as I am.

Maybe she's watching out for him? Maybe she thinks he only picks crazy chicks – like Am.

'Could you tell Jack to stop following us?'

'Uh?'

'It's really getting on my nerves.'

'She's hardly ever around, Charley.'

'I told you, she creeps after us!'

'You,' he leans up close, 'have a seriously screwy head.'

'You,' I lean even closer, till our noses touch, 'have a seri-ously nosy sister.'

'Not-possible. I-keep-telling-you, she's-at-surf-school-all-day, and-then-out-shopping-with-Mum, all-night probably.' He licks my lip every time he makes the 'l' sound.

That sentence had a lot of 'l's, real and imaginary, and by the end of it I don't really care if Jackie's standing on the rock filming us, I'm having too much fun.

'This is the best summer ever,' I say a bit later.

'Really?'

'Yeah, but there's only a week left.'

'Right.'

'Am I just a summer crush, then?'

'No!'

'So?'

'Let's just chill, Charley, we've got time.' And he stretches out on the sand as though we have all the space in the world – but that's just not how it feels to me.

How can he be so cool? He can't possibly feel the way I do.

'They won't just let me get on a bus to your place, you know.'

'No?'

'No!'

'No chance of Glasto in a tent together next summer, then?'

'Oh, Pete!'

I can't bear the thought of us parting, can't imagine not waking up with the sun on my face and the sea in my ears, can't imagine not sitting in the starlight.

Me and Pete.

There's nothing like it, me and Pete wrapped up together in his old coat, whispering together in the dark, hummed at by the waves, hidden by the rocks.

'I don't want you to go, ever,' I say one night.

'Let's run away and set up a surf school in Mexico,' he says.

'Yeah, let's,' and we imagine it, and how we'll do it: I'll steal a credit card, we'll book a flight over the net, we'll live in a shack on a beach, in the endless sunshine, with no one to stop us being together all through the night, 'till morning, and sleeping late.

'Bagsy you cook breakfast.'

'Bagsy you never wear clothes till lunchtime.'

'Bagsy first Mexican wave.'

'Oh no!'

We both know it isn't real, that it can't happen. I don't really want to run away, I can't wait to get back and give

Jenna and Sal all the goss. It's just that I wish Pete was coming with me.

There's a light somewhere far out on the rocks, a fisherman. The light of his lamp shines yellow under the white stars. There's the sound of something shifting on the slipway behind us, a cat perhaps.

'Jack?' I whisper, and Pete laughs.

'Talk about obsession.'

'You're my only obsession,' I murmur, pressing up against his warmth, and feeling his hair tickle my forehead. I can't bear the thought of not being near him; can't imagine a day when we don't kiss, can't look into each other's eyes, can't touch.

'Let's spend a whole night together,' I hear myself say. In my head we're on a beach in Baja, or maybe at the Beverly Hills Hotel, with huge pillows made of goose feathers, great for fighting with, and we've just surfed all day, and there's champagne in ice buckets all over the floor. The bath's the size of a whole bathroom, and rose petals are chucking out scent off the top of the water.

'How will we do that?' says Pete.

'No idea,' I mumble. 'Maybe you could win the lottery?'

'What? You want money?' He laughs.

'Eh?' Then I tell him what's in my mind and we laugh, and he says he can't afford the Beverly Hills, and his country house is only a tenant farm, so what'll we do?

'I'll sneak out. We'll go to the house in the woods, at night! Come on, your family are camping kings, don't try to tell me you can't nab a few mats and bags from some-where.'

I wait for him to say no again, to say, why now, Charley, when we've got all the time in the world to get to know each other. I watch him as he thinks about it.

'Oh, Charley!' he says. 'There's no hurry; we can still see each other after the summer. They can't stop you ringing, can they?'

And something in me just snaps – all the fear of feeling watched, and the waiting, and the not knowing why he doesn't want me – it all just rises right up in me and snaps the elastic.

'Pete! The summer's ending, all of it! And you'll be gone! Can't you see that you don't KNOW what it'll be like once you get home? Neither do I!'

I don't know what's got into me. Why am I shouting at him?

Someone's walking over my grave . . . whispering at me . . . telling me, now, now, now.

And all I know is this urgency. This feeling that all I have is now, right now, and I can't make him see or hear me. I can see the haven in my mind, all shut up for winter. The empty grey waves all high and clean and perfect and we're not here to use them . . . I'm trying to tell him, but all that comes out is . . .

'Now, Pete!'

'What?' he asks, holding my hands between us. 'What is it, Charley?'

'I need to be with you NOW, Pete, not next week, or next year, but now. I want us to be together for a whole night. I want to see what happens!'

'Hey!' He holds on to me, as shaken and surprised as I am.

'Listen, I didn't say we couldn't spend the night together, I just don't want you to feel . . . I dunno . . . that you have to . . . or that it's too . . . sometimes it's not . . .'

'I want to!'

'OK, OK!' he says. 'Let's spend the night, see what happens!' And we're holding each other and laughing, and I'm saying, 'Was that the wrong way round?' and he's laughing back, and his voice is so surprising as he says:

'No, Charley, that was the right way round!'

And then we kiss, and slip apart, feeling the cool night air come between us. As we leave the beach something slips and slides. I swear I hear a smothered sound.

'Weirdo!' says Pete, as I jump and turn. 'Jack is just not that interested.'

But then who can it be?

Charley: Hospital. Now.

Who was it? Who stood and stared and watched and followed?

The room outside of me is silent and empty, night-time.

Outside is the starlight.

Mum will be getting off the train.

Here the night is orange and noisy. Behind the windows cars swish, but there it's so black and silent that I could almost hear the

stars shine. It's so dark sometimes that you can't see your hands
before your eyes . . .

Hands before your eyes . . .

So dark . . .

A memory . . .

Fear, heart-pumping, armpit-prickling fear, star-less and
shadow-less . . . alone in the inky blackness, arms outstretched and
finding nothing.

'Where am I?'

Somewhere in the darkness a fire explodes, orange light against
a black sky, like a dawn before its time . . .

'Who's there, who's there?'

'Hal, where are you?'

Hal. Now.

'Who's there?'

The question comes at me, in Charley's voice, and I find
myself looking around me, wondering what's real – the
whole world feels suddenly unsure and dangerous. Even
the village, so peaceful in the sunshine, looks different. The
camp site isn't just colourful any more, it's crazy. People
there do drink and drugs and beating, and Am's big grey
house up on the cliff isn't romantic any more, it's just lonely
and desolate and worrying; why is Am so strange, and what
did she think of Charley and Pete? The whole world's
shifting again, showing what's underneath.

Nowhere's safe.

And Jack? I dunno, I just know I can't give her up yet, but I'm thinking about it. I need her, that's the thing – she's the link between this year and last year, and she can find things out – things I can't.

I don't see her coming, just hear her voice, and I can't help what my body does when it hears it; the sound of her is like a life raft, full of normality, holding the fist of fear at bay.

'*Who's there?*'

'I think I've got something, Hal!' Her eyes are alight with excitement; they almost glow.

'Can you see in the dark?' I ask.

'What?'

'Your eyes, when you're excited they gleam in the dark just like a cat's.'

'Yeah, right!' She brushes me aside; I just love that she does that. Every other girl I know, including Charley – ESPECIALLY Charley – would say, 'D'you think so?' and then want to know a hundred reasons why, but Jack just runs right on.

'Listen, I heard Pete on the phone to Am, they're getting together sometime today, only I don't know where. Do you think he means it about Am leaving here?'

'I don't know!' I say. She looks so worried and pale, as though she's trying so hard to be the old Jack, fun and feisty, but it's only a skin she's wearing, an old skin she's put on, that doesn't really fit any more.

'He hasn't packed any stuff, or anything,' she says, and she clings to me.

'What if he goes, Hal? What if they DID do something?'

And I feel great – shit, isn't it? – but I feel just fandaby-dozy, because at last it's me she's hanging on to, not Pete; at last it's me who might have the answers.

I smile, I can't help it.

'Let's see if they're on the beach!'

He's there. The waves aren't great, but he's making the best of it. We watch, and I can't help but see a shadow beside him on the waves, a skinny black shadow, with red hair in wet rats' tails, and eyes that are always the colour of the sea. Her face always had grains of sand clinging to it, clinging to her cheekbones and nose. The wind is warm and strong; it breaks the waves up, making them choppy and tight, and difficult to do anything with.

I feel the breeze sweep across my face as my eyes begin to close, and I can hear Charley's breath again, as endless as the sea, but without any life in it.

In. Out. In. Out.

'Who's there?' she calls out, in fear.

The sound of her voice seems to merge with the sounds of her breath, and the sea, and the thump of her frightened heart – all rising and falling together. The blood in my ears begins to thump, before falling away from my head – the sound of her heart beats inside me, until the sea and the sand, and even the girl beside me, all disappear.

'Who's there?' I hear it again, and then I'm slipping and sliding, slipping into the deep dark chasm where Charley lies, as still and lifeless as the ghost doll in the deserted

house. She's calling me. She's calling out of the darkness to me, with every pumping beat of her fearful heart.

'Hal?'

I try to call back.

'Charley!' But my voice doesn't make a sound, is swallowed up by the deep blackness, and vanishes without a trace.

I feel the fear in her blood bump and prickle, as it moves around her body; and then, out of her fear and sadness, a picture begins to form. A picture of our house in the woods, only it's dark, as dark as a moonless night. I take a step towards it. I see the black empty window of the cottage, I reach out and try to move closer, but there is no light, anywhere, no light anywhere at all.

'Pete!' The sound of his name echoes inside me, knocks against my bones.

I can't see my hands before my face. The icy fist in my gut is back, clenched tight and ready to strike. I take a step forward into the unknown, and that's when I hear her scream.

'No! Pete!'

And it's as though my whole body's made of glass, and her voice has just hit perfect pitch. I feel like I've been blown across the beach, into a thousand pieces.

'No!'

Her voice rings and shivers inside me, and then suddenly it's like the world's in rapid rewind, and all the pieces fly back together as the thoughts fade away . . . and I'm back on the beach, watching Pete on the waves, as though nothing at all has happened.

Except for the fact that Jack's looking at me a bit weirdly.

'Well, do you?' she's asking.

'Do I what?'

'Want to learn to surf?'

'No,' I say, trying to pick up all the pieces inside me, and make sense of them.

'Because of Charley?'

'Uh?'

She looks at me and snaps her fingers.

'Wake up, duh-brain. You're the one who just said her name – when you were looking at Pete on the waves.'

'Yeah, so?'

'And I asked if the thought of her made you want to surf?'

'Right, and I said no.'

'No you didn't, Hal.' She's staring right at me, as though she wishes she could see through my skin and bones, right to my marrow. 'You didn't say that, Hal,' she says.

'Didn't I?' and I can feel myself shaking, and I know she can see it too.

'No,' she says slowly, 'you know you didn't, so why are you pretending?'

'I don't know, Jack.'

She shakes her head, as if to clear it.

'You shouted, "No! Pete!" You yelled it, just as Pete went

for that wave, but you weren't looking at Pete, were you?'

'Are we playing fifty questions?' I try to make her laugh. 'C'mon, Jack.'

But she stares at me. She looks worried, like she's wondering if she can trust me after all, and I know just how she feels. I don't want to talk to her about what I see any more, about Charley; she's still Pete's sister, and I know whose side I'm on, so why shouldn't she feel the same?

I look away. Out on the waves there's no Charley-shadow beside Pete. There are only the waves, and the sea, and the sky.

I shiver.

Someone's walking on my grave.

'It's happened again, hasn't it?' she says after a while, and I don't have to ask her what she means. I nod. I'm so scared that she'll think I'm crazy. No, I'M so scared that I AM crazy.

'I don't want to think about it, Jack.'

'Are you all right?' she asks after a while. But she doesn't come near me, and I know she's scared too, only this time maybe she's angry with me as well, scared and angry. Because we just can't get round Pete and Charley, and I think he's a first-class knob-head who messed with my sister, and she still thinks he's perfection.

'Look!' I begin. 'It's just that I miss her, all right? That's what Mum says it is. And when I saw Pete on the waves just then, I imagined she was with him, where she should be. That's all.'

'Yeah, right! Whatever!' She turns away.

'Jackie, don't do that!'

'What?' She's still not looking at me. 'What am I doing?'

'Pretending I'm not here, and that you're not interested,' I tell her.

'Well don't give me all this "it's normal" crap, then!'

'I'm not!'

'And stop blaming Pete for everything, he's—'

'He's what? In love with my sister? By her bedside every day? Not responsible for hitting her so hard she doesn't work any more?' I'm choking on the words, can't believe that they're finally out there, in the air between us. But Jack's shaking her head, holding back the tears, and her fists, too, maybe, by the look on her face.

'I don't care,' she yells. 'I don't give a fuck what people say, he didn't hurt Am, he was set up, that's what I reckon—'

'Oh, right, Jack, yeah, and who by, eh? Al Capone in Cornwall last year, was he? Taking his hols, maybe? Perhaps he threw Charley in the sea, and then came back later and took the concrete off her feet! Like fuck!' People are beginning to stare at us, but we don't notice.

'He wouldn't! He wouldn't . . . OK, he loses it sometimes, he's been in fights, but he wouldn't hit a girl, Hal, it's just not Pete!'

'And that makes it all right, does it – I mean, as long as it's not girls? Get real!'

'He didn't do it!' She's stony-faced now, her arms crossed over her body, and she's set straight, not budging. 'He didn't hit Am, and he didn't hurt Charley!'

'Who did, then? Or are we back with me as prime suspect?'

'No! NEITHER of you could do it!'

'So who, then?'

'I don't know, Hal, but I've been thinking, I've been thinking all year, and I've got an idea . . . I just . . . oh, I dunno . . . it's a bit . . .'

'What?'

'Well, you know Am's dad?'

'Not that again!' What the hell is she on?

'Well, he's a freak-out, you know, stay away from him if you're a girl on the beach, rumours about what his hand's doing in his pocket, about how he treats Am – dragging her off the beach, smacking her around for nothing . . .'

'What has this got to do with anything, Jack?'

'Well, what if it was him who hurt her?'

I begin to laugh. 'Oh, right, so it's not anyone who actually KNOWS Charley, or spends any time with her – like Pete, say? Not anyone she might actually want to be alone with in the dark, oh no, it's just some poor local who happens to have a bit of a rep as a weirdo! Good one, Jack! Always go with your prejudices, that's what I say!'

And she's had it. I dodge her palm as it flies past my face.

'Like brother, like sister!' I say as I grab her arm, and she just falls apart.

'I'm not!' she cries, trying a left hook with her free arm, but I'm ready for her.

'Are!' I hold her wrists.

'Aren't!' She shakes free.

'Are!'

'Oh no I'm not!'

'Oh yes you are!'

We start to laugh – or are we crying?

'Oh yes it is!'

'Oh no it isn't!'

'That's the way to do it!'

'Oh, Hal!' she says.

'Oh, Jack!'

And we fall to the sand and lie in each other's arms. After a while we start to kiss, and there's nothing, I mean nothing, that I love more in the whole wide world than kissing Jack – except, perhaps, knowing what the hell is happening with my sister. And that's the problem.

We watch Am, who's miles down the beach, talking to an Aussie-looking lifeguard type. Suddenly I can see her and Pete together. It's bizarre, like there's something about people that gorgeous, like they belong together or something.

'I bet she looked good with Pete.'

'Not to me,' she says, thinking. 'You know, he was always kind of hanging off her arm, a bit like being the tail end of a comet. I dunno,' she almost whispers, 'it was like he was her thing . . .'

'Yeah, but you know what I mean . . . you just look at them and they're kind of so . . . so . . . equally gorgeous.'

'Yeah, but it went wrong with them, really it did, Hal!' and she looks at me as though she's really thought it through and got it right. 'I mean, when you look at it from the other side, all the pieces do fall together, if it was her dad . . . I mean, people joke, don't they, but really it's about all the stuff we never say, isn't it?'

I don't know what she means. I don't want to know what she means. What stuff we never say?

'OK, OK. All I meant was, I just – I can sort of see them together. I can see how they fit just to look at, I mean. I can see why she might want to be with him.'

She stares at me.

'Arm candy!' she mutters, and we start to laugh again.

We watch Am all day. She smokes non-stop, one after the other, her fingers fluttering, striking matches one after the other, staring at the waves, and at Pete.

Why aren't they ever together in public? What are they hiding?

After Pete's gone she stops staring at the waves and lies back in the sand, as still as a lizard in the sun, staring at the sky instead, and apart from the smoke rising from her fingers, she could be dead. The odd guy tries his luck, and when she can be bothered to reply, to sit up, her whole body twitches, moves, taps against the sand as though she's always running.

'Am, Am, Am,' mutters Jack. 'She never DOES anything!'

she groans, piling up another mound of sand and beginning to shape it. She's already made a long line of turtles climbing in and out of sand holes.

'How do you do that?' I ask. 'How do you know what shapes to make?'

She shrugs. 'I just do it.' I could watch her for ages; it's amazing the way she digs and builds and piles, and then just smoothes away at the surface, making curves and hollows until a shape emerges, as though it's always been there hiding in the sand, just waiting for the right pair of hands to discover it. She makes a figure, a figure of a girl curled up in the sand. She's naked, lying on her side and her hair stretches away in waves and rivulets, merging with the beach.

'Wow!' I say, sitting up. 'I didn't know you could do that!' She smiles and pats the sand, firming it, adds another rivulet to the hair, sharpens the profile.

'I've always done it, ever since I was a kid, just didn't stop.'

'Mmmm.' Her hands are so sure of what they're going to do next, I lie down again and begin to imagine them making shapes with me.

'The trick is to dig down deep to the damp sand. Can't work with trickly sand,' she mutters, still shaping and smoothing.

'Finished?' I ask, and she looks up. She has sand across her cheekbones and forehead, and I delete the image that comes to mind; the image of Charley's face dotted with sand and freckles. Jackie nods.

'Cool. It's great,' I say, and it is. There's something lonely and sad about it, a small girl lost in all this sand.

'Think so?' she asks.

'Yeah. Can you make shapes out of just anything?'

'Whaddya mean?'

'Well I could do with a bit of definition here,' I suggest, pointing at my chest. She laughs and piles sand on my body, and her hands feel gritty and damp as she smoothes them against my skin. Her back's so sun-warm and smooth and it is such a pain having to glance over her shoulder all the time just to make sure Am hasn't left the beach.

'Just keep still!' she laughs to herself, and when I look down at my chest I laugh too.

'From "Hey, Arnold!" to "Hey! It's Daniel Craig!"' She smiles, so do I, and I flex my arms. My whole new sand chest is as muscled and tight as a boxer's.

'I wish!'

'I don't. It's gross!' She flicks it all off, and I'm back.

'Much better,' she says.

The sun is stretching itself out into long afternoon shadows by the time Am finally gets up and makes a move. Jack's added a dolphin and a boy to her collection. The sand turtles are being swallowed up by the sea. People stop to watch her, kids try and copy her. I wish Sarz was with us.

'Will you show Sarz how you do that?'

'Some other time, sure,' she says, and I hold that to me. Some other time, I think, and I wonder when, if ever, that time will be.

We get up and trail after Am, along the beach. Just as we stand up, a huge dog runs on to the sand. Everyone looks up, mums grab their children. Dogs aren't allowed on the beach in summer, and this one's huge; huge and black, and loose. Its owner appears over the cliffs yelling at it: 'Pippy! Pippy!'

Me and Jack laugh, because it's a crazy name for such a monster-dog. But we soon stop, 'cos the dog's heading straight towards us. The owner's still yelling her head off, but the dog pays no attention. Its lead's flapping in the breeze and it's as free as air.

We stand completely still, and the dog races right past us, straight towards Am. It's as if it's got a fix on her or something, and the whole beach just freezes, staring, like the whole thing's happening in slow, inevitable motion. Am stands completely still too, and stares at the dog as it heads straight for her, and then, just as it leaps right at her, she growls at it! It's unbelievable, she doesn't move, doesn't blink, just flicks her arms up, dodges, and growls at it, and the dog turns in the air mid-leap, and goes right past her shoulder.

My heart's thundering, and the owner is apologizing, gasping; but Am's voice, when it comes, is as cool as ice.

'Animals should be kept under control,' she says, and it makes me go cold, the sound of her stiff, held-in, angry voice, as though she knew all about control, and animals.

She sees us and smiles, not a nice smile.

'See you at the barby!' she says.

We get off the beach, and sit under the oak trees.

'Shit! Did you see that?' I whisper, but Jack just looks troubled.

'She wasn't scared!' she says. 'She wasn't scared, Hal!'

'I know!' I say.

'Perhaps there's something else she's scareder of?' she says, and I manage not to say what's on my mind:

Yeah, and perhaps that someone is Pete?

After a while we run out of talk, and then there's absolutely nothing else to do but kiss, and touch, and lie in the dappled light under the oaks, with the breeze and our hands running over each other, smoothing us both down.

And just for a while, there's no one else but us.

Charley: Hospital. Now.

'Who's there?'

Someone's there.

'Pete?'

There's no answer, only the black blanket of darkness.

A shadow shifts.

'Who's there?'

I know someone's there, right there on the very edge of my vision; only if I turn, whoever it is might disappear; if I turn, I might see . . .

'Pete, please! It's not funny . . .'

And at last he's there, in my mind's eye. I can't see him, but I can feel him, holding me, and I can feel the total wonder of it, the part of me that was always waiting, waiting for him to say, 'Yes, Yes! Let's be together.' My whole body's humming, swaying to the music on the beach . . . I couldn't see the darkness watching and waiting, rising behind me . . . I was blinded by my eyes . . . could only see . . . Pete . . .

Charley. Then.

My back feels so warm, leaning against his chest. His arms are hugging me and rocking me to the music as we chat.

'Oh please, don't you rock my boat!'

We laugh as I whisper my lyrics in his ear: 'Oh please, will you rock my bo-o-at?' I'm happy. And Pete seems to catch the happiness, like it's flowing right into his hands, and he feeds it right back to me, fixing my hair, holding my hands and touching just about any part of me that he can get away with, given that we're sitting in the middle of a huge group of people, chatting. He gives me secret looks and squeezes. I smile back, a little fizz of fear and excitement inside. We're here, in the same place at last, wanting the same thing: each other. It feels so good I smile at him, and he smiles right back.

I'm happy.

We're happy.

Together.

I look over at Am, waiting for the old stab of pain to kick in, but for once it's like she has no power over me. He's going to be mine, I think, all mine, and then it's as though she suddenly hears me thinking, and her head turns to look at me. She stares at me, and I hold my eyes up, even though it's hard, even though my eyes are begging to be lowered and put away. I make them hold on. She smiles, a sudden, surprising smile, as though she can see what's in my mind. As though she could take it all away from me and make it her own, any time she likes.

I lower my eyes.

I shiver.

Someone's walking over my grave.

When I look back she's not looking at me any more, she's looking at Pete. I hold his hands hard, so hard that he whispers in my ear, 'Hey! Lighten up!'

'Later!' I whisper.

At ten I stand up and yawn.

'Knackered!' I say. ''night, everyone.'

'Early bed for growing girls!' says Am, with a strange smile, and I have to cross out the sudden feeling that she knows exactly what's happening.

'Stuck record, Am,' manages Pete.

'Surprised Mummy's let you out to play this late!' She gives me a sharp look, and my heart sinks. Does she know that Mummy doesn't? And if she does, what's she going to do about it?

'Whatever!' I barely bother to look at her. 'See you tomorrow, guys.'

'Sleep well.' And from Bella, 'See you tomorrow.'

Tomorrow, I think, it'll all be different by tomorrow, and

I hold that thought to myself, scared, excited.

'Yeah, like you need your beauty sleep,' slurs Em.

Pete kisses me and whispers in my ear.

'See you later.'

I hug him.

'Can't wait,' I whisper.

And I can't.

Hal/Charley. Then.

'Hey, Hal!'

'Uh!'

'Are you asleep?'

'Yeah!'

We giggle. I'm so happy, wired, and he can sense it.

'What's up?' he asks.

'Nothing!'

He turns away, angry that I can't share any more. What am I meant to say? 'Hey, Hal, tonight I'm gonna sneak out and spend the night with a guy!'?

I'm scared. I'm excited. My body's humming so hard I think he might hear it! I listen to his breathing in the night, angry at first, but slowly it grows soft and steady, and asleep.

'Shit!' I've been asleep too, and now I'm wide awake, and my heart's beating like a hammer. I've been dreaming.

'It's all right, I'm awake now,' I whisper to myself, and I am, even though the house is still swaying with sleep. I look at the clock. 12.16. Hal's breathing is slow and sure over by the door. It calms me as I listen to it, mingling with the sound of the waves and the creak of the floorboards. Slowly my own breathing matches his, and I can sit up and look out of the window, where I can see Pete's shadow on the slipway, under the orange street light, waiting.

I get up, and as I walk past Hal I drop a kiss on him. I don't know why, all I know is that he looks just like an angel, a sleeping angel, all innocent and happy. His arms are flung out wide and open, with his palms resting upwards by his cheeks: he looks like an angel drying his wings.

'Bye,' I say. 'I'll be back,' and I wish I hadn't hated him so much, just for wanting me around; but it makes me feel so bad sometimes seeing his fed-up face.

I creep past Mum and Dad's room. They shift, someone murmurs. I creep on, down the stairs, over the third step that always creaks, and through the kitchen. I pick up my wet suit off the back of the door, so I can say I went for an early surf. Who knows, perhaps we will — surf, I mean, up with the dawn, tomorrow, just the two of us. Changed.

Different.

The night feels as deep and warm as dream-darkness. The poplar tree's inky black leaves rustle and sway in the warm salty breeze, its leaves singing like a spring river.

My legs feel as heavy as lead.

My heart feels as light as air.

'Hi!' he says.

'Hi!' We hug each other, and smile hidden smiles in the darkness.

'All right?' he asks.

'Cool!' I say, and we set off together, alone, into the night.

Hal. Now.

The early evening is sleepy and golden; the wind's dropped and everyone's heading for the rocks. It's gonna be a warm, warm night, and the excitement of it hangs in the wind, drifts on the smoke. Warm night means music and bodies, bodies dipped in sand and each other; but all I can see is the dark, all I can feel is the way my head turns sometimes, turns towards the photo of Charley, only now it turns to this feeling in my gut, a feeling of darkness and danger . . . and I remember our last words to each other, that night when she never came back.

'What's up?' I asked her.

'Nothing,' she told me, but I didn't believe her then, and I don't believe her now. What happened?

Why didn't she come back to us?

I can see Pete coming down the hill. He hasn't got his board with him, and that looks weird, very weird, a bit like suddenly seeing someone without any hair on. Pete's ALWAYS got his board with him, just in case. He heads straight for the barby rocks, where someone's already got the coals going, and the smell floats across the sand.

'Hey, Pete!' everyone calls out, pleased to see him around. He's been out of the loop all summer, disappearing off the beach with the waves, as though dealing with people is way more than he can manage.

Em goes up and gives him a big hug, someone hits him on the shoulder. I can't hear them from here, but I can feel them all gathering around him, protecting him, pleased he's back.

Why do they all like him so much?

I shiver.

Someone's walking over my grave.

I feel Jack's hands over my eyes.

'Hi, one brother, delivered as requested.' She looks great. Her hair's pushed back behind a bandana that makes her eyes look even greener than ever, and there's a gorgeous gap between her T-shirt and jeans. Hard as I try, I can't be angry with her; I just want to wrap myself around her and hold on.

'Hi!' I say, and we look over at the guys.

'How is he?' I ask, still watching.

'Jumpy as a cat flea,' she says. 'Did you see he didn't bring his board?'

'Yeah.'

She sits down next to me, and we look across the sand to where they're all standing and chatting. It feels so good to just sit back and watch for a bit, and that's how come we both see Am first. From where we are, we can see the path to the beach, but the others are right up under the rocks. When she comes into view, it's like a ripple goes through the whole group, and they turn, like a swarm of fish in harmony, and look at her, as she walks across the beach, and then they all turn back to Pete.

The excitement on the smoke drifts higher.

'Let's go!' says Jack, and she's up and across the beach in seconds, standing right next to Pete.

'Beer, Pete?' Mark holds out a bottle.

'Yeah, thanks,' and he reaches out and takes it, and the chat begins to cover up the looks that are spreading around. He's got his tight little group of friends with him, Em, Bella and Mark, and they're wrapping the chat around him, talking about some surf stuff, but Pete, he's not there. I can tell. He's like Charley was nearly all last summer, like I am these days, when I'm home. His mind's somewhere else, and he's just going through the motions. His eyes keep slipping across the beach, to that lonely figure, smoking on the rocks.

I look up, and my stomach drops when I realize where she is. Am's right near where I found Charley on the rocks, as close as you can get to the very spot, given that the tide's coming in. I realize, suddenly, that everyone here – everyone that knew Charley – stays away from that bit of the beach. Only day trippers and families, and people who don't know, only they ever go over to the far right-hand side of the beach, where the rocks hide just under the waves, where I found her.

'All right?' whispers Jack, squeezing my hand.

'Yeah.'

Everyone's whispering:

'What's SHE doing here?'

'Probably hopes her luck's in, now he's available.'

'No chance.'

'Well wouldn't you, if you had a chance?'

'S'pose.'

'God, poor Pete.'

'Nice to see him.'

They grow quieter when they see me near them. They can't help it, it's as if I'm endlessly connected to something I can't even see, or understand, but know the names of: Am, Pete, Charley. It's like they're the tips of a triangle, and the feeling comes again: the feeling that they all know something, the whole gang of them, something that connects the three lines to make a whole triangle. Only they fall silent when I'm near, and it makes me feel sad, sad and alone.

'I'm going to tell her to fuck right off!' That's Em, she makes me smile.

'Don't!' Bella grabs her arm. 'Wouldn't she just love the attention?'

'Yeah, but she was such a bitch to Charley.' She turns and sees me.

'Hi!' She gives me a sickly smile.

'Hi!' I say back, and vaguely wave my can at her.

'Burger?' she asks, and I shake my head. I'm looking at Pete, and pretty soon everybody else is too, because he's heading across the beach. In full view of everybody, he's walking across the sand, deep and golden in the last of the evening light.

And he's heading straight for Am.

Everybody falls quiet, waiting and watching to see what'll happen next. Even the people on the beach seem to sense that the conversation's stopped, and they look over, and then follow our eyes back to Pete, before carrying on.

'Go Pete!' says Em, ''bout time somebody told her where she's not wanted!'

'Shit!' says someone else. 'Why did she have to be here?'

'Thought she'd finally given up on us,' says Bella, staring after Pete.

'Yeah!' says Mark. 'Too big and cool to play with us kids.'

'Doesn't take after her daddy, then,' says Si.

'Stop it!' snaps Bella, and my gut just turns right over. I think of Jack's words: what does Daddy do when his hands aren't in his pockets? I feel sick. I'm grateful to Bella for shutting them up; it isn't funny.

I look around for Jack, but can't see her anywhere, and then I hear her voice.

'Why can't you all just leave him alone?' she asks quietly, sadly. 'If he wants to talk to Am, it's his business, right?'

What? I'm thinking. C'mon, Jack, he's just shown us his colours, he's just told the whole world where his feelings lie. What about Charley?

'And he's had a tough enough time, so just get off his case for a bit, you lot.'

'Yeah, but Am!' moans Em. 'Christ, after what she drove him to. I thought he was picking up some taste when he was with Charley—' She turns and looks at me, and gives me that sickly smile again.

'It's all right, you can say her name, you know,' I tell her.

'Hey, Em!' says Si. 'Maybe Pete didn't drive Am to any-thing; maybe he just can't keep his hands or his temper to himself.'

Bravo Simon!

'No way,' yells Em, looking straight at me, as though it was me talking. 'NO WAY Pete ever touched Am – well,' she says a bit drunkenly, doubtfully, 'I mean in "that" way, like beat her up. It was a set-up; didn't you hear what it's about? She's a . . . total tart . . . it was a set-up and Pete's just too—'

'Jeez, Em, find yourself a movie to be in!'

'Hey!' she yells after me. 'I liked Charley!' and I nod. Why, I wonder, why do so many people feel they need to tell me this?

Jack's heading across the beach, and I catch her up.

Pete and Am.

They're sitting on the rocks. In front of them the sun is a beautiful, perfect circle of deep red fire, but they're not even looking at it, they're too busy looking at each other.

We can hear the hum of their voices, in between moments of silence. His sounds worried, low and angry, hers is clear and definite, but we can't hear what they're saying. It's maddening; the wind blows only the odd word to our ears.

'Look, Am, you have to go . . . if you're not here then nothing can . . .'

'Not without cleaning it up . . .'

'Am, it's not the place that needs . . .' and then there's an agonizing growl from Pete, and the sound of her laughing, and then she asks something, and he leans towards her, closer and closer until his arms are around her shoulders, and their faces are almost touching, and Jackie's holding on to my arm, gripping it so hard that I think it might actually snap off if she doesn't stop soon. From here they look just like a couple, any normal couple, pulling on the beach.

'Bitch!' from Jack.

'Bastard!' from me.

'What's going on? There's no way he'd . . . just no way . . .' mutters Jack. But it's there, right in front of us, Am and Pete, chatting and pulling, and looking great – together again.

'What about Charley?' I want to scream at him, and the answer is immediate, a physical pain at the sight of them together, as though a burning blade is slicing through the seams, just where my heart joins itself to veins and arteries and begins to live. I gasp, and this time the falling isn't in my head, it's in my heart, as though it's falling out of my body, right through my feet; and I'm no longer rooted to the earth, because my heart's too busy falling through the earth's crust and hurtling towards its centre. And then my feet give way and my face is in the sand, my head skimming backwards to Charley.

'Charley!'

Charley: Hospital. Now.

'Hal!'

The pain's like having my heart cut out. There's a terrible lurching moment, just before you've realized it's happened, and then there's the searing, severing, slicing agony of burning pain, that wells up before the emptiness begins.

Pete and Am . . . I knew it . . . I knew it . . . I see the wristband on my wrist . . . Always, it says, Forever . . . only the words weren't meant for me . . . they were for her . . . she gave him the band! He only passed it on . . . to me . . .

Hal. Now.

'Charley!'

It's her pain I'm feeling, and it's beyond the power of my own breath.

I can see her body, so dead to me, and yet so full of this burning pain.

'Why, Charley?'

In answer I see Pete and Am in front of me, together on the beach, arms wrapped around each other.

But how can Charley see that?

Where is she?

'Here, Hal, I'm here!'

I hear her voice inside me, and then I get it. She can't see Am and Pete, not now. It's a memory she's seeing, a memory that's filling us both with this terror.

'Stilettoed.'

'Where are you?' I call to her, but I can only feel her stunned breathing, not regular now, but ragged and scared.

'Pete!' She calls out his name in an agony of terror, but there is no reply; the sound of his name spins and whirls and falls into the empty blackness.

'Charley! Charley!' I whisper her name aloud to myself in the darkness. I stretch out a hand, and as I do, I feel her coming closer . . . closer . . . and with her is the darkness . . . the fear . . . I hold myself still, try not to turn away . . .

'Hal!' She calls my name . . . and then . . . she is reaching out . . . reaching out . . . until the fear and cold are almost upon me . . . and . . .

. . . our hands touch . . . and her fingers feel as fragile as sugar-spun frost, as pale and insubstantial. Whispering over my skin they turn me pale and cold, asking for my warmth, but I hold still. I hold on, knowing that there is only one way to find the answers – this way.

We can't do it alone.

We can only do it together.

'Hal?' she whispers – asks – as her coldness begins to seep beneath my skin, like sea-water.

I'm so scared: what if I lose my mind?

But already I'm whispering her name like a 'yes', and already I can feel her sigh of relief, her sense of wonder as her mind comes alive inside me, and for a moment we're together and whole again. And then, somewhere out of all the fear and the blindness inside of us, a kind of sense begins to emerge, a sense of place . . . a memory. For a moment it's as if Charley's actually with me, inside my mind and body.

I see a sudden flash of light. Am and Pete are etched in blazing light against a wall; his hand is sinking into her hair.

Where are they?

'The house,' she sighs, *'that house!'*

And I hear her mind uncurl, begin to stretch away from me. She doesn't want to let go.

I can feel it in her, flowing through me, her longing for the warmth of my living body. I can see the picture it makes in her mind: a deep red flower, alive and unreachable.

And then, somewhere in the dim distance, I hear my own self sigh with the blessed relief of her releasing me, freeing my mind.

I can hear my own breath now, panting to catch up with itself, blowing in and out fast, the way that women do in films when they're having babies.

'The house.' I hold the words to myself as I feel her hands dissolve, the white hard frost melting as the warmth of my body returns.

'Hal!' I hear Jack calling. 'Did you pass out? Hal, are you OK? What's happening?' Her voice is frightened, urgent.

'Jack?'

When I come to, my head's in her lap and her hands are stroking my hair. But we were sitting behind a rock. How did I end up here?

'Hal, please!' She sounds so scared that I open my eyes, just to reassure her.

'They've gone, Hal!'

I sit up.

'I know where.'

'The house?' she says.

'How d'you know?'

''cos it's what you said: "Where are you?" And then you answered yourself, "the house." You were scared, Hal.'

Her eyes are wide, huge, and it's not just the fading light; we're both scared now.

'I can FEEL her, Jack,' I say, still shaking.

'Who?' she asks, but we both know who.

'Charley. I can feel her like she's inside me.' She nods.

'What happened?'

'I don't know, I think she was in the house, a deserted house we used to go to, and she was searching for something. I think . . . I think it was Pete. Or she'd seen something – Pete and Am, I think. She was scared, Jackie, so scared.' And I feel my own heart begin to beat fast again with the blood-fear, and my whole body begins to shake.

She nods again.

'Jack, are you all right?'

She nods, shaking, and we cling together. 'It's so scary, Hal, when you do that, you look, you look—'

'What?' I swallow.

'You look possessed, half dead, like . . . like you might never come back.'

I can't speak then. I can only hold on to her harder, because I know exactly what she means. She's describing

294

the way I feel when I look at Charley, like she's gone away forever, to a place we can't follow, a place she'll never come back from.

'And your breath goes, like you said, like it's not you, like it's mechanics, and I – I'm—'

'You're scared I won't wake up, ever,' I finish for her, and she nods.

'I know!' and I have to hug her, because she's so warm and alive and here, and so am I, and it makes me glad.

'Which way did they go?' I ask after a while.

'Off down the lane to the woods.'

'Shit!'

I don't want to go down there. The idea of the dark, down there amongst the trees, it scares me shitless right now.

A weird picture flashes through my mind, a picture of myself stretched out in bed, and Charley's voice floats through my head.

'Spread out like an angel drying his wings.'

Will she ever let me go? Will she always be inside me?

I wish so much that I was asleep in my bed, deep asleep, with the sound of Charley snoring, and beyond her, through the window, I could hear the endless rhythm of the rise and fall of the sea, sending me back to sleep every time I nearly wake.

But I'm not asleep. I stand up.

'C'mon, Jack,' and I hold out my hand. I pull her up.

'You're always saying that,' she says.

'Let's go home,' I say, 'early night. I'm knackered.' I wonder if she'll fall for it. I yawn, and it's not hard to be convincing; I am seriously knackered. Jackie walks along until we get to the street light, just by the camp site.

'You mean we're not going to follow them?' she asks.

'Gimme a break, Hal.'

'Do I look like I care what happens to Am?' I ask, and then I deliver the killer blow. 'Or Pete, for that matter? Especially if they were playing some pervy couple game with my sister. Look, Jack, seems to me they deserve each other, and me and Charley, well, we're just riddled with imagination, that's what Mum says. Seems like she's right.'

She stares at me, unconvinced.

'I've had it, Jack, honest. 'Night,' I say, and I wrap my arms around her, sink my head into her hair, and breathe her in, as though I could hold the smell of her inside me forever, keeping me safe.

'I love you,' I say, and as soon as the words are out I realize that they're true. I mean it. I love the way her hair's so straight. I love the way her eyes don't change colour, ever. I love the way she scratches her arm when she's thinking. I love the way she kisses. I love the fact that she can build things out of sand, and that she looks so brave, when really she's so scared.

She looks a bit like that now.

'Don't be scared!' I whisper, but she just stares at me, as though she's waiting for something I haven't said yet.

'Jack?'

'Mmm?'

'I said I love you.'

'Do you?' she says, and she gives me a quick strange hug. 'See you, then.' And she disappears quickly, swallowed up by the shadows at the edge of the field. I stand there for a bit, feeling sad that she's angry, wondering if she'll try to follow me, but I'm scared enough on my own, I'd be terrified for Jack. I can't think about her now, I'm scared enough just trying not to think about what I know I'm about to do.

I set off across the pub car park, and down the lane that leads over the bridge and into the woods. I'd like to whistle out loud, I'd like to pretend I'm brave, like Charley, but I can't. It would only give me away – and anyway, I know I'm not.

Charley: Hospital. Now.

'Hal . . .' I call him, my body calls him, we can still feel the wonder of me being in his mind, alive again . . . the warmth of the air upon his skin whispers to me with memory . . . and with it the other memories begin to stir, no longer as stiff and immoveable as my body. No longer invisible under the dark moonlit water, they are shivering, and the surface of the water begins to rise with them . . . we're waking up, Hal.

The memories follow him, as he leads us back to where they began, down the lane and into the darkening woods . . . to where the house is . . .

297

Charley. Then.

It's such an amazingly warm night; even the breeze that lifts and drops, bringing in clean air from the sea, is warm tonight. In the woods, the silence is only broken by the trees singing in the breeze, like glasses, each one filled with different amounts of water, each one singing its own tune. Their black shapes wave in the air above us, dancing against the stars. Animals rustle in the undergrowth, an owl calls out, and something screams across a distant field in the darkness. I jump, holding on to Pete.

'Like a jack flash,' he says, and stops me on the pathway, soothing my hair over my head, calming me. 'Do you want to go back?' he asks. 'Sit on the beach for a bit?'

I shake my head, but he's right: the wood feels closed-in, claustrophobic, like it's taking my breath away, like there's not enough air beneath the close canopy of the trees for me to breathe.

'I'll be all right when we get there.' My voice sounds so sure and confident, but my body can't stop twitching and turning, looking back and wondering why there always seems to be a rustle behind us. It's such a relief when we finally get to the house.

'C'mon.' Pete heaves me through the window. He lights a fire, and lifts the rucksack off his back. He begins to empty it, and we laugh in the shivering candlelight, because it's like the Tardis, he just keeps pulling things out of it, until we're surrounded by food: olives, wine, beer and crisps, and chocolate, and a huge blanket, and two fantastic roll mats that self-inflate, and Pete's grinning at me from ear to ear and nodding his head, like he's really, really pleased with himself, and the rucksack is finally empty.

'You didn't get all this in the haven!' I say, and he grins, so pleased I asked, just so's he can tell me.

'No way! I got Brooke from the Cabin caff to get it all, she said the wine goes right well with the olives.'

I smile; he sounds just like Brooke, yet another woman who'll do anything for Pete.

He picks up the wine, but then his face falls and he says, 'Oh no!'

'No corkscrew?' I ask, and I realize just how fully lovely he is, making me smile, easing the nervous fizz inside.

'Aha, screw-top.' He taps his head.

'Very clever!' I say. He laughs and cracks a beer. It sounds loud in the quietness, and I jump. He hands me a glass, a real glass, carefully packed in paper. I hold it in my hands, and wonder how I could ever, EVER, have doubted him.

The wine is a New Zealander, just like Brooke: Withers Hills. 'I'm impressed,' I say.

'Thank Brooke.' He laughs.

He taps his tin cup against my glass.

'Cheers.'

'To . . .?' I ask.

'To you. Nice to meet you, come here often?' and he takes a mega slurp from his tin.

'All the time,' I say. 'How'd you find me?'

'I haven't found you yet,' he whispers, and I shiver, and

he smiles a secret smile, all to himself.

I'm singing like the trees. We're here, we're here, we're finally here!

Alone.

Together!

Why can't my body stop shivering?

'Olive?' he asks.

'Please.' He picks it up and holds it to my lips.

'Thank you,' I say, and then he kisses me until the stone swaps mouths.

'That's disgusting!'

'Yeah, it is,' he says, 'but nice.'

Charley: Hospital. Now.
The memories are coming too fast, I can't make shape of them, can't control them.

Charley. Then.
Oh, God! It's like being on a slide, and once I'm over the top I can't stop. The feel of his hands slipping over my skin like waves, lifting me up and up and up, until I'm gasping for air – and somehow we fit, just like dancing. I reach for him and . . . I stop.

I can't believe it. The world's appeared again, right over his shoulder, and my head just gets right in the way, tells me it's impossible, this thing we're doing, it can't happen, it's terrifying. I see Am, dancing in the air above me, laughing.

'It's easy!' she says.

I pull away.

'Aarggh!' His groan is awful, as he curls up and away from me.

'Sorry, sorry, sorry, Pete!' I whisper.

'Charley?' he asks, and his eyes are huge and black, like he's swallowed the night sky. 'What is it?'

'I can't,' I whisper. 'I don't know what it is.'

He sits up, and puts his head in his hands, still and quiet, thinking for what feels like ages, before he finally makes words.

'Why?' he asks at last. 'Are you scared?'

'Yeah.'

'Of me?'

'A bit.'

'What've you heard?'

'Nothing!'

'About me and Am, I mean?'

'Nothing, I just imagine her, Pete. I imagine her, so much better than me, and it gets in the way. It's weird, like she's actually here, watching us . . .'

He looks up, sharp and quick, and then he laughs.

'Talk about a mood dampener! I dunno, Charley, maybe you do need to know . . . maybe you can sense it all, inside me, getting at me?' He says it almost to himself, and my heart turns right over at the way he says my name, and it beats, hard, because I know I'm right, there is something, and he's finally going to tell me what it is, that shimmering shining thing that lights up the air between them.

Am and Pete.

'I wouldn't hurt you, whatever you've heard.'

'What? What do you mean?' I ask slowly. This isn't coming out right.

He takes my arm and shakes it.

'Whatever anyone says, I couldn't, wouldn't hurt you Charley, I—'

'What do you mean?' I say again, but he doesn't answer, and the last bits of the wine seem to float right out of me, and the air is cold. I'm scared now, really scared; why is he talking about him? I thought this was about Am.

I realize how far away from home I am. It dawns on me that no one knows I'm here. When his hand reaches for my face I flinch; I can't help it.

Bad move.

'You have heard!' he says. I shake my head.

'It's not true, Charley, I didn't hit her, not once.'

'What do you mean?' It's all I can say, like my brain's stuck in some awful loop it can't escape from, can't take in new information – what it might mean.

I'm cold now, shivering with fear. I reach for my T-shirt, scared he might stop me, but he just goes on.

'It wasn't me who hurt her, Charley. It's her dad, he treats her like an animal. Oh, God, Charley . . .' And it all comes spilling out of him, like sawdust out of a scarecrow, and slowly the words begin to piece together, to make a horrible, dawning sense. How they had to hide all over the peninsula so her dad would never find out that they were together, and that's how Pete knows all these secret places.

'Urgh, you've been taking me to the places you've shared with her,' I can't help yelping.

'And he found out – her dad, I mean. I thought I could talk to him, you know – make him stop, do something – but it wasn't like that. She hadn't told me all of it, I just thought he was . . . violent . . . but it wasn't just that . . . oh, God, Charley . . . as soon as he thought she was old enough, he . . . and she HATES looking so gorgeous . . . really, it just . . .'

And he looks at me, his eyes full of horror and memory, and it's nothing like I thought at all. This thing between Am and Pete, it's not all Brad and Angelina at all, it's not perfect couples and beauty and pure longing at all . . . it's abuse and horror, and I feel sick. I can feel it rising in my throat.

'I don't want to know, Pete. No!' And he turns away from me, like he might chuck up himself, but he doesn't stop, can't stop, the words go on and on, how he thought he could make it right for her . . . I can hear the stream outside running over the rocks, and I wish I was lying in it – under the cold dark stars. I wish the sound of it was drowning out his voice as it washed me clean.

'I think people round here knew, Charley. Not just that he beat her, all of it . . . that he . . . he . . .'

'Abused her.' I whisper it, it's the only way we can say it.

'I think Simon's mum might know – anyway, someone finally reported him. He went mad when he found us,

Charley. God! It was the first time he hit her where anyone could see, I think that's what made them tell, and Am said it was me who hurt her . . . God, her face, I couldn't do that . . . but I felt like it was me in a way . . . if I hadn't met her . . . if I hadn't gone along with her . . .'

'What? Why . . . why didn't she get him put away?'

'She was scared. She said,' and he's almost crying now, 'she said he was her dad, the only one she had. It's weird, Charley, she really loves him, he's her dad; and so she said it was me who did it, she said it to protect him.'

'But that's so sick!' I shout. 'Why did you go along with it, Pete? My God! I didn't know,' I whisper to myself. 'I thought she was so amazing and fascinating and gorgeous and I was jealous of her!' But even as I'm talking I can see it all beginning to make sense, like pieces falling into place: all Am's wild don't-give-a-fuck-ness; not because she's full of Pete at all, but because she's so hurt already. All the horror and hurt and guilt and messed-up longing between them . . .

But not love, it wasn't love!

'Can you see, Charley?' he asks. 'I didn't want you to . . . to feel you had to . . . don't you get how much I want to be with you? What a relief it is to just be with someone normal? And I didn't, don't, want us to rush, it's not . . .'

I hold his hand, I hold his head. We rock together for a bit, taking deep breaths. We talk and talk and talk.

'I said I'd never tell,' he whispers. 'Every time you say you think Jack's following us I think it might be her . . .'

I shiver and look up.

'It's OK, she doesn't know this place,' he says.

'Unless she followed us,' I say.

'I said things to her, Charley, I said we could run away together, I said I wanted to save her . . . I said I'd never, ever tell anyone . . .'

Run away to where? Mexico?

'It's OK,' I tell him. 'I never heard a word.'

And I wish I hadn't.

Pete gets up and takes out a penknife, and I watch as he carves our names above the fireplace, and the date. He does it slowly, beautifully, so that we are wrapped around each other in letters; I run my fingers over it and we chat, drink, touch as he shapes our names in wood.

And then, we can't help it, we're kissing.

'If I could make things,' he says suddenly, 'like Jack can, in the sand, I'd make you.'

I notice I'm shivering in the cold. It must be nearly dawn.

'Still scared?' he asks. I nod.

'But not of you,' I say.

Someone's still walking over my grave, in slow, sure steps, I can feel them . . . coming closer . . . I hold on to him, tight. I'm shivering and holding on as though even time couldn't tear us apart.

He laughs, a small laugh, and it's as though he's heard me.

'We've got time,' he says. 'We can work it out with your parents, we can phone, we can wait. Hey!' He laughs. 'I can work on the farm until I've got enough for that posh hotel!'

I can't stop shivering.

'You're cold!' he says, and he holds me right back, rocking me in his arms.

'We don't.' I hear the words come out of me, cold and definite. 'We don't have time, Pete.'

Footsteps coming closer . . . I can hear them . . . feel them . . .

And we hold on to each other, we kiss until I begin to unwind, until I begin to feel safe and warm, until the wanting him begins to lick away at my bones, lighting fires inside me.

'What's it like?' I ask. 'Why is it so scary?'

'Like I should know!' he laughs, and it sounds so wonderful, his laugh.

'Tell me, though, Pete,' I whisper. 'Tell me what it's like.' That's what I say, but what I can't seem to say is that I'm cold and scared and that I need a story. That I can feel the night unfolding, loosening us from each other, and that I need to hear his voice . . . slow and steady, like a night-time story, a story that goes on and on, without ever ending . . .

'I think – I think it's like surfing,' he says. 'You know how crap it is for ages, you can't get the board straight and then you can only catch the surf in the shallows.'

'Yeah.'

'And you just keep on hoping, yeah?'

'Yeah.' I smile at him.

'And you keep on trying, and you can see it, in your

head – how it could be, catching that wave, "the one",
yeah?' he asks.

I nod.

'It's just . . . it's just like that, I reckon. Only it takes a long
time to get it.' He grins at me, spreading his lovely hands
and shrugging his shoulders. 'A good ride, I mean.' And he
smiles that smile, the one that comes out of the corner of
his mouth, all embarrassed and wishing it didn't exist, the
one that I love so much.

'And you have to wait for the right wave,' he goes on,
'and you fall off a lot. 'S what I reckon, anyway.' He shrugs,
as though he doesn't want to admit that he can actually talk
for that long, or think that much, and I wonder where all
the thoughts have suddenly come from, where they've
been hiding – or perhaps I was just never ready to hear
them before.

'So it's not that great, then, I mean, at first?' I ask. 'Not
like all soft focus and goose-down pillows?'

'No.' He shakes his head.

'And that's your story?' I ask.

'Yeah, that's what I reckon, only maybe . . .'

'Yeah?' I ask, and the sudden hope is so hard and painful,
like a knot in my heart.

'Maybe it's different when you've had a bit of practice
. . . and when . . . when you're in love,' he says.

Hal. Now.

I'm standing on the bridge over the stream, wishing Jackie

was with me. If I walk over the bridge and along the pathway, the last houses in the village will be on my left. By the time I get there they'll already have an orange glow behind the closed curtains. The sun drops early behind the cliffs, and the shade will lie deep on the valley floor.

Beyond the houses the road runs out of tarmac, turning to dust and pebbles. The valley seems to rise up and close the trees in. The road stops. There's a gate, a rusty five-barred gate that no one but me and Charley ever seemed to use. We never opened it, not once. We vaulted it, squeezed through it and clambered over it, but we never opened it. Beyond the gate there'll be deep shade under the trees, no street lights, just the wind in the leaves, and the lonely, growing darkness.

'Don't want to,' I hear myself mutter at the thought of it, and then I hear Charley's voice, as though she's calling to me from the past.

'*Come on, Hal,*' calls the memory of her voice. She sounds irritated, the way she always did – held up by me. She makes me want to hurry on. I take a step towards the road.

'*Hurry up,*' she says, and the sound of her voice disappears into the trees, as though she's running way ahead of me, caught up in her own thing, and I'm left behind again, alone. I so want to follow her. I don't want to feel alone and scared, I want to be with Charley. I take a step forwards . . .

'*No!*' Her voice is immediate, present, physical, heart-stopping.

'She's not here!' I whisper to myself. 'She's in a bed, in Oxford.'

Something rustles in the undergrowth, along the stream, and I wish that I was an otter or a fieldmouse, an owl or a stoat – anyone, or anything, other than me, Hal Ditton, trying to grow enough courage to go into the woods and face the darkness alone, without my big sister.

What are they doing there? I ask myself, because I'm sure that's where Am and Pete are, and I'm sure that if I can only go into the darkness I'll find out why.

I set off.

The dogs are still barking, long after I'm through the farmyard and on the path that stretches down the hillside. It makes me feel followed, but when I look back the lane's empty. Up here there's still some light, but the path goes down steeply, and soon the trees begin to block out the last of the sun. They sigh in the evening breeze, and the boughs crack and creak as though they're sad at giving up the day's heat and light, sad at having to settle into the cold and coming night.

I don't know where I'm going. The track becomes harder and harder to see as it slides deep into the valley. I stop and listen for the stream, but all I can hear is the wind in the trees, and invisible animals that rustle and sniff.

A fox breaks cover and dashes across the path, making my heart pump. Yellow eyes turn towards me, glow, and disappear.

'Shit!' I whisper.

I can hear the birds and bats shifting in the trees above me, taking flight and landing, flitting black shadows inside the rapidly darkening patch of sky above. One of them sings, each note sharp and sweet and sudden. The wood is alive with itself, but I don't belong here; I'm clambering down the path, disturbing everything. It's a long time before the silence settles behind me, as though my own shadow – or something else that follows behind me – is stretching itself out, confusing everything, long after I'm gone.

At first I'm not sure it's a light at all. It appears and disappears between the twists and turns of the covering trees on the path, but it always reappears; and even though it scares me, knowing that I'm right, and that there is someone in the house below, it also means that I'm on the right path, and that I know where I am.

I can hear the stream. The small flickering light disappears as I reach the path beside the stream, blocked out by the house.

I stop.

I'm here.

I don't know what to do.

What would Charley do?

She would hold my hand tight with excitement, and she would creep down the path, dragging me along in her wake.

I go the other way, climbing through the undergrowth and into the garden. This way – my way – I can get right up to the wall of the house under cover. I take a deep breath and remind myself that even in the dark there's a good chance that I can find half a dozen hiding places, that I know this ground better than anyone else in the whole wide world, except Charley.

Up against the warm brick of the house I hear voices, voices that carry in the night, out into the still air under the trees.

'OK, Am?' Pete's saying. 'We're here now, so what is it you need to do before you leave?'

Am's muttering to herself, almost like he's not there. 'What if she wakes up and remembers?' I hear her say. 'That's what'll happen, she'll remember, and then they'll come here, and they'll see! We've got to get the place clean, Pete, scrub it, scrub it.' Her words sound weird and disconnected.

'WHO'LL come here?' he says. 'Look, Am, why scrub the place clean? There's nothing here for anyone to see.'

'What's here for you, Pete?' she sneers at him. 'You tell me. What do you see?'

There's a silence. I hold my breath and my heart stops to listen: what will he say?

'You already know why I come here . . . I come here because it's the last place I . . .' He stops. 'It's not really any of your business, Am.' He sounds so tired, I think, tired and sad – but Am's voice livens right up, switches a gear.

'It's nice here, really, isn't it?' she says suddenly, as though she was in some posh house, not a dark deserted ruin in the middle of the woods. I get a sick feeling inside when I hear the sudden change in her voice; a feeling of madness and danger. Pete doesn't even bother to answer. I try to picture them. He must be standing somewhere near the window, because his voice sounds low but clear. She's further away, but her voice is much louder.

'Did you play house here? We could play house here too, Pete.' And I can't work out what's happening to her voice; it sounds teasing now, teasing and sharp and desperate, all at the same time.

It makes me feel sick and sad and weird inside.

'No, Am,' says Pete, and I wonder how his voice sounds so calm, but then I realize that it's not so much calm as kind of dead, as though nothing in the world could possibly ever interest it any more.

'Why not?' Her voice is quiet now, quiet and truthful; it throws me again.

'Oh, Am!' he replies.

'Why?' she wails at him. 'Why did you tell her? You promised me, Pete, you said you'd never tell. You said you'd always be there for me . . .'

'I said a lot of things, Am, and I meant them – but things change and I had to tell Charley, you know that!'

I hear her turn away from him, and her voice when it comes is cold and hard, spiteful.

'So you come back here,' she says, 'for the memories? Good memories, are they, Pete? Enjoy them, do you?'

He doesn't answer, but the air itself seems to gasp.

'We have to go now, Am,' he says. 'You said if we came back one last time you'd leave – well, we've done it . . .'

'You'll visit her if I go, won't you?' she says.

'What does it matter?' he asks. 'What if Charley does remember what happened? If you're not here, then—'

'This house remembers!' she says suddenly. 'Pete, we've got to clean it, clean it all up, before it tells.'

'No! Am, there are only four people who know what happened, and only two who can tell, and that's me and you, so—'

'Help me! Help me clean the house and then I'll go anywhere you want, I promise!' she says, but her voice is sly and secretive now.

'Am,' he says, and he sounds desperate to get through to her. 'You can spend all night spraying surfaces if you want to, but you can't wipe away what happened. Let's go.'

'What did happen?' she says suddenly. 'You tell me!'

And my heart begins to quicken. I'm going to know; I'm going to find out what really happened.

'Do you think I don't know what else happened, Pete? Did you think I couldn't see you both?' she asks.

'You're imagining things, Am.' Pete's voice blocks her right out.

'Am I?' she laughs. 'Am I imagining things? Like Charley?' she asks. 'Was she imagining it?' And she laughs again, and I go cold, she sounds so crazy, completely mad, but Pete's answer is quiet and sad.

'You know she wasn't, Am. You followed us, you

followed us, and if you hadn't—' And then his voice stops dead, as though he can't bear to think of what might have been. It's a while before it starts up again. 'You do know, don't you, that if you hadn't followed us she might still be here?' he asks her, and it's weird, as though he's talking to a child, the way I talk to Sarz when she's done something wrong but can't see it. But he isn't getting through, and Am just goes right on, as though he'd said nothing at all.

'You were the one who *left* me, Pete . . . you were the one who told her! And you promised, you *promised* me!' she says, and even I can tell that she's clinging to the memory of that promise so hard that she can't hear a single word he's saying.

'It's not the telling that's the problem, Am, it's what happened!' And I wonder how he can just go on trying to explain, when she's slipping and sliding and changing tack all the time.

'Do they wake you up at night, Pete,' she asks, 'the memories?'

'Don't!' he finally snaps. The word's a whip-crack, lashed out of him, followed by a heavy, sudden silence.

And I feel the air move, move as though it can sense the slow curve in time, stretching out as it describes an endless circle over the last year, that finally finds its edges meeting.

Charley: Hospital. Now.

Hal! He's there . . . where the memories wait . . . in the darkness . . . where Pete is. Pete! . . . oh, he's near him, near him, near him and my heart begins to sing ... my arms reach out to be where Hal is ... wishing I could have his eyes and arms and fingers, so that I could feel and touch ... and my fingers begin to stretch ...

'Oh Hal!' I curl around him like smoke, begging him to breathe me in ...

Hal. Now.
'Oh, Hal!'

She's here. Charley ... and she's muttering my name, reaching out for me, touching me with her thin, cold fingers, and brushing up against my brain with her memories and longing.

'Oh, Pete!' she whispers, and I can feel her longing for him rock within me, knocking me sideways.

'No, Charley!' I shout, but the pictures are already tumbling from her mind and into mine, even as I try to push her away, to hold on to the feel of the warm red bricks at my back ... but it's all slipping out of my grasp, images colliding. I see Pete in the oak grove last summer, on the waves, under the stars and in the warm sand ... I feel her longing begin to whisper in my bones ... to lick at me ... and I am lost in the curling fog that suddenly surrounds me, filling my lungs with cold dank air ... or is it water?

'Oh, Hal! Please ... oh, Pete ...' Charley whispers.

'Pete!' I cry out, only it's not my voice that comes out of me. With a shock as sudden and cold as sea-water I realize

it's Charley's voice coming out of me.

'Pete!' I hear myself cry out again with Charley's voice, and then he's there, at the window, his face shocked and white and suddenly small in the darkness.

'Hal?' he asks. 'You sounded so like . . .' He holds out his hand and helps me over the windowsill. Am's face is shocked and silent beside him. She stares at me as though she expected someone else too, and is checking me out just to make sure.

'*Oh, please, Hal!*' Charley whispers inside me. '*Let me in,*' she begs, and I feel my mind slipping from me, just stepping aside to make way for her, the way it always has, and my body begins to slip too, I'm falling . . .

'*Oh, Hal,*' she whispers, '*thank you,*' and her cold blood shivers within me as she slips beneath my skin, and the last thing I feel is the strange strength of Pete's arms, and his warmth, as he catches my weight, our weight, steadying us both before my limp body hits the floor.

Charley. Now.

I'm here, in Hal's body, and oh, I'm so close to Pete, as close as the breath of his voice on my cheek, and the feel of him next to me carries me back to last year, to where the memories lie hidden in the walls of the house. I stretch out within Hal, reach for his mind that isn't lost and alone and in darkness; for his body that isn't immovable . . . like mine in its hospital bed.

His warmth is delicious . . .

'Oh, Hal!'

Like floating in the Mediterranean . . .

'Thank you!' . . . and Hal's body falls away from him to me, is mine . . . and his mouth shapes itself to my words. I feel his chords vibrate to my tune, my voice, my words . . . and at last, I can speak . . .

'I'll tell you a story . . .' I say, and I hear the words with Hal's ears, but the voice is mine . . . my voice! And I remember that they're the same words I whispered to Pete, here, in this house, last year, when I thought we were alone together.

'Tell me a story, a story without ending,' I whispered to him, and I know now that I whispered it because my own end felt so close that night . . . even though I didn't know why . . .

And now I'm finally here, back with him, where our last, long night began . . . the memories come, unravelling at last, rising from the mute darkness . . .

I can feel Pete's arms around me, shaking with confusion at the sound of my voice in Hal's body, but he holds on . . . I am held, in Hal's body, within Pete's arms, held safe where the memories can finally be shared . . . can be remembered.

At last the pictures begin to form behind my eyes, jagged at first, and red and black behind my lids, fragments of a life . . . but then they steady and begin to flow, to stand out whole and clear, heading towards their ending . . . I was here in this house and I was . . .

I was smiling . . . that's what I was doing!

I have my voice . . . I'm ready to tell my story . . . but right now I'm lost in that last perfect moment . . .

Pete!

Charley. Then.

I'm smiling. Smiling and shaking with the strange shock and pleasure of it all. I am looking into Pete's eyes and they are liquid and light. They come closer and closer as he kisses me, and then they retreat, so that we can stare beyond the surface, deep into each other.

'Different?' I ask, and he smiles, gives me the whole of his lovely lovely smile, and I smile back.

'Some wave,' he whispers.

My eyelids flutter and fall. I'm so tired. Game over. I'm home.

That's what it felt like.

'Charley.' He whispers my name into my hair, into my ears, into my skin, over and over again until it sounds like the beat of my own heart, until I fall asleep in our warmth.

Absence.

Air.

Those are the first feelings.

I'm cold.

I'm alone.

And he's gone.

My heart breaks and jerks, as I remember that not all stories have a happy ending . . .

I reach out into the dark, but there's only the shadow of his warmth left beside me, and a swift-moving silence in the darkness, a tremor in the air.

Danger.

Charley. Now.

'Pete!' *I call his name, hold him close and real, and he gasps at the sound of my voice, holds me closer.*

'Charley?' *He looks into my eyes. I look into his.*

'Charley!' *he says after a long, long while, only this time it isn't a question, it's an answer. Even dressed in Hal's body, he knows me.*

I smile.

'What happened?' *he asks.* 'What do you remember?'

It's so hard to pull my eyes away from his, to turn them back towards the past. I stretch within Hal's body, gaze at Pete, touch his face, and I so want this one small moment we have to be like a frozen wave, no past, no future, only now — but it isn't. The past rolls on towards us, over us, asking to be told.

'Tell me,' *he says again, and I close my eyes, feel the tide of memories surge inside me, and the need to tell them. Feel the eyes of Pete and Am staring at me, and Hal's mind, so full of questions. Hal, who's fought so hard to get us all here, back to where it all began, still waiting for his answers.*

What happened that night?

I begin to speak.

Charley's story.

When I woke up, Pete, I knew you were gone. I was alone in the darkness, and then I heard you say her name . . .

'Am?' you said, and I felt my heart drop, fall straight through my body, fall right through my feet and sink deep into the earth.

I sat up in the dark. I sat very, very still and I waited.

There was no answer. No sound at all, except the sound of the wind in the trees.

I listened.

I listened the way I'd been listening all summer, practising for this moment, as though I'd known, somehow, all along, that it would surely come. All summer listening to the sound of twigs cracking and boughs shifting, listening to the sound of the world around me, and knowing that there was someone else out there, listening right back at me.

It was deep night. Do you remember, Pete? And the cloud covered the moon over so tight.

'Come back,' I whispered to you, but there was only a rustle by the window, a stifled sound. My heart was beating so hard I wanted to scream and run. I wanted to laugh.

'I want my mum!' I shouted out loud. I said it to break the silence, to make whoever was out there laugh, to make it all normal again; but the moment the words were out of my mouth I knew they were a mistake. They sounded so loud in the silent dark. They didn't sound funny at all, they sounded like truth.

The moon sailed out from beneath a cloud just as you reached me. I saw you hold out your hand for me, you were so much closer than I realized in the darkness . . . and behind you was a huge shadow, a shadow that stretched itself out across the wall from the empty window. The cloud shifted, but not before I'd seen Am's face at the window.

I yelled out her name.

'Am!' I said.

And the moon disappeared.

Dark.

I have to stop, to open my eyes and know I'm not really still trapped in the past. When I look at the room it's hard to believe it's the same place. The torches and candles glow in the dark, and light up her face. Am's face, as white and cold as the moon. She strikes a match and lights a cigarette. She picks up pieces of paper and shreds them with her nervy fingers. Her eyes are locked onto Hal's body, limp in Pete's arms. Her ears are listening to my voice, like I'm simply telling a story . . . any story, nothing to do with her at all, as though the sound of her name spoken in my voice means nothing at all . . . but we both know different, and I'm telling the story now, the truth. Am stares . . . waiting . . . watching, as she always has, like a cobra, waiting to strike . . .

I turn away from her. I turn to Pete . . . I go on . . .

Do you remember the darkness, Pete, do you remember the fear?

'Shh,' you said, and you lifted me up and away, back around the table, shifting and shuffling in the silent darkness. You wanted me to be quiet. I knew that straight away: it was in your hands and arms, even in your breath, and even though I was scared, I was so thrilled that we could talk in that new and silent way, with our bodies.

Pete's hand tightens in mine. He does remember . . . and so does she, Am . . . a red-hot flicker of anger rises and dies in me. She was there, always there, watching, waiting, following. We were never really alone . . . and then, in the flickering torchlight, I remember the rest of it, and the anger fades and dies.

We stood so still in the darkness, didn't we, Pete?

He nods.

We listened together, trying to feel the slightest movement in the air. I'd never noticed how dark the dark was, this deep in the wood, in the night. So dark that when I held my hand inches from my face I couldn't see it. I knew it was there, but I couldn't see a thing.

Silently, slowly, you eased me down. You wanted me under the table, hidden and safe. I wanted it too, but I was scared, scared by how scared you were. I wanted to find the torch and shine a light on everything. I was so sure that if I could only find some light to shine on us all, this crazy game would stop. We'd laugh and feel ashamed. Am would say, 'Made ya look!' and we'd say, 'God, you scared us,' and it would all be over.

Then I was alone under the table, Pete. You'd gone. There was a cold hole in the darkness where a moment ago there'd been warmth. I was alone in the dark and the silence. I listened. I listened with all my senses. I listened so hard that I found I was even listening with my skin. There was a movement, a movement by the wall. I didn't hear it so much as feel it – a disturbance in the air as it shifted. It wasn't big enough to be you, Pete. It was Am, she was by the door.

By the door.

I sent the words to you silently, willing you to hear.

I felt you step back.

Oh God, not quiet enough.

Thoughts chased each other through my mind.

What's she doing here? What does she want? Why are we so scared?

My skin was leaping with fear. I remembered the empty wine bottle on the edge of the table with the candle in it. I listened and slowly, in a darkness so deep that it felt like nothing could ever exist again, I managed to move. I found the table leg. I reached up, skimmed the table's edge until I felt the cold clean glass in my palm. Slowly, soundlessly, I lifted it into the air and out over the edge.

I sighed with relief.

Somewhere in the dark room, a body moved towards the sound I didn't even know I'd made. I remembered I didn't have any matches to light the candle, or even a lighter.

I remembered that I was naked.

Pete is holding me now like he could reach back in time and clothe me.

I touched the wristband you gave me, Pete, wrapped my palm around it and twisted it, feeling it biting against my skin, painful enough to stop me screaming.

I stop, I have to ask him a question. I open my eyes and look into his.

'Why did you give it to me, Pete?' *But he shakes his head. I know then that Am hasn't told him; he still doesn't know it was a mistake, giving me the band.*

Am shifts on the table, lights another fag, stares at us through the smoke.

'It was mine,' *she says.*

And we stare at each other across the room. Her hands begin to tremble. I close my eyes, make myself go on, to the next bit, to what I did . . .

A voice screamed a name. It came in through the window from the woods, like the wail of an animal.

That isn't Pete, I thought, *I know it isn't Pete,* and my heart stopped beating.

Something crashed through the trees.

Animal?

'Am! Am! Where the fuck are you?' It was a man's voice. The sudden torchlight in my face was blinding in the dark. I heard my scream deafen the silence. The light swung away from me, and I saw you both, trapped against the wall, blinded by the beam. Am wrapped around your body, Pete, and you holding her so close and tight. In that moment I saw everything so clearly. I saw your long fingers tangled deep in her hair, I saw the longing and fear on her face.

I thought you were together.

Still together.

And then . . .

'No!' Pete began yelling, holding Am back, behind him, shading his eyes from the light.

Where did the light come from? There was a huge shadow behind it.

'Here! Now!' said the shadow, like it was calling a dog, but it was you, Am, who moved. And your voice, Am, it sounded so small and scared and sorry . . .

'I'm coming, please, Daddy, don't, I'm coming . . .'

'You, out of the way!' The man spoke as though you were a piece of shit, Pete. He was wrong.

'No!' Pete yelled again, and he held you back, Am, even though he was shaking with fear, even though you tried to push past him, towards the man.

'You! Here! Now!' And you tried to pull away from Pete, pleading with your dad, but Pete held on to you, even though he was shaking as much as the shivering, drunken torchlight.

'You saved us, Charley,' *says Pete.*

Did I? And for what? I close my eyes again, turn back, slowly, reluctantly. I see it, tell it, remember what I did . . . the horror of it . . .

For a moment then, everything went still.

Stalemate.

And then Am's dad moved. He grabbed hold of you, Pete, and shook you. The torch fell to the floor, and there was the sound of something banging against the wall, crashing into it . . .

'I-told-you-to-stay-away-from-my-daughter!' he yelled, banging your head against the wall with each word.

Your hands were up, trying to fend him off, and Am whimpered pointless, barely audible words.

'No! Please, Daddy, no!'

Terrified.

And Pete, you were so helpless.

I felt the cold green glass in my hands, I remembered it. I stepped out from under the table, and I swung the bottle as hard as I could. I swung it at the dark shadow's head, and I heard the bottle crack and shatter in the air, and then my hands were empty, and I was swinging at nothing.

'Dad!' Am screamed.

'Am? Am?' he called, a blind searching cry, like the sound of blood in my ears.

I open my eyes. There's a silence in the room. 'Oh my God,' whispers Hal within me. 'Way to go, Charley!' and suddenly, even in the memory of the fear and the horror, there's room for a smile.

'What happened then?' he asks, the way he always has.

Me and Hal turn to look at Am, together, but she's still silent. Silent and shaking. She lights one fag from the stub of another. She strips newspaper between her fingers and shreds it as though she wishes it was the words I'm speaking that were being ripped to pieces, as though she wishes she could strangle the slow, sure sound of them, coming through Hal's lips, and out into the wait-

ing silence . . . but she's listening . . . hearing how we felt as scared of him as she did . . . so I go on.

Pete was holding me, muttering incoherent words.

'Oh whoa, oh fuck, oh shit, Charley!' We were clinging to each other in the dark, turning away from the circle of fallen torchlight, and the suddenly still shadow within it.

'Is he alive?' I whispered. 'Are you OK?'

'Yeah, shit, Charley!' and we clung to each other.

I don't know how long we stayed like that. We stayed until our hearts had stopped beating so hard that we thought they might burst against each other. We stayed until we'd stopped shaking and didn't have to hold each other up any more.

We stayed until we saw that your dad was climbing out of the window, swearing and stumbling – and when he'd gone I began to cry, I couldn't help it. I clung to Pete and cried like I never knew I could, and he held me and handed me my clothes, and helped me get into them whilst he whispered sweet, funny things to me.

'It's all right now, Charley,' he said. 'He's gone. You decked him, great left hook, way to go, wonder girl!'

I open my Hal eyes and turn to Pete.

I look up at him, at Am.

'You know how that feels, don't you Am?' *I ask her.* 'Pete making you feel better?' *and she sighs, a small sigh. A sound I don't think she knows has even escaped her.*

A sound of longing.

He holds me even tighter and I smile, he knows what I'm try-ing to do, to help Am . . . he knows silently, the way he always has . . .

I tremble. I feel my own longing rise. If I could just let myself sink into the warmth of Hal's lips and lift them up to him . . . I could feel the skin of Pete's cheek . . . and then Hal will be gone, and it will be just me and Pete . . . me and Pete . . . forever . . . always . . . no Hal . . . no Am . . . that's what I wish, that's the story I want to tell, but that's not the way my story goes . . .

And then we saw that you were gone, Am.

'Where's Am?' we asked together. We searched the whole cottage, creeping through the rooms with our shivering candle, whispering your name . . . but you were gone . . .

'Pete.' I was shuddering. 'I can't bear to think of her with that man, what if he's got her?' I could see it all, Am, him dragging you up the hillside, trailing you after him, your terrified whimpering in my ears.

'Pete, we've got to get help, now! I'll go and get my dad, you go and find them.'

He holds on to me, hard.

'No way, I'm not leaving you alone.'

'It's not me he wants to hurt, though, Pete, is it? It's you, you and Am. Don't let them see you, Pete, just find out where they are, wait for me and Dad, OK?'

I open my eyes. Am stares and shivers, but her fingers are finally still, her whole body as frozen as stone, trying not to be noticed.

'It was all I could think of, Am – my dad, my safe boring dad, and his crummy jokes. I wanted him there. I wanted to know he was as real as your dad. I wanted him to wrap his arms all the way around me and make it all better – the way he always has.' *Am stares, the only life in the glowing tip of her fag, undragged in her still fingers. So I continue.*

'OK, OK,' said Pete. 'I'll find them, but we stick together till you're home.'

We climbed through the window and stood in the black night, leaning against the wall of the cottage, shaking. I was shaking so hard that my arms and legs didn't even feel like mine. We stood there until the trees began to make sense again, deep black shapes waving their tendrils against the sky. And then we ran, we ran along the stony stream path holding hands, our free hands held out wide into the night for balance. We ran together, stumbling and expecting to be stopped, to run into something – or to fall.

When we finally made it into the village it didn't feel possible that the street light was still lit, or that the village, sleeping in its faint orange glow, was exactly as it'd always been.

It was like waking up and finding your whole life had been a dream, a good one, until now, until the nightmare.

I nearly killed someone. The words repeated themselves, over and over inside me, unreal, but true.

And then I saw the white surf glowing in the darkness. Like a promise . . . a promise of a place where there was nothing except the lift and fall of the waves, and the longing for the next one.

No past, no future. Just now.

And I thought of you, Hal, of you still sleeping, like an angel drying his wings, and of the impossible truth, that we had just lived through the same night, the same hours, under the same sky. I tried to think of anything other than the sound of a bottle crashing into bone. Anything other than the sight of your face, Am, as you hid behind Pete. And the clean white surf beckoned, like a promise of change and something new . . .

'I'll watch you to the door of your house,' said Pete.

I open my eyes.

'That's what you said, Pete, and if I could change time, if I could rewrite that moment, that's what I'd do. I'd walk up to the old oak door of our house, and push it open . . . but I didn't, did I?'

Pete shakes his head and holds me so close I can barely breathe.

'You wanted to be in the waves,' *he whispers with a smile in his voice.* 'It's what you've always wanted.'

The waves called me, promised to wash me clean of all the shit and horror, just a few minutes, that's all I wanted, that's all I thought it would take, a few minutes . . .

'Go on then, weirdo!' you laughed, Pete. 'And don't get into any fights without me, will you!'

And we kissed . . . a quick, brief kiss . . . the kind of kiss you give each other when you think there's another day, or week, or maybe even years . . .

I open my eyes. I'm here now, at the crossroads of the story, and soon, Pete will leave me, will walk away up the cliff. Looking for Am, like I asked him to, and I won't see him again, not with my own eyes, not till now.

'We didn't say goodbye,' *I whisper.*

'And I didn't say I love you,' *he tells me.*

'You didn't have to.'

I go on.

The waves gleamed in the night, fine white lines shining out, fighting against the dark with a promise of dawn. And I could hear them calling me, the way they always had, whispering my name. Slowly I walked towards them. The sea was warm against the coming-dawn chill, warm like a smile, warm like belonging. I walked beyond the surf, and lay down in the sea. It lifted me in its arms, lifted and dropped me, lifted and dropped me, without ever allowing me to fall. The way it always had.

Until now.

In. Out. In. Out.

With the rhythm of the waves.

Like the rhythm of you and me, Pete.

Being together.

I lay there for a long time. I lay there until I felt the tide turn, and the rhythm of the waves change as they turned towards land. They were huge and grey and weirdly out of rhythm, and just for a moment I felt afraid of them, of their ease and power.

Just then a light shone out from our house on the cliff, like a lighthouse, a beacon of safety. I looked up, and that's when I saw you.

You were standing under the street light, Am, staring at me.

And then the light went out.

I watched from the waves as you stepped out from beneath the shadow of the street light, and walked across the beach, alone.

And I thought, you're alone! You're OK! That's what I thought, Am.

You sat on the sand trying to light a cigarette, and I watched as you tried to strike the matches in little flares that caught and died and failed to ignite. I got out of the water and walked towards you. It was cold out of the water. You looked so small on the beach, so small and lonely, and I wanted to say how sorry I was that your life had been so shitty, but when I got to you, you just stared at me, so I took your cigarette, and lit it, handing it back to you.

'Am,' I asked. We were both shivering. 'Where's Pete?'

'Gone.'

'And your dad?' No answer.

'Am, we'll help,' I told you. 'My dad and mum'll help. You . . . you've got to get away from him, he's evil!'

But you just looked at me, didn't you, Am, the way you're looking at me now. A clear steady gaze, as you drag on your fag, like it could save you, like it isn't killing you with every breath, just like your dad.

'What?' *says Pete.* 'You were there, you saw each other?'

We don't answer, we stare at each other, as we did then, as we always have, wondering who'll be first to look away. And I remember what you said.

'What do you know about anything, Charley?'

'I know that your dad's a frightening bastard.'

'You don't know anything.'

'You need help.'

'What do you know? What do you know about me, or Pete, or my dad, or anything? How can anyone help? Does knowing stop you being with Pete? Does it stop me being here without him? Does it stop my dad being a crazy bastard over and over?'

I tried to put my arms around you.

'Oh, fuck off! If you tell they'll just take him away, or take me away, right? And then I'll have no dad as well as no mum!'

And you stood up and walked into the sea.

Good, I thought, good, it'll help you wash it all away too. But you were right, Am, I didn't know anything, because you didn't even try to swim, you just went on walking, right under the waves as though they weren't even there, until your head was just a speck, until suddenly I realized I couldn't see you any more.

I ran into the sea and reached for you, but the waves were heaving in the grey light, and then a wave hit me, picking me up and rolling me over, and I hit something hard. You. I grabbed you and held on tight, and when we came up I had hold of your arm. You looked dead in the half-light, but then you spluttered and coughed, and your eyes opened, and you saw me.

God, you were angry.

But I didn't know, Am! Couldn't even imagine wanting to die.

You were livid, and the waves were dragging us back into the sea as you struggled to get free. I couldn't tell if I was fighting you or the waves, it felt like the same thing, and then you were leaning over me, right over me, and a wave lifted us off our feet, and I felt my neck hit a rock.

As soon as I landed I knew I was hurt.

'Oh, Charley, Charley, Charley,' *Pete calls out, as if he was there with us both struggling in the sea. Finally, Am leans forward and stubs out her fag, her hands gripping the edge of the table* . . .

'Charley, what happened?' *asks Pete.*

'She saw the wristband, Pete.'

I lifted my hand up for help, and the white band glowed on my wrist in the half-light.

Always, it said on it. Forever.

My little piece of you, Pete, only it wasn't mine, was it?

'It was mine,' *says Am.* 'I gave it to you, Pete.'

He turns away from her, to me.

'You tell me, Charley,' *he says again.*

I was drowning in the sea. I made a grab for Am's hand and she caught my wrist, trying to pull me up, trying to help me, and we struggled against the tide and the waves.

And then she saw the wristband.

She shouted something, but I couldn't hear it above the noise of the waves and the drumming in my ears. She let go of my hand and grabbed at the band, trying to pull it off my wrist, but it wouldn't come. She pulled and tugged until the band snapped, flipped up and flew off my wrist, and I fell back onto the rock.

The band disappeared into the sea.

And Am snapped, too, she went mad. Her rage was like something elemental, like thunder and lightning, raining all around me.

Unstoppable.

And I couldn't move, couldn't fight back. I wasn't working, something in me was broken, and all I could do was call her name, trying to remind her that I existed and that it was me she was hurting.

'Am! Am!'

But she couldn't hear me.

And then I called you, Pete, and at the sound of your name, she stopped.

'His name,' *Am interrupts.* 'You said his name!'

I go on.

I felt her try to lift me up, to help me this time, to take me away from the suddenly too-cold water and the hard rock. It was a struggle, I couldn't move, and we pushed against the waves together, in the cold, grey light, until I fell from her hands and hit my head again, hard on the rock.

'I can't,' she said. 'I can't!' and she called your name, 'Pete!' but there was no answer and the tide was rising up, covering us.

'Pete!' she yelled into the waves and shattering surf, and time seemed to stop. She disappeared beneath the waves, came up.

'Your ankle's stuck, pull, Charley. Pull!' But I could barely hear her now, her words were far away and fading as the cold gripped my bones, and the white lines of surf were far beyond us, heading for the beach, and the swell was lifting me and dropping me. I looked up at Am, a shadow looming over me, eyes a deep bruised blue. Her face filled my whole world, and then there was darkness.

And the next time I looked, I was alone.

I was alone.

'Pete!'

I tried to shout your name, but no sound came out. Only the beginnings of the sun answered. Its rays shone on me as though it could lift me up. As though it could somehow share its warmth, reach right into my bones, and save me.

I looked up towards the house, shining and white, sudden and bright in the first glance of the rising sun, but the windows stayed covered, dark and empty.

I was alone.

When I open my eyes, the room is silent.

'Is it true?' *asks Pete. Am nods.*

'Why didn't you get help?' *he asks. And I wait for her answer, the answer I've come so far to hear.*

'I thought you'd blame me,' *she says.*

And Pete holds me in his shaking arms.

'It's over, Pete,' I whisper, and I feel Hal begin to breathe again inside me, because the story's told, and we're here, where the past and present meet, and the future's unknown.

And I'm scared.

'I'm here, Charley,' says Pete. 'You're not alone now.'

And Hal speaks in his own voice.

Hal. Now.

She's so scared, scared of the growing cold and numbness in her body, scared that she's dying with only the sky and sea to hold her. Scared of whatever it is she'll find when she leaves my body.

'You're not alone any more, we're here, it's OK,' I say, hearing Mum and Dad in my whispered words.

'*Hal!*' she whispers. '*Pete!*' and I feel her breath grow strong and steady within me, feel it merging with the wind in the leaves outside in the black night. I feel it flow right down to the edge of the sea, and pick up the endless rhythm of the waves. Her breath carries us down to the very end of our story, to the rocks, where I found her. And I close my eyes and her memories come, clear and clean within us, rising like waves, just waiting to be ridden. And there amongst her final memories at last, we all look out together, through her dying eyes which she can barely open.

'*Don't leave me!*' she whispers.

And we don't leave her, we hold her tight. We look out with Charley, at the growing dawn spreading across the sky and into morning. We watch the images flit across her rapidly failing mind. She sees Mum's face in the growing clouds, and feels Dad's arms around her, his beard prickling her face. She sees me, 'like an angel drying his wings'. And she reaches out for a memory of Sara. She sees her, face intent, bent over a pool of water, watching, as a flower-red sea anemone slowly opens up its petals, readying itself to swallow.

The sky is rose and gold, and for just a moment the beauty of it fills her mind, holding back the pain, until there is only the push and pull of the waves as they gather and retreat, holding her to them and letting her go, holding her to them and letting her go.

Charley. Now.

They are with me in the waves, Hal and Pete, holding me close, stopping me shivering in the sea, stopping me sinking back into the dark place beyond memory.

Hal. Now.

And now that we are with her, she can reach up for the sun, feel the deep red beauty of it. She remembers her longing for a bright red flower, impossible to reach, and yet her hand reaches out, stretches closer and closer across the clouds, until her fingers seem to touch the sun, and somewhere in our minds a deep red flower falls from a tree, from the sky, straight into the palm of her waiting hand.

Charley. Now.

I'm dying, looking up at the sun, as it dawns, filling another day . . . and I take a breath . . . I take a breath and reach up to it, reach up to the sun, to its warmth and life, stretch up for the deep red flower that is always just out of reach.

And.

The dark is gone, the cupboard door lies open, a pathway of shining sunlight hovers beneath my feet, out and away from me, across the sea.

I take a step.

I am on a high wire of light.

They hold my hands.

Hal and Pete.

I take another step, and slowly, so slowly, I let their hands fall and hold my arms out wide to the waiting sea, and air, and sunshine.

I am balancing.

Between life and death.

In my left palm lies the deep red flower. I hold it to my lips, so close that I can smell my longing for its deep red warmth . . . for all the stories, as yet untold, that lie in each tightly curled petal . . . it is life, but not my life – it's Hal's.

My life, my story, is in my other hand.

And when I turn to look, I see that it is empty . . . or is it?

I look closer, the lines of my own palm stare up at me . . . I take another step . . .

. . . and find that they are full of the unknown.

For one long moment I balance, face up to the warm air, until I know, and then I take a step . . . on my own . . .

. . . and at long, long last, I feel my body in its hospital bed take a breath. A real breath, full of sweet, sweet air – full of holes, and ragged struggle.

And I let myself begin to fall.

Every story has an ending . . .

Hal. Now.

I can feel something pushing against the air, taking up space. It's me! My body. I know it's there because Jack's all over it, pushing and prodding and holding on to me as though she thought she'd never get me back. She followed me!

I open my eyes. Pete helps me up.

We grin at each other.

Was that weird or what?

And then I feel it, the empty space inside.

She's gone.

I'm crying. The tears are falling out of my eyes and down my face without pause for thought, without stopping.

Pete nods, his own tears as surprising as a rock crying, like a granite cliff just cracking open and oozing tears, standing motionless as the stream runs down its sides.

Am stares at us silently, wary.

'Where is Charley?' she asks, looking around as though she might appear through the walls.

'She's gone,' I say, and I watch as Am's eyes lose their frozen glassy surface and fill with tears. I can't believe how blue her eyes are, their colour is indefinable, like turquoise mixed with sapphire dust.

'I'm sorry,' she whispers. 'What did I do?'

Pete and Jackie both look at me; they all look at me, as though they think I might have an answer. But if I do, I can't find it.

'I don't know, Am,' I say, 'but I know you tried to save her.'

'It was an accident,' I hear myself say, and I realize that maybe Mum's words are true: that maybe sometimes we just die. We die for all kinds of weird reasons – because some-one got angry that morning, or we went in the sea at the wrong time, or we walked in front of a car. It doesn't make any sense, it never has and it never will; it just happens.

Endings.

'Let's go,' says Jack, and she wraps her arms around me.

Am is the last out. She stares into the house through the window, and then she lights a match and throws it in, and all her shredded pieces of paper catch light and glow a deep steady red, before bursting into flame. She turns to us, her beautiful face all lit and glowing by the flames she's made.

'I'm never coming back, Pete,' she says, her face shining. 'Never,' she whispers to herself, as though she can hardly believe it. 'And he can burn in hell!' She smiles suddenly. 'Without me,' she says.

Pete holds his hand out to her and she grasps it.

We stumble through the woods, along the same path Charley took, last year, to the sea, and when we get there, out on to the beach, under the clear, starry night sky, the waves are huge and swelling shadows. We sit on the rocks, shocked and silent, and stare.

All together.

All alone.

Perhaps we can all see her, dancing on the waves – or maybe it's only me. A deeper shadow, hanging under white curls of surf, a shadow that seems to turn and wave, before turning back and disappearing into the dark depths of the sea and sky.

'Hal?'

The voice is so soft and gentle, it sounds like it has seeped out of the very darkness itself, slipping out of the sea, and the wind and the waves, to find me. It feels so much a part of everything around me that at first I can barely hear it calling.

'Hal?' it says again, behind me, and I realize that I have never noticed, until now, how much Mum sounds like Charley.

'Mum?' I whisper back, turning from the waves and the wind and the dark, racing, moon-struck clouds, towards her.

'Hal,' she says again, and I feel her hand on my shoulder, soft and steadying, holding me ready, speaking to me before the words do.

'It's time to come home now, Hal.'

I nod, and manage to stand.

Jack and Pete touch me wordlessly on my way.

Am stays silent and still as she stares up at us, me and Mum, with something like longing.

Charley's earring snags against my hip as I stand. I take it out of my pocket and hand it to Pete. He folds it into his palm where I know it is safe, and I turn towards Mum and start to walk.

Epilogue.

Our house is like a 1930s house; it rises up out of the darkness, like a ship on the waves. A ship that rocks and steadies itself in the wind, a ship that's built to last.

In the kitchen there are photos, photos of all of us as we grow older. I am looking at the last photo of Charley, but I don't really have to look at it any more, because I have so many pictures of her within me, where her memory lives.

Mum puts her arms around me. Dad's eyes close as he stretches out his arms to fit us both within them.

'Hal,' they say together. 'Oh, Hal.'

And there's a soft pull at my wrist, where Sara struggles to join us, slipping gently into the circle of Dad's arms without breaking it.

'I know,' I say, not wanting to hear the words, and I feel my own eyes close against what's to come.

'Hal.' Their arms hold me up, lifting me from the ground until I feel like I'm floating and held, safe and ready.

'She's dead, Hal,' they say, and I feel my head fall to my chest with tiredness and relief, and they carry me upstairs to bed in the darkness.

I feel my mind close down; I feel myself float right out above my limp and lifeless body that lies on the bed filled with relief and exhaustion. Somehow I'm both awake and asleep, watching my parents watch over me together, and I try to tell them what's happened, my mum and dad, but I'm not sure that they can hear me.

It's OK, I whisper, she can never truly die because she's inside us, and I know that wherever she is, whatever darkness she faces, she's not alone either, because we're inside her too.

I look down at them, Mum and Dad, as they hold hands together across my sleeping body, and wipe each other's silent tears from their faces, together and alone.

'Beautiful boy!' whispers Mum. 'Only-boy!'

'Sleeps like an angel drying his wings,' says Dad, and I feel myself smile, and I wonder if they know where the words come from. If they, too, can feel the faint wisp of air and memory that floats in from the sea, and finds its way in through the window to echo in his ear.

I see Charley's face; her eyes are as huge and blue as the summer sky, and her lips are as soft as cloud-linings, as they whisper to me.

'Thanks, gravy-bum!' she says.

'Sayonara, sis,' I reply.

And from somewhere deep within I feel her finally fade away; fade far, far away into the unknown, where I know that I can no longer follow her.